TRUFFLE HOUNDS

SANDY ST. JOHN

SOUTHPAW PRESS

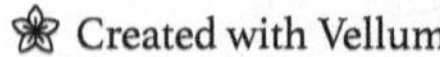 Created with Vellum

For my friend, Evan

Whose kind heart helps soften the hard edges of the world

I wouldn't say I'm a jealous person. In fact, I hardly remember ever being jealous of anyone. Okay, once in third grade, when Meagan Mahoney got a horse, and my parents refused to let me have one, I was definitely jealous then. But for the most part, it's not something I experience. I grew up in a pretty affluent family and had everything I needed—except the horse. I'm not that impressed by flashy things. I have my own house, a reliable car, and good relationships with people who matter to me, *and* I'm even starting my own business. So there's not much for me to be jealous about. Okay, I'm not married. I don't have a boyfriend. I don't even remember my last date—but I'm not jealous of cutesy couples.

My name is Jessie Gallagher. I am the proprietor of Barker Street Bones, a gourmet dog biscuit company. Starting this business has been keeping me busy. I also have a handful of regular dog-walking clients to help bring in some extra money. See? I'm quite busy. That's why I don't have a boyfriend. Or a husband. I certainly don't begrudge other people having those relationships. I don't. I'll get around to finding someone.

It was late Friday afternoon, and I'd finished my dog-walking rounds. I was picking up dog food for my friend Evan's dog when I ran into his neighbor, Kip Willetto, perusing the cat food aisle. Evan is my best friend, and we know essentially everything about each other. Okay, maybe not everything, but we know the big things, and I know for a fact he doesn't have a girlfriend.

So then, what was this?

"I saw them together," Kip said, nearly buzzing with excitement when he saw the disbelief on my face.

"You must be mistaken," I said.

"I wasn't sure if I should say anything," Kip said, leaning close and speaking in an exaggerated whisper. "I wasn't sure if you two were—you know, together. As in the biblical sense, in which case, I'm sorry to bring this up."

"No, no, Evan and I are just friends," I insisted. We were. Evan and I had been friends for years, so I found it impossible to believe he had a girlfriend I didn't know about. The sudden, odd humming feeling in my chest was strange, though. It's not like he *shouldn't* have a girlfriend. We were just friends. Why shouldn't he have a girlfriend? But why wouldn't he have told me? Evan was my best girlfriend, only he wasn't a girl.

"Well, *that's* good," Kip said, patting himself on the chest in relief.

I stood silent, trying to digest this news. Would we still hang out like we do now? Why hadn't I considered Evan dating before? Visions of tagging along on his dates gathered at the periphery of my mind.

"Honey, are you okay?" Kip reached over and gently patted my shoulder. "I shouldn't have said anything. You have feelings for him, although I'm not sure why." Kip grimaced almost imperceptibly. Kip and Evan had never exactly gelled. Mostly, they ignored each other in passing.

"No, don't be ridiculous," I said. "It's fine. I'm surprised, is all. Are you sure? Maybe it was someone from work."

He arched his perfectly sculpted eyebrows and looked away. "How about you?" he asked. "Have you met anyone recently?"

I had had a boyfriend, but I wasn't even sure what year that had been now that I thought about it. My parents had loved him, had set us up, in fact, but he was pompous and self-important, and I'd finally realized I didn't even like him. When we broke up, I was relieved more than anything. Then I'd gotten busy at work, and life rolled along, and now here I was. Alone. While Evan had a girlfriend.

"No, not exactly." I trailed off, feeling pathetic. "Oh wait, I almost went out with one of my dog-walking clients last year." As soon as the words were out, I was sorry.

"Almost? Last year?"

I sighed. "He was super cute, but he moved to Dubai. Anyway, what's this girl like?" I smiled, my dry lip catching on my tooth. I hated myself for even asking. If Evan wanted me to know about his girlfriend, he would tell me.

"Well," Kip tapped his lip with his forefinger, staring down the aisle as if conjuring her image. "I wasn't close, but she looked very young."

"Maybe it was his cousin or something." I tried to remember if Evan had any young cousins but was coming up blank.

"No, I don't think so. Well, if he's from Appalachia, maybe. The way she was all over him—clutching at his arm, fiddling with his hair, I don't think this was a relative. Do you have any relatives that bite your earlobe?" A fluorescent light flickered above us, making me feel slightly dizzy. He leaned forward and touched the space between my eyebrows, rubbing in a gentle circle. "Sugar, if you don't stop frowning like that, this line is going to be permanent."

"What line?" I stepped back and felt along the skin where he'd been rubbing.

"It's just getting started," he said. "I have some cream that can help, but you need to stop frowning that way."

Okay, this was not that big a deal. I was happy for Evan. And as for me, this was simply a wake-up call—another area of my own life that needed a little attention. We moved down the aisle away from the flickering light.

"I know what you need!" Kip said, visibly brightening.

"A man?"

"Well, obviously, don't we all? But no. I know how we can help you find the *right* man. Not just *any* man."

"Oh no, I'm not doing one of those online dating apps."

"Of course, you're not. You'd probably be matched with a hatchet killer."

"Thanks."

"You know what I mean. Those sites are a hotbed of psychoses. Trust me, I know."

"Then what?" I asked, not entirely sure I wanted to hear the answer.

"I am going to make you an appointment with my friend, Bertram." I stared at him, waiting for a little more clarification. "Yes! This is perfect. He's just starting out, and I'm sure he'll give you a reduced rate because you're my friend."

"He's starting out as what exactly?" I could feel my frown line redeveloping.

"He's a psychic. He can help you find your person." He fished his phone from the leather crossbody man-satchel resting on his hip. "Let's see if he's online. Maybe he can fit you in today."

I glanced at my watch as if I needed to be somewhere, but truth be told, I didn't. The only thing on my agenda was dropping off the food I was buying for Evan's dog, Henry. I'd volunteered to pick it up since he'd been so busy at work this week. Or at least that's what he'd told me.

"I'm not sure I need a psychic," I said. I probably just needed some time to digest this news.

"Honey, you're not doing that well on your own. If you don't act soon, everyone will be paired up, and then what?"

I flashed back to a Noah's Ark toy I'd had when I was little. I was maybe five then, and that Ark and I were inseparable. It had a little handle on top, and I carried it around, bumping its heft against my hip like an overstuffed suitcase. I was enchanted by all the animal pairs and spent hours marching them up and down the ramp, side by side. I loved that thing. It felt right that everyone had a special friend to travel with.

Kip sighed and slipped the phone back into his purse. "Sadly, he's not online. But I will track him down tonight, and we'll set up an appointment for you pronto." He leaned forward and gave me a little air hug. "Don't you worry. Kip's gonna take care of you."

It's amazing how one little conversation can change the trajectory of your day. I'd waltzed into the store, nothing more pressing on my mind than hoping they had the right brand of food, and I left feeling as if everyone in the world was pairing up, like my little ark animals so many years ago. Two by two. Except for me. I was one.

CHAPTER TWO

I hadn't expected Evan to be home yet, and I'd planned to drop the dog food on the porch, so imagine my surprise when I saw Evan's car in the driveway. I felt unaccountably nervous as I hoisted the bag onto my hip and made my way up the creaking porch steps. Henry, the canine recipient of the food delivery, recognized my footsteps, and his sharp little barks were peppered with whines of excitement. His nails clacked against the hardwood floors inside as I approached the door.

I stood for a moment, expecting Evan to open the door. He had to know I was there. A sudden flush of uncertainty washed over me. What if he was in there with his new girlfriend right now? I considered dropping the food and running, but finally, the door swung open, and Henry rushed out.

"Hey, buddy," I said, reaching down for the whiskey-colored furball as he danced around my legs. I glanced sideways at Evan, ensuring he was presentable. "I didn't think you'd be home from work this early." He looked terrible, pale with dark circles under his eyes, and I sensed I'd woken him up. His dark hair was mashed flat on one side, and he wore an undershirt and khakis, both creased with wrinkles.

"Yeah, I wasn't feeling great, so I left early. I brought my computer home. I'll have to work some this weekend." He yawned and rubbed a hand across his face. Noticing the dog food, he reached out and took it from me. "Thanks for getting that. I was almost out. Let me know how much I owe you."

I entered the living room and looked around, wondering if I'd see any girl paraphernalia. It looked the same as always. It actually looked better than it had when he first moved in. At least now he had some decent furniture and a giant screen TV, not to mention way more gaming consoles than he needed. But even with the new additions, he still had a lot of work to do.

"Hey, you doing anything this weekend?" I asked, my voice squeaking unnaturally.

"Yeah, there's this thing. I was going to ask if you wanted to go—" His phone began bleating an unfamiliar ringtone, and he immediately grabbed it, his energy level zooming from half-dead to full-on. "I gotta get this," he said, shooing me gently to the door with ever-frantic movements. "I'll call you later," he said, shutting the door behind me with a decisive bang.

That was rude. I could only assume that was the new girl-friend. I drove home feeling untethered. How had things changed so fast? An hour ago, I was looking forward to the weekend, unsure what we'd be doing, but assuming my weekend would be like most others—hang out with Evan doing whatever, maybe spend some time with my grandmother. You know, the usual stuff.

Once home, I drifted into my house, where my dog Addie greeted me with her traditional fanfare. Her idea of a hearty welcome involved bouncing up and down repeatedly, ominously close to my face, like a black and white basketball. I guided her to the living room, where she hurtled up next to me on the couch and settled down. I told her about Evan's new girlfriend, but she didn't seem concerned. Flopping back against the cushions, I explained it again while she rolled over for a belly rub. My phone rang, and I reached for it, convinced it would be Evan, ready to tell me about his new girlfriend and finish whatever he'd been planning to ask me to do this weekend. But no, it was Frances, my grandmother.

"Hi, Frances," I said, rubbing a hand along Addie's pink belly.

"Jessica, how are you, dear?"

She and I generally get together every week, often on Saturday night for dinner—yet another sign of how pathetic my love life was. But I enjoyed my dinners with Frances, I reminded myself. A lot.

Only she wasn't calling to confirm our unofficial Saturday night dinner. Instead, she was calling to let me know she had other plans this weekend.

"Oh, of course, that's fine," I said, knowing I didn't sound completely sincere.

"Is everything okay?" she asked, immediately picking up on my tone.

"Yes, everything's good," I said, trying harder. "Are you doing anything exciting?"

She paused for the merest fraction of a second before replying. "Actually, an old friend of your grandfather's is in town. They worked together in the early days of their careers. I haven't seen him in many, many years."

"Frances, you have a *date*?" What was going on here? My grandparents had been married for fifty-eight years before my grandfather passed away. Frances had never so much as looked at another man as far as I knew.

"It's not a date. It's a dinner with an old friend." She sounded very matter-of-fact and very much like she wouldn't entertain any more questions about it. "At any rate, I wanted to let you know so you could make other arrangements. Perhaps you and Evan could do something fun tomorrow night."

Perhaps. But the evening dragged on with no word from Evan, and I began feeling an unaccustomed dread over the looming weekend. I ran listlessly through a litany of options to fill my time. I could make additional dog biscuits for my business. I could look into building the website I needed to grow my little enterprise. I needed to do an inventory of my supplies. I didn't want to do any of that.

It was a very long evening.

I awoke way too early on Saturday morning, particularly since I didn't have anything planned all day. Addie bounced around the bed, digging at the blankets and poking me with her nose, trying to convince me to get up and play, but sensing defeat, she finally rolled over and went back to sleep. I wished I could get back to sleep. Instead, I spent some time trying to picture how things would be now with Evan's new situation. Maybe if this girl were really cool, it would be okay. But then I put myself in her shoes and tried to imagine my new boyfriend's girlfriend, or rather, a friend who was a girl, hanging out with us, and it seemed unlikely.

I gave myself a mental shake. What was I doing? I was totally overreacting. This could easily be a casual thing; for all I knew, he hadn't told me because it wasn't a big deal. I would let it play out. In the meantime, maybe I did need to start thinking about getting out there myself. I'd always assumed I had plenty of time and that things would work out. But thinking about it now, time was slipping away. If I didn't find someone soon, all the good ones would be taken. I should welcome this as a wake-up call. Although, the thought of actively trying to find a partner seemed as appealing as having my teeth scaled.

I did what any rational person would—I shoved it out of my

mind. I took Addie for a walk, then cooked myself a giant breakfast of bacon, eggs, and pancakes. I'd just finished putting away the leftovers and cleaning the dishes when my phone buzzed. It was Evan.

"Hey!" I said, inordinately happy to hear from him. "What's going on? I made a huge breakfast, and I have leftovers if you want to come over."

"Cool," he said, "but I can't." I could hear background noise as if he were in a crowd. "I'm at this dog festival right now over at Allen Parkway. I was going to see if you wanted to go—" He was suddenly muffled as if he'd put his hand over the speaker.

"Evan?" I asked.

"Yeah, I'm here," he said. "Anyway, it's called Bark at the Park. They've got all kinds of dog things. There's this lady you've got to see. She's an artist who does pet portraits, and Jess, it's amazing! She's raffling tickets to do a custom painting of your pet, and I'm getting some tickets because Henry would be so cute, but Addie is so pretty I wasn't sure if you'd like to do this too?"

"Yeah, that sounds awesome. Are you going to be there for a little while? It'll probably take me about half an hour to get there. Can you wait?"

He went muffled again, and I could tell he was talking to someone else.

"I think so. I'm actually here with a friend of mine. We might go look around a bit. This artist lady is my friend's aunt. I *know* you'll want to do this. She does drawings too, and watercolors if you don't win the painting. They're not as expensive. But, yeah, definitely come down. I'll look for you."

We disconnected, and I hustled to my closet to change. I'd never seen Evan interested in art before. He had nothing on his walls except some hideous wallpaper left by the previous owner. If he did buy a dog painting, I figured it would be more like Dogs

Playing Poker or an incandescent dog portrait on black velvet. Hopefully, this artist wasn't like that. At any rate, it seemed I was about to meet this mystery woman of Evan's. My stomach clenched slightly as I raced to get ready.

CHAPTER THREE

I arrived at the park less than half an hour later, but finding parking proved challenging. After multiple passes, I eventually lucked upon a pickup truck backing out of a prime spot in one of the small lots directly off Allen Parkway. I nosed in and got out of my car, quelling the nervous sensation in my gut as I looked out over Buffalo Bayou. Houston has four major bayous running through the area and more than twenty-two smaller tributaries, earning it the nickname Bayou City. This particular area was close to where I'd been forced off the road last month and had nearly drowned in the raging water. I was lucky to be alive. My previous car had not survived. Today, the water dozed stagnantly between the banks, a warm, gentle incubator for mosquitos, not a surging, violent channel that could sweep you to your death.

I shook off the memories and quickly texted Evan as I trotted down the grassy embankment toward the crowds. At least two dozen tented tables had been set up in raggedy rows, along with a handful of food trucks and two air-conditioned trailers holding an assortment of hopeful canines looking for a good home. There were quite a few families in front of the trailer, and many of the dogs were romping with gleeful abandon, happy to be out of their crates. Hopefully, all the dogs would find homes today.

A breeze tickled the tree tops but didn't dip down in the shallow basin beside the bayou, and the rising humidity made it feel like a Turkish bath. A sheen of perspiration popped out along my forehead and upper lip. I slowed down, studying the tables of delightful canine-themed items for sale while simultaneously scanning for Evan and his friend. There were so many things to tempt a dog lover: dog apparel, blankets, bowls, booties, toys, and homemade treats. I stopped and picked up a bag, impressed by the packaging. I should have set up a booth myself. Why hadn't I known about this?

"Can I help you?" asked the woman behind the table. "Those are our most popular treats—chicken pot pie biscuits," she said, smiling a grandmotherly smile at me. I glanced at the ingredient list: ground yellow corn, corn gluten meal, rendered fat, soy flour, corn syrup, propylene glycol, and a host of other items I'd never heard of but were likely waste products from the back end of a chemical plant. I looked up as her cherubic face beamed at me.

"This packaging is so cute. Do you make these yourself?"

"Everything here is made with love," she said, treating me to a non-answer.

"I don't see any chicken in your chicken pot pie biscuits," I said, causing her eyes to narrow menacingly at me. A lady next to me flipped over the bag she was looking at, squinted at the label, and thumped it back down on the table before walking away.

"Look here, young lady," the woman hissed at me. "I don't know what your game is, but I won't let you bad mouth my product."

"What's hexame...hexametap," I stumbled, trying to pronounce the word.

"Hey, there you are!" Evan grabbed my arm and pulled me toward the path. I tossed the bag of toxins back onto the table. "You gotta come see this." I looked around for his friend, but he appeared to be alone.

"This is so cool," I said. "I didn't know about this event. I should have set up a table for Barker Street Bones."

"Right?" He led me through the crowd, steering my elbow like a rudder. "There is so much here. I got the cutest stuffed dinosaur for Henry. He's going to love it."

"You didn't bring him?"

"No, it's too hot. I don't want him to get sick." I smiled. Evan had come a long way as a dog dad.

We approached a tent set up under a tree and slightly apart from the others. A small crowd stood watching as a middle-aged woman sat on a stool in front of an easel, her hand flying across a piece of paper, bringing a small fluffy-white Maltese to life in shades of charcoal. The woman holding the Maltese beamed, cooing at her dog while smiling shyly at the people watching. It was astounding. The artist managed to capture not only the physical likeness of the dog, but somehow, you could see the dog's sweet personality emerge on the page.

"See?" Evan whispered. "Imagine what she could do with Henry and Addie." Other works of art hung along the sides of the tent. Watercolors, acrylics, graphite, and colored pencil drawings featured beautifully rendered dogs, so lifelike I expected them to run off the page. We moved closer, mesmerized by the furry subjects. I was admiring the intricate brushstrokes of a Bernese mountain dog's fur and imagining how beautiful a portrait of Addie would be when I felt Evan jostle against me.

"Bae, what took you so long?" A small, dark-haired young woman had shoved into him from the other side, apparently catching him off balance. She sidled against him, inserting herself under his arm and smacking a stuffed dinosaur against his belly. "Here's your toy." Her eyes slid to me, and I felt a jolt of something. Not anxiety, exactly. Not jealousy, I didn't think. But something vaguely unsettling.

"Hi." I smiled and did a gawky wave. "I'm Jessie." I suppressed the urge to grab Evan's other arm. He repositioned, trying to relocate her out from under his armpit.

"Jess, this is Gabriella Goodman. Gabriella, this is Jessie Gallagher."

Her dark eyes looked me up and down, and she burrowed closer to Evan, marking out her territory like a cat rubbing her scent glands all over him.

"Nice to meet you," I said, trying to mean it. Even the way Evan said her name was irritating. *Gah*-briella. I mean, I get that's how her name was pronounced, but it sounded pretentious coming from Evan.

She ignored me and looked up at Evan through the thickest eyelashes I'd ever seen. Kip was right—she was young. Very young.

"I'm bored," she said. "And it's getting hot. Aren't you ready to go yet?"

"Yeah, sure," he said. "I wanted Jessie to see your aunt's work."

"Yeah, I guess it's pretty cool. You can't bother her while she works, though. She doesn't like it." She finger-walked her hand up Evan's chest before booping him on the nose. "Let's go." She sounded like she was five, but, in reality, she was maybe twenty or so. I wondered if she could even drink legally. Where in the world had he met this creature? And how had they gotten together? Rumpled Evan and the sex kitten. This was perplexing.

They walked away together, Gabriella clutching Evan's arm while he nervously flapped the dinosaur in his opposite hand. Just before they disappeared into the crowd, she craned her neck to peer at me over his shoulder, narrowing her eyes and giving me a small smile. I tried to smile back, but my face felt frozen.

I turned around, unsettled. By way of distraction, I went to examine the raffle display and a price list of other mediums offered. If I didn't win the raffle, maybe I would get a pencil drawing of Addie done. The more I studied the pieces around the tent, the more I wanted one of Addie.

"Hello. Do you see anything you like?"

I looked around, surprised that the crowd had melted away. I was now alone with the artist.

"Oh, hi," I said. "Everything here is incredible!"

We studied each other, and it was like when you meet someone you feel that you've known before. Her energy was balanced and appealing, and her frank gaze was nothing like her niece's. She was fiftyish, her brown hair beginning to show glossy streaks of white, pulled back by a loose silk scarf. Her eyes were light and curious, studying me with an intensity that I imagined she used on all her subjects. She was probably trying to establish if I would look better in watercolors or black ink. She'd dressed in flowing layers that lifted and floated with every movement. She reminded me of an upscale hippy.

"Thank you," she said. "I love what I do, but hearing when someone likes it is always gratifying." She moved back and began gathering up the charcoal sticks she'd been using and arranging them in what appeared to be a specific order. They all looked the same to me. "I'm Christine Wagner, by the way."

"Jessie Gallagher," I said.

"Are you in the market for a pet portrait?"

"I wasn't until my friend called me to come check this out."

"Ah, was that your friend with my niece?"

"Yes, that's Evan." I hesitated half a beat, wanting to pump her for information about Evan's new girlfriend. I liked Christine Wagner on sight. I had the feeling I wouldn't like Gabriella Goodman at any time. "I met your niece for the first time today." My voice rose in a half-questioning tone, and she slid me a look but simply nodded. I stepped over to a display featuring a series of bloodhounds captured in various poses. It looked to be the same dog in all of them. I glanced at Christine. "Yours?"

Her face lit up, a genuine smile highlighting narrow laugh lines near her eyes. "Yes, that's Lucille." She focused on a pencil drawing showing a giant, wrinkled head drooping over a sofa's padded arm. "We found each other a couple of years ago. It's rather clichéd, but I was going through a bit of a life crisis." She opened a blue cooler behind the table. "Would you like a water?"

She took one for herself and handed me a bottle, cold water dripping off the sides. She sank back onto her stool and gestured for me to take a seat on the cooler. We sat in the warm, still air, sharing stories about our dogs—the funny, charming, outrageous things that dogs are inclined to do. We chatted for a long time, taking short breaks while Christine interacted with the customers who came and went. One thing about talking to another dog lover is that you can share a thousand stories and not get bored. I've noticed that non-dog people allow you one anecdote before zoning out. By the time we started slowing down, the crowds had dwindled.

"So, what do you do for a living, Jessie?"

I launched into a brief account of my fledgling attempt to start a business after departing a job in which I'd never felt fulfilled. "This motivates me, though," I said, looking around the tent. "You've made a business out of doing what you love. It's inspiring."

She smiled and set her empty water bottle on the table behind her. "I've only been doing this for a couple of years."

"What! No way."

"Believe it or not. Don't get me wrong. Art has always been a passion of mine. But I married young—I was still in school, studying art. He was in a medical residency. I ended up quitting and going to work while he finished his program." She glanced toward the front of the tent, but the couple walking past didn't stop. "And, eventually, he was a big-time thoracic surgeon with a non-profit on the side. I went to work for his non-profit, and the years went by. We never had kids; we worked; we lived. I thought we were happy." She fiddled with the edge of her skirt. "I'm not sure why I'm telling you all this," she said.

I wasn't either, but I said, "I'm guessing this is the lead-up to the life crisis you mentioned earlier."

"Ah, yes," she said, nodding. "And, also, how my business came to be. I never gave up my art entirely, but my ex-husband didn't encourage it." She stared away across the grass toward the bayou. "He didn't *discourage* it exactly, but he made it clear he thought it was a *nice hobby*." She looked up and met my eyes.

"Ouch. That sounds dismissive," I said. "And ex-husband."

"Turns out, there was someone young, pretty, and smitten with the great doctor. Like I said, cliché. We'd grown a little apart, not so much that I saw this coming. The kicker was that she worked at the non-profit too, so when he left me for her, well, it was a colossal mess. I couldn't bear to keep working with everyone whispering behind my back. Well, I could have, but it was incredibly toxic. So, I quit. Lost my husband and my career just like that."

I could feel a trickle of sweat rolling down my back. Here I was, determined to start out on my journey of love, and this was depressing me.

"So you went back to your art?"

"First came Lucille," she said, the corners of her mouth turning up. "Michael, my ex, hated dogs. He said they smelled and were dirty."

"And you stayed with him for as long as you did?" I smiled as I said it, but this solidified my need to find a guy who loves dogs.

"Can you believe it? Anyway, one of my friends who works with a rescue called and asked if I could foster a dog they'd gotten in. She was big and scared and needed someone quiet to give her a safe space until they found a suitable home. She'd come from a pretty terrible situation." A fly buzzed past, and she waved it off. "She was a mess. She was filthy, and she smelled. Michael would have hated her on sight. She was underweight and scared of random things—her food bowl, a Ficus tree in the corner, a chair scraping on the floor. I was a mess all my own, so once I got her cleaned up, we took refuge together, hardly leaving the house other than to go to my studio—and that's in the backyard, so it was like we were in our own world."

"She's a lucky girl," I said.

"I was lucky to get her. She was younger than the rescue had thought, only about a year old, but so calm that she seemed older. I'd been feeling useless and ugly, and this big, drooly dog looked at me like I was the center of the world. It didn't take long before I started drawing her. It was like a part of me reawakened. I started doing some artwork for the dog rescue, attending adoption events with them, and offering a sketch of the dogs as they were adopted. People loved it."

"I can imagine." I thought back to the day I'd adopted Addie. I had some photographs from that day, but most were blurred, and she didn't look her best in any of them.

"From there, people started asking me for custom pet portraits, and here I am."

"That's a great story," I said. "Well, except for the bad parts."

"Sometimes it takes a major shakeup to get you on the right path," she said. "And it's rewarding to make money from my *little hobby*." She stood up and began fiddling with her art supplies as if embarrassed. "Sorry to drone on. I don't usually overshare that way."

I rose from the cooler, twisting a kink from my back. "No, don't worry about it. It's been great talking to you. I would like to buy some raffle tickets before I go."

She picked up a business card, flipped it over, and wrote something on the back.

"Forget the raffle. Why don't you come by my studio? Bring pictures of your dog, and we'll see which medium is best for her." She handed me her card. "I usually don't have people come to the studio; most of my work is done via online transactions. Since my studio is in my backyard, you can't be too safe, right? But I'd love for you to meet Lucille. And we could talk about possible synergies between your biscuit business and the rescues."

I glanced at the back of her card, noticing her address was only a short distance from my parent's house. I speculated that she'd gotten her house in the divorce.

"My ex is hosting a big fundraiser for his non-profit tonight, and I'm just dreading it. Having you over will give me something to look forward to. We can have breakfast and maybe some mimosas." She laughed, a guarded vulnerability softening her edges. "Depending on my evening, maybe a lot of mimosas. I believe in rewarding oneself for doing necessary but unpleasant things."

"Why don't you just skip it?" I asked. I like rewards too, but sometimes it's easier to skip unnecessary drama.

"I would if I could, but they're honoring all the work we've done over the years. The one thing Michael's always done well is to give credit where credit's due, and it would look churlish if I didn't attend."

She suggested I come over around nine, and I agreed, a mild anticipation running through me at the thought of making a new friend. I tucked her card into my purse. Maybe this new girlfriend thing of Evan's wouldn't be so bad after all.

CHAPTER FOUR

When I left the park, I felt more balanced again. Evan had thought of me when he saw Christine's art, so it wasn't like he was going to blow me off suddenly. And I was looking forward to seeing Christine tomorrow. My weekend was definitely looking up. I decided to swing by to see Frances. It was early enough she couldn't possibly be getting ready for her non-date date yet.

My parents live in the upscale neighborhood of River Oaks. It's close to downtown, swanky shopping, and a world-class medical center—and that proximity makes it unaffordable unless you have a great deal of money, which they do. Some parts of River Oaks are more posh than others, namely the areas closer to the River Oaks Country Club, where lush estates nestle on oversized lots. My parents live on one of those streets, and my grandmother lives in a guesthouse behind the main structure. The arrangement works out well for all involved. The only downside, in my opinion, is I can't hide out with Frances without my parents knowing I'm there.

I rolled down the driveway, stones crunching under my tires, and proceeded straight to the guesthouse. Frances was striding toward her door, apparently having come from checking on her chickens. The chickens were a new addition to her list of hobbies. Despite my parents' initial objections, she'd steadfastly refused to budge. She lit up when she saw me, and I trotted over for a quick hug before we headed for the door.

"What a wonderful surprise," she said, kicking off her shoes on a small mat. "Come in and sit down. I need to wash up. It'll take but a minute."

I went down the small hallway I'd traversed thousands of times into a sunny kitchen that always made me feel I was home. Taking two tall glasses from the cupboard, I opened the refrigerator and pulled out the omnipresent pitcher of iced tea. I added ice, cut a lemon from the bowl, and was placing the glasses on the table when Frances reappeared.

She squeezed my shoulder as she slipped past me and into her usual chair. Her cheeks were pink, her hair slightly windblown, and she looked as happy as I'd seen her in a while. These chickens had brought her out of a low spell and had given her something she enjoyed again. Or was there something else behind her cheery glow?

"Ready for your date?" I asked.

"Jessica, I told you, it isn't a date. I'm merely having dinner with an old friend of your grandfather's." She took a sip of tea, dabbing at the condensation dripping from the bottom of the glass.

"Where are you going?" I asked, studying her closely to see if I detected any new vibes coming off her.

"We're going to a new little Italian restaurant off Post Oak. If it's good, perhaps you and I can go sometime." She sounded very pragmatic. I waited, hoping for a little more information. She met my eyes and stared back at me before shaking her head. "Jessica, you are becoming almost as nosy as your mother."

"No, I'm not," I protested. "You're going to a new Italian place. That's great." I swiped at the drops on my glass.

"He was a friend of your grandfather's," she said. "It will be nice to catch up with him. Someday, you'll realize how valuable it is to have people who remember the same generational references—the shows, the news, the music. Word from the bird, it'll razz your berries."

My mouth dropped open. "It will *what*?"

She smiled. "Exactly. How about you? Are you and Evan doing something this evening?"

I sighed. "Not exactly."

"Oh, dear. Is anything wrong?"

I gave Frances a quick run-down of Evan's new girlfriend. I did an excellent job of being nonjudgmental and neutral in my description. Still, I noticed a sharp, almost minuscule twitch of her eyebrow when I told her how grabby and possessive Gabriella had seemed.

"I imagine it would be difficult for most women to understand the close friendship you and Evan share," she finally said when I wound down. "Perhaps she needs a little time to grow accustomed to it, and maybe she'll warm up to you when she understands that you two are genuinely just friends?" She'd raised this statement at the end into question form, as if not sure Evan and I *were* just friends.

"Frances, we *are* just friends," I insisted. "But still." I connected two water droplets on the tabletop with my finger, twirling them into one bigger drop. "But still, this is going to change things."

"Change is inevitable," she said gently. "You know that, sweetheart. But you and Evan have been friends for a long time. That aspect doesn't have to change. Although it might take a little adjustment on both of your parts. Have you talked to him about it?"

"No. I just found out about it." I connected a third water drop to my tiny puddle. "I need to hurry up and find someone too," I finally said.

She put a hand over my mine. Her fingers felt cool and smooth. "Jessica, this is not a competition."

"I didn't say it was."

Her fingers tightened a shade. "You will find the right man at the right time."

"What if I don't? It seems like everyone has someone, and suddenly, I look around, and I don't."

She released my hand and straightened her shoulders in a look I knew all too well. Frances generally didn't meddle. She wasn't nosy about my life. She never told me what to do. She would ask me leading questions or tell me relevant stories to get me pointed in the right direction. But sometimes—sometimes, she felt the need to give me what she considered to be unadulterated truths. There have been some instances where maybe I didn't want to hear her truths, but once she had this look, there were no options but to hear her out. I sat back in my chair.

"It seems to me that this is the first I've heard of you actively wanting to find a beau," she began. "I seem to recall your mother asking about several young men she knew that might be perfectly suited for you, but you had neither the time nor the interest to get to know them."

"Frances—"

She held up a hand. "And suddenly, Evan has found someone. Whether she is the right someone for him or not remains to be seen. But he is actively seeking a partner, which is more than you have been doing. I'm not saying you are wrong in any way. I understand how hard you've worked to make your business successful. That, in and of itself, is admirable. But you can do both. You can be a successful business owner and have a happy relationship. You have, instead, chosen to focus on your other interests over and above finding a husband at this point in time."

I wanted to argue with her, but there wasn't much to dispute. "I know," I said, caving more quickly than usual. "But now I feel like I'm behind. Everyone is paired up. What if I'm left with the squashed and rotted avocados at the bottom of the pile? The ones that should have been thrown out five days ago, but the produce guy was too lazy to do it, and now they're oozing brown goop all over." I thumped my head down on the table.

Frances smiled. "You most definitely have a way with words, and most assuredly, you will find the right someone. I think it's safe to say you will not end up with an old oozy avocado."

I didn't know how she could be so sure of that. Then again, she always tended to be very optimistic about my future. I guess we'd see.

On my way home, a thought drifted up from the recesses of my mind, and I turned it over, trying to decide how I felt about it. Frances was right—my mother had asked me only two weeks ago if I would go out with the son of one of her friends who'd recently moved to the area. Her friends had moved here several years ago, but their son had gone to school elsewhere, taken a job in LA, and recently relocated to Houston. You know, not a date, she'd said, more like a friendly welcome to Houston kind of thing. Of course, I'd immediately said no. Maybe this was the kind of thing I needed to stop avoiding. Maybe he was a nice guy who would appreciate being shown around his new city. Then again, he was a grown adult whose parents had lived here for years, so it wasn't like he was brand new to Houston. But still.

As soon as I got home, I dialed my mother before I had a chance to change my mind.

"Hey, Mom," I said when she picked up. "I was wondering..." I hesitated, feeling a sudden recoil. I ignored it and pushed on. "Remember a couple of weeks ago, you mentioned that your friend's son had just moved to town, and you said he'd appreciate someone showing him around? Um..." I petered out.

"I'll call her now," she trilled. "His name is Chaz, and I'm sure he would love to meet you. I'll ring you right back." She hung up before I had a chance to change my mind. I'd changed my mind. I redialed. This was a bad idea. I didn't want to meet someone named Chaz. My call went straight to voicemail.

"Mom, it's me. You know what? Never mind. This is a bad idea. I don't want to meet this guy. So, call me back, okay?"

I closed my eyes and rubbed my temples. Addie, who'd been trying to greet me since I'd walked in, was still cavorting around, refusing to be ignored. I picked up one of her favorite ropes, and we ran upstairs to play tug-of-war on the carpet without her slipping. Tired of that game, she ran and got her favorite plastic carrot, which she dangled enticingly in front of me, squeaking and pulling away as I lunged. Those snow-white paws moved fast. We were still playing when my phone finally rang.

"Hi, honey, it's me. I wanted to let you know I passed your contact information to Chaz's mother. We think you kids will have a great time together. She will get it to him immediately, so expect a call!" I breathed quietly into the phone. I didn't want to do this. "Jessica? Are you still there? I also got your message about changing your mind. Don't be silly. It's about time you started looking for someone appropriate to date." She paused, listening to the squeaking. "Anyway, let me know how your date goes."

"What do you mean, someone appropriate?" I asked.

"I don't mean anything. It's just that you spend all your time with your friends and dogs, and it wouldn't hurt you to start meeting some men that could be potential husband material."

Right about now, spending the rest of my life hanging out with Evan and the dogs seemed preferable to going out on setups and blind dates.

CHAPTER FIVE

I had a general idea of where Christine lived and found her street easily. Her house was adjacent to a park that we'd always referred to as Pumpkin Park, so called because of a pumpkin carriage on the playground that has enamored little princesses for years. I couldn't remember the last time I'd been here.

I'd arrived a few minutes early, so I drove slowly, looking for house numbers. The street was Sunday morning quiet, and hardly anyone was up and about yet. Newspapers rested on newly watered lawns, and a gentle breeze blew through the live oak branches shading the street.

I noticed two people standing outside the front door at the last house. There was something about their body language and demeanor that seemed off. The man had a phone pressed to his ear, and even at a distance, I could see his mouth moving as if he was yelling into the phone. I pulled along the curb, scraping my tire halfway up it, so absorbed was I in watching them. The number on the house indicated that this was Christine's. It wasn't until I turned off my engine and opened the door that I registered the mournful baying of a dog that seemed to be playing on a loop from somewhere nearby. Ah-woo-woo-woo. Ah-woo-woo-woo. Ah-woo-woo-woo. It gave me chills.

I looked at the people again, wondering why they weren't doing anything about the dog. The man on the phone was older and wore a private security uniform. The other was a woman in an expensive-looking dressing gown. She clutched the edges of her robe tightly across her chest, holding them together as if the security guard might try to forcibly expose her. They took turns peering through a vertical window beside the door before turning away and walking in tight circles.

They watched as I approached, but no one said anything. Finally, the woman let go of her robe with one hand and held the free hand to her ear as if that could block out the sound of the dog.

"Is everything okay?" I asked, stopping short of the front stoop.

"Stand back, Miss," said the security guard. Up close, I could see the hand holding his cell phone was trembling badly. "We're waiting for the police, and I need you to clear away."

Ah-woo-woo-woo. Ah-woo-woo-woo. Ah-woo- woo-woo.

"Is that Lucille?" I asked. I moved towards the door, inserting myself between them, and approached the window. "Is Christine okay?" The glare rendered it impossible to see directly inside, so I did like they'd been doing and leaned close to the glass, shading it with one hand.

"Ma'am. Ma'am, I need you to step back," said the security guard. His voice rose to a high-pitched warble that shook as significantly as his hand.

Through the window, I could see a long, dim hallway leading toward the back of the house. It was wide enough for twin console tables overflowing with large vases of fresh flowers. A grand staircase rose away on the left with a wide landing midway up. What lay at the bottom of the stairs caused my heart to jump nearly into my mouth. On the hard marble floor lay a woman. I couldn't swear that it was Christine because her head was turned away, but judging from the heartrending sounds coming from the bloodhound by her side, it had to be.

I turned to the pair beside me, my breathing speeding up to match theirs. They looked at me like small children, hoping I was the adult sent to handle this scary situation.

"Is she…" I took a deep breath, trying to get control. "Did you call an ambulance?" I turned and peered back through the window. The woman was dressed in a flowing formal gown. The bloodhound was lying beside the woman, her giant head resting on the woman's hip, lifting every few seconds to bellow her mournful dirge.

"Can we break in? We need to check on her. Someone needs to get the dog." My mind had already skipped past the idea that Christine could be dead, caught instead on the heartbreaking loop of grief that made me want to cover my ears and hum loudly to block it out. That anguish was nothing like I'd ever heard before. We needed to get Lucille out of there. I grabbed the door handle and was shocked when the lever yielded to my touch. "It's open! We need to go check on her."

The security guard turned towards the street, scanning for backup.

"He already went in," said the woman. "She's…she's passed." Her fingers grasped her robe so tightly that her knuckles went white. Up close, I could see the burgundy material was silk, covering what looked to be matching pajamas. Her feet were shoved into black leather slippers, several sizes too large. She was in her sixties, her skin a pale, papery white in the morning light. The lack of makeup made her look vulnerable and surprised.

"We need to get the dog out of there," I said, holding my hands to my ears, trying to block out the rhythmic lament. Both of them ignored me. At the next Ah-woo-woo-woo, I seized the handle and pushed, stepping into the cool air of the entry.

"Miss! You can't go in there. It's a—we need to wait for the police," said the security guard. I wondered how many days he'd put on his uniform and trundled off to work expecting to chit-chat with residents, pick up papers for folks who were out of town, and maybe, on an exciting night, chase off kids intent on toilet papering someone's yard. Judging from the sheen of sweat on his alarmingly pale face, finding a dead resident wasn't something he'd planned on this morning.

The bloodhound didn't even register my presence.

"Lucille? Lucille. Hey, baby," I said in my softest, most soothing voice. She was unresponsive—lost in a world of desperation. As I edged closer, I could see the woman's hair escaping from a complicated chignon, strands caught in pools of coagulated blood as sticky looking as tree resin. Red smudges dotted the hallway, but I couldn't determine if they were footprints or pawprints. It seemed unlikely that Christine had moved since she landed where she now lay. As if the dog's reaction hadn't been enough, a quick glance at the profile confirmed this was Christine. At the bottom of the stairs, one high-heeled shoe rested not far from the foot it once held.

I dropped into a low crouch and wiggled closer to the dog. "C'mere, baby," I coaxed. Lucille didn't even look up. Her long, silky ears brushed against Christine's body every time she raised her head to howl. Half-closed red eyes were ringed with black fur, and folds of skin drooped along the sides of her jaws. She took quick, shallow breaths between cries, her cheeks fluttering in and out as if she could hold onto Christine by drawing in her scent.

It looked like she'd been there for a long time; long strings of drool dripped from her jowls, creating a crosshatch of puddles and streaks across Christine's teal dress. I inched closer. Lucille was on the far side of the body, and I hesitated. I needed to work my way over and snag her collar, but I didn't want to track through the blood. I finally got up and edged around, crossing near the feet, taking care not to disturb the shoe on the floor. The other shoe was still on Christine's foot, although the heel appeared to be caught in the fabric of her dress—a long gash visible along the skirt where it had ripped right through.

Near the bottom of the stairs lay a large nylon dog bone, nearly a foot long, the ends chewed to frizzled knots. I closed my eyes and tried not to think about what had happened. I needed to comfort Lucille. My heart pinched as I wondered if dogs felt guilt. It seemed entirely possible that Christine had tripped over the dog toy, but would Lucille understand that? *Could* a dog understand that?

Her vocalization had quieted from a loud, mournful baying to a soft, snuffling cry. I leaned over and snagged her collar, giving it a slow tug. "C'mon, baby," I said softly. "Let's go outside." I wondered what was taking the police so long to get here, not to mention the ambulance. Not that Christine needed an ambulance, but still. What if she had?

Lucille didn't budge, and I wondered how I could move her nearly ninety pounds if she didn't want to go. I held the collar with one hand and put pressure on her shoulder to help get her started. Finally, she stood, allowing me to lead her to the front door. She walked, or rather, crawled, with her belly nearly touching the ground as if the weight of her world collapsing was unbearable. Tears clouded my eyes, and I squinted into the sun as we exited the door.

"You shouldn't have gone in there," said the security guard, stepping back and grounding himself with the scolding. "Don't you go far. The police will want to talk to you. You can explain to them how you messed with the scene. I told you not to go in. You heard me tell her, right?" He turned to the woman beside him.

I could hear sirens approaching, and I led the dog a short way onto the grass, where she hunched and relieved herself. The stench nearly made me retch.

"Oh, heavens," said the lady in the robe, holding a hand to her nose and turning away. "Oh, that is appalling." She stepped off the porch and made her way several yards across the grass, moving away from us. I can't say I blamed her. The poor dog must have been holding this in for hours, and the stress had created a toxic brew that could clear a crowd. Even the security guard's thin chest shuddered with a dry heave, and he turned away, holding his palm against his lips.

A Houston police cruiser pulled to the curb and shut off the siren. Lucille finished, and I led her upwind to a spot under a tree closer to the street. Neighbors began drifting out of their houses to see what was happening. This was a part of Houston where police sirens usually passed through on their way elsewhere. Once they saw the lady in the robe, they gravitated toward her to get the news. The police officer made his way to the private security guard, and they put their heads together, whispering quietly.

No one paid much attention to Lucille and me, and for that, I was thankful. I didn't know if dogs could go into shock, but this one seemed close. Her eyes had a vacant look, and she didn't seem to be focusing on anything or even notice the activity beginning to buzz around us. A low moan reverberated in her chest as she pulled her breath in and out. I rubbed her neck and murmured her name, telling her it would be okay. It was not going to be okay.

CHAPTER SIX

I'm unsure how long we sat there, at least long enough for a group of ants to find us and begin crawling up my leg. I hopped to my feet, wishing I had a blanket or something else we could sit on. I brushed at Lucille, ensuring the ants weren't crawling on her too. The security officer, who'd been on the scene when I arrived, tottered past, hunched over and unsteady on his feet. I hoped he would be okay—judging from his pallid face, I wasn't sure. Another man approached me, leaving the clutch of people still milling near the door.

"Hi," he said, his glance alternating between Lucille and me. "I'm David Pierce. I live next door. My wife, Irene, found..." he stopped and closed his eyes briefly. "She found Christine this morning when she heard the dog barking."

"I'm Jessie Gallagher. I was supposed to meet with Christine this morning. I met her yesterday, and she planned to show me her studio." I stopped myself before launching into mindless babble about how I wanted a painting of my dog, how I'd liked Christine on sight, and how I'd thought we might be friends. None of that mattered.

David Pierce looked to be in his early sixties. His hair was predominately gray, precisely cut, and a near-perfect match to his eyes that looked sad behind their silver wire-frame glasses. He was good-looking in an understated, classic way. Judging from his clothes and cleats, he'd been pulled from a round of golf. He squatted on his haunches and reached out a hand to Lucille. "Hey, Lucille." Her head hung down, and she didn't respond.

"I'm a little worried about her," I said. "I've never seen a dog this distressed before. Do you know if there's someone that can care for her?"

He blinked slowly, his eyelids on a delay. "She was Christine's baby," he said. "She and Michael never had children, but when this dog came into her life, she poured her heart into her." He ran gentle fingers down Lucille's ear, and she shifted as if recognizing the touch.

"She seems to be responding to you." I let my sentence drag out.

"She's a sweetheart," he said, rising to his feet. "But Irene... Irene has cats." He brushed at his pants even though they'd not touched the ground. "Let me see if I can find anything out. We've been neighbors with the Wagners for years, even before they divorced."

"She mentioned her ex hates dogs," I said. "I can't imagine she would have wanted Lucille to go to him."

He affected a laugh. "Yes, Christine's ex-husband would not want Lucille. I think she had a sister, though. Let me check with my wife. Is there anything I can bring you? I'd invite you in, but as I said, Irene has cats and some expensive crystal collections." I wasn't sure what that had to do with anything. Noticing my look, he continued. "Lucille can be a little bit clumsy."

"Maybe you could bring her a bowl of water? And do you have a towel or something we could sit on? There are some ants around here."

"Let me see what I can do," he said, giving Lucille a final rub before moving away.

I stood and pulled Lucille around the yard as much as I could. She was heavy and had no interest in walking around, so in the end, we only moved about six feet before she threw herself down with a groan. At least we were still in the shade. David Pierce returned several minutes later with a large mixing bowl half full of water and a heavy blanket that he spread out for me. We coaxed Lucille onto the blanket, but she showed no interest in the water. He told me the police were in contact with Christine's sister, and they expected her to arrive as soon as possible. I didn't know if that meant in minutes, hours, or days, being that I had no idea where she lived. David wandered away as if afraid I might stick him with the dog if he lingered.

I knew the police would probably want to talk to me since I'd barged in and changed their crime scene by removing the dog, and I was surprised no one had come to question me yet. I changed positions, trying to get comfortable on the lumpy ground. Several police cars had arrived, and all the officers remained on site. They'd put crime scene tape up, blocking off the entrance, and one officer stood outside, keeping the neighbors away. An ambulance had come and gone, replaced by a white panel van that said Harris County Medical Examiner on the side. The neighbors congregated at the house next door, and the crowd grew as the morning went on.

I'd grown weary of watching and was contemplating my options when a shadow fell across the blanket. I squinted and held a hand over my eyes, trying to make out who was standing in front of me. The sun had moved, and I was looking directly into the blazing orb, unable to discern more than it was a medium to tall man. My eyes watered, and I looked down.

"Excuse me," he said. "What's, um, what's going on here?" I tried to look up again, but the sun was too harsh.

"Could you move a few feet one way or another?" I asked. "It's extremely bright."

He took three steps to the right, moving into the shade of the tree. Beyond the dots still dancing in my eyes, I saw a guy, probably in his early thirties, dressed in boring business casual and clutching a manila folder to his chest like a high-school girl would cradle a book. He flicked one thumb back and forth along the edge of the folder and jerked his chin towards the activity near the house.

"What's going on? Is everything okay?" His voice rose and cracked a little at the end.

"And you are?" I asked. I couldn't tell if this was some looky-loo or if he had genuine business being there. Then again, I wasn't the official gatekeeper. What did I care?

"Martin Amos," he said, acting as if that alone should tell me everything I needed to know. His eyes flitted to Lucille, then back to me.

"Hi," I said. "Do you know the homeowner here?"

"Yes, I work for the estate attorneys handling her business. I'm supposed to drop off her signed paperwork."

For a minute, it flashed through my mind—wow, these guys move fast, before I realized he probably didn't know Christine was dead yet.

"You might need to go talk to that officer up there," I said, gesturing towards the front door. He gripped his folder, curling it into a cylinder and bopping a hand against the end.

"Is Christine okay?" His face had a slightly soft, pasty look, broken up by faded pink acne scars.

"Did you know her well?" I asked, hoping he was a disinterested document runner. He didn't look wholly disinterested. More pink bloomed on his neck, and streams of sweat ran down his temples. His armpits were already dark with moisture, and I worried he might start hyperventilating. "Do you need to sit down?" I asked.

"What do you mean, did I?" he asked. His folder was now rolled tight, and his fingers continued their relentless twisting. Whatever documents he had in there would need to be steamed and pressed with a hot iron to get them to lie flat again. "What happened?"

Lucille had finally relaxed, or collapsed, into a semi-slumber. Her head lay heavy on her paws, and her breath came in deep quivering puffs. I ran my fingers gently along her head and down her neck. "It looks like she fell down the stairs, I think."

"And? And is she going to be okay?" I could tell by the pitch of his voice he already knew the answer.

"No. She's gone." I looked up at him. He was staring at the front door, his mouth moving silently as if having a conversation with himself. "Are you okay? Did you know her well? The neighbor told me her sister will be here soon. Maybe you should give her the documents? Or you could give them to the police?"

His attention swung back to me. "Uh, no. I should probably call my boss. I'm not sure what they'll want me to do with this." He looked down at the folder in his hands. "Oh, crap." He unrolled it and tried to roll it in the opposite direction, only making it worse. "I was supposed to deliver these yesterday. My boss is gonna kill me."

I tried to think of something encouraging to say, but he was making a total mess of what I presumed was Christine's final will and testament. Then again, what's a wrinkle or two so long as it's still clear who's getting what?

A man in a suit approached us from the front door, holding a notepad and a pen. Based on prior experiences I'd had, I presumed that this was a detective. Finally. I could give my statement, and if someone would take Lucille, I could get out of here.

The document runner wandered slowly away as the investigator approached.

My conversation with the detective was succinct. I'd expected a lengthy interview or a lecture on ruining their crime scene. But he seemed pretty blasé about the whole thing. From what I could discern, they appeared inclined to believe this was a tragic accident. I ran him through what I knew, why I was there, and why I'd gone in, even knowing I shouldn't. He knelt down and gave Lucille a sympathetic rub, leaning his face against the top of her head.

"Real shame about the dog," he said. "People never think about the heartbreak pets go through in this kind of situation, but I've seen it so many times. You can't explain stuff like this to an animal." I searched his left hand for a wedding ring. This was my kind of man, but alas, someone else had already snapped him up. "The victim's sister should be here soon. We appreciate you looking after the pooch. Think you can stay a little while longer till she gets here?"

I assured him that wasn't a problem, although I didn't want to face Christine's grieving sister. I wondered if the sister was Gabriella's mother or if there were more siblings. A knot of anxiety started to form in my gut. He wrote down my information in case they had additional questions, then disappeared back inside the house.

Now, I found myself on high alert, watching for approaching cars. There wasn't much traffic on this road, and most cars stopped at the far end near the playground. The joyful shriek of children was a blessed burst of ordinary clamor helping offset the radio static of the emergency personnel moving in and out of Christine's house.

I saw the car as soon as it turned the corner. The knot in my stomach tightened, and Lucille scooted closer as if sensing my apprehension. A nondescript, white four-door sedan made its way through the tangle of emergency vehicles and pulled to a stop two doors down at the first empty stretch of curb. I could see two figures inside. They were still for a moment before leaning together for an embrace. I looked away from the tenderness of it, wishing I was anywhere but here right now. I had no doubt Christine's sister felt the same.

The middle-aged woman leaned hard against a man I assumed was her husband as they shuffled toward the house. He steered her gently, her head half buried against his chest. She looked enough like Christine that seeing her walk down the street was slightly disconcerting. I saw Christine's limp body in my mind, then looked again at this discernably alive version. On closer inspection, it was clear that the sister was shorter than Christine, with a plumpish ring around her middle that matched her husband's. Her features were similar but slightly off. She wore dark purple scrubs and rubber shoes, making me think she'd run out of a hospital setting to be here. Her husband wore baggy shorts, a faded bowling shirt, and white gym socks pulled up his calves.

A small contingent of women from the neighbor's house motored off the porch to intercept them before they reached Christine's front door. They surrounded the couple, fussing and clucking, reaching out for ungainly pats and hugs. Lucille and I stayed where we were, but I got to my feet, feeling it showed disrespect to remain lounging on the blanket.

The next-door neighbor, Irene, had dressed, spruced up her

hair, and now took her place as chief information purveyor, pointing and gesticulating toward Christine's front door. Her voice rose and fell as if telling a story, and I couldn't imagine how the sister must be feeling. I was relieved when one of the officers walked over and retrieved the couple, shooing the flock of women away.

I settled back down with Lucille, still dreading the handoff. Lucille was awake, pitiful little whimpers sounding deep in her chest. I focused on her, running my hand along her side and murmuring soft words of comfort. It wasn't the first time I'd had to lie to a dog about everything being alright, but I still felt terrible about it. This wasn't even the first dog I'd dealt with whose owner had died. The last one had been Henry, and that, at least, had had a good outcome. The difference was he hadn't seemed overly attached to his previous owner. Lucille, on the other hand—well, her heart was breaking in front of me.

It wasn't long before the sister and her husband came out of the house and approached me. I popped to my feet again, clutching the leash in a sweaty palm. Lucille didn't even raise her head.

"I'm so sorry for your loss," I said.

"Thank you," said the woman. Her eyes were red, and her nose was puffy. She clutched a tissue in one hand, and several more peeked from a side pocket of her purse. "I'm Christine's sister, Penny, and this is my husband, Bill."

"I'm Jessie. I met your sister yesterday, and she invited me to see her studio this morning. I can't imagine what a shock this is. She seemed like a remarkable person."

Penny gave me a weak smile as tears spilled onto her cheeks. Her husband pulled her against his chest while she tried to collect herself.

"The officer said you've been taking care of Lucille," Bill said.

"We very much appreciate that. We know how much she meant to Christine."

Penny took a deep breath before sinking down next to the big dog. Bill knelt too, but he stayed near the edge of the blanket, giving his wife a little more space. Penny reached out a trembling hand. "Hey, Lucille," she said softly. Lucille lifted her head and stretched her neck forward, her bloodhound nose moving slowly up and around Penny's hand. Penny's hand continued to shake, but she held it as still as possible while the dog inhaled her scent. When Lucille finished sniffing, she scooted closer before dropping her head onto Penny's lap. Waves of grief collided and merged between the two, rolling outward nearly physical in its intensity. Emotions that I'd glossed over since I saw Christine's body swelled in my chest, and a sob choked in my throat.

I felt like an intruder at such an intimate and private moment until Bill reached over and squeezed my shoulder, his warm brown eyes radiating sympathy and inclusion. I wasn't sure why I felt so emotional—I'd only met Christine once. I was probably being affected by the dog's grief. And, of course, Penny's. I'm not good with others' sadness. I gave him a watery smile before looking away.

After a few minutes of sobbing over Lucille's head, Penny fought for composure. Bill rubbed her back and murmured soft-nothings until she finally raised her splotchy face and fished around her purse for another tissue.

"I'm sorry," she said, presumably to me. She blew her nose loudly and wiped the back of one hand across her eyes. "This has been such a shock."

"I can't imagine," I said. "I wish there was something I could say or do."

Penny slipped one leg sideways, trying to get more comfortable under the weight of Lucille's head. "This poor baby. She was so devoted to my sister. I don't know how she will adjust."

"Dogs are resilient," I said, although looking at the devastation that was Lucille right now, I wasn't sure that that was always the case.

"Do you know much about dogs?" she asked. "We've never had a dog, but of course, we'll take Lucille home and care for her." I was happy to hear that. These seemed like good people, so at least I wouldn't worry that Lucille wasn't being loved.

"I'm so glad you're going to take her," I said. "I can definitely give you some pointers. And I can give you my number, so if you have any questions or need help, I will do whatever I can."

We ran through some of the most pressing basics I could think of for people who have never taken care of a dog. I recommended they find Lucille's food in the house and keep her on that since a sudden food switch can cause digestive upset in dogs. I told them she was already having some issues due to the trauma she'd experienced, so they shouldn't be surprised if those issues persisted. I felt better when they told me that Penny was a nurse, so at least she'd be looking for dehydration or other complications.

Bill said he would gather as many of Lucille's belongings as possible to take with them. They told me they lived out in Cypress, about twenty-five miles northwest of Houston. I had no real idea how to help a traumatized dog other than to offer love and give her time. Bill plugged my phone number into his phone, and I entered both of their numbers into my contact information. They would have a lot to deal with over the next few weeks, and I could only hope they would all adjust as well as possible.

I was home shortly after lunchtime, a swirl of emotions. Addie intuits my moods so well that I wasn't surprised to see her ordinarily animated energy turn subdued as she settled quietly beside me. I rubbed her mindlessly with one hand while hitting Evan's contact with the other hand. I hoped Gabriella wasn't with him because I didn't think news of her aunt's death should come from me. While Penny and Bill hadn't said anything specifically, I hadn't gotten the impression they had children, so I speculated Gabriella wasn't theirs. Then again, who knew? It wasn't like we'd talked about anything besides Lucille.

Evan answered seconds before my call went to voicemail. "Hey, Jess, what's up?" He sounded rushed.

"Hey, Evan. Is Gabriella with you?"

"No, why?"

I gave him a brief rundown of my morning, and when I was through, there were a couple beats of silence.

"Evan? Are you still there?"

"Yeah," he said. "I'm just thinking how weird it is that you keep finding dead people and their dogs."

"I don't keep finding dead people and their dogs," I protested. "I mean once."

"Okay, and now," he said. "If I didn't know you better, I might be scared."

"Evan!"

"Sorry, it's still pretty weird."

"So anyway, I didn't know if Gabriella knows yet. I didn't want her to find out from me. I wasn't sure how close she was to Christine, but I'm sure it will be a shock." Evan was quiet again. I could hear a tapping sound like keys on a keyboard. "Evan?"

"Yeah, I'm here." He sighed. "I should call her, I guess? But I'm so far behind with work."

"Well, you don't know if she knows or not. Maybe don't call and let her reach out to you?"

He groaned. "This isn't great timing. I told you I'm already behind on that project. I've got to catch up on some stuff." I didn't think Gabriella would find this response to a death in her family very supportive. Who would? But it wasn't my problem.

I spent the afternoon feeling listless and fretful. I tried to forget my morning. I tried to forget the sound of Lucille's keening and the way she'd lain over the body, faithful companion till the end. I tried not to think about how Christine had died or what she might have gone through. I pushed away thoughts of what Penny was dealing with—the emotional over-load that pulsated from her as she tried to comfort her sister's dog while working to reign in her own shock and distress.

None of these thoughts were leaving my head willingly. I finally put on my running shoes and fought through the mental exhaustion that made me feel leaden. I left Addie with a treat-filled Kong and headed out for a run. It took me several blocks before I could convince myself to build up momentum and run, and even then, it was more like a slow jog through the oppres-sive afternoon humidity. Large clouds were blowing in from the Gulf, and every time one crossed the sun, I got a slight respite from the heat. Sweat beaded my skin, sticking my hair to my neck and streaking my t-shirt in ever-widening splotches. But, in the end, the endorphins did their thing, and I arrived home slightly calmer than when I'd left.

I checked my phone and grabbed a cold bottle of water from the refrigerator. Judging from the rapid-fire succession of texts that had come in while I'd been gone, Evan hadn't managed to morph into an intuitive, caring boyfriend.

Gabriella's here, and she's really upset about her aunt.

Her parents had a big fight, and her mom left.

She's crying. What am I supposed to do?

I leaned against the counter, took a long drink of cold water, and stared at my phone. Surely, he didn't need someone to tell him what to do in this situation. Or maybe he did.

Evan, just be supportive.

The reply was immediate. I had to assume he wasn't hugging and holding her.

What does that mean?

I sighed. *Hug her. Hold her. Listen to her.*

I waited for his response, but when none came, I headed for the shower. Maybe he had taken my advice to heart. I took a long shower and then stretched, knowing my muscles would likely be sore even from that short run. I got a lot of exercise on my dog-walking rounds, but it had been a while since I'd gone for an actual run. When I rechecked my phone, there was another chain of messages from Evan.

I tried supportive, but she got mad at me. Why is she mad?

Where are you?

I told her you were there this morning. Now she's mad about that.

Do you think it's okay if I ask her to leave?

I flopped back on the floor and stared at the ceiling. I wasn't sure how I felt being Evan's love coach. Although, upon consideration, this was more akin to rudimentary human coaching.

My phone buzzed again.

She wants to fix my place up. What do you think?

It sounded as if their conversation had taken an odd turn. How did they go from family tragedy to redecorating Evan's house? Frankly, I thought it was a terrible idea. From what he'd told me not long ago, he'd tapped out what was left of his savings on a roof replacement.

After writing and deleting several responses, I decided on: *If that's what you want to do, it might be fun, but I thought you were going to wait awhile since you just got the roof replaced?*

I waited for him to reply, but he didn't. When my phone finally rang later that evening, I snatched it up. It wasn't Evan; it was Kip.

"Sweetie, hi. Sorry I didn't get back to you sooner, but Bertram was nearly *impossible* to track down. I finally heard from a friend who heard from a friend that he was down in Galveston. As if there's no cell service in Galveston." He took a breath. "Anyhoo, I guess his phone was turned off or some such nonsense. I don't believe that for a minute. Who turns their phone off? I hope he wasn't avoiding me. I can't imagine what I could have done to offend him. But, good news, he can see you tomorrow!"

I had forgotten entirely about Kip and his psychic.

"Kip, I don't know. I appreciate you going to all that trouble, but—"

"No, Jessie. You are not going to bail out on this."

"It's not that. I've got a lot going on right now. Something happened this morning, and it's thrown me. I found someone dead." I told him about my morning, but he didn't seem interested or concerned beyond a few speculations about Gabriella's possible role.

"Jessie, there will always be something going on in your life. Wouldn't having a man to share these things with be wonderful?"

"I'm sharing it with you."

"That's not what I meant, and you know it. I've already said yes, so we're doing this."

I don't know why I'd thought this was a good idea. I'm not even sure I *had* thought it was a good idea. What if this psychic told me I would end up old and alone? What if he saw all kinds of horrible things in my future? Worst yet, Frances was no spring chicken—what if he said something upsetting about her?

"What if he tells me something bad?" My voice was quiet, and there was sudden silence on the other end of the line. "Kip?"

"I'm here," he said. "Look, Bertram is just starting out, so I can't guarantee that he will or won't see anything bad. Or good. But he's given me some practice readings, and, honey, he's gentle. He didn't tell me anything bad. Okay, he did tell me I was going to meet a two-faced loser, and it wouldn't work out for me, but I always meet guys like that. Also, who wants it to work out with a two-faced loser? If you're worried about a general reading, I'm sure he can limit it to your romantic life. And since that's already dead, you have nothing to worry about. Right?"

It was hard to argue with that logic.

CHAPTER EIGHT

After Kip's call, my newly found endorphin-induced calm left me. I found myself filled with an apprehensive excitement—like the night before sleepaway camp, when you want to go and will probably have a good time but are filled with nameless misgivings nonetheless. At any rate, it was better than the darker feelings I'd been experiencing earlier. Not surprisingly, I didn't sleep well and awoke feeling vaguely testy. I was irritated that I'd never heard back from Evan. Why bother me for advice in the first place if you're only going to leave me hanging.

Kip had told me my appointment with Bertram was scheduled for six-thirty. He'd given me his address and said he would meet me there. It was hard to concentrate on my existing business. Still, I can only ignore my biscuit baking for so long before I start running low on inventory. I tried to settle into my comforting routine as much as possible, but my mind was abuzz, and I had to recheck myself constantly. I couldn't afford to make any mistakes with my biscuits; a few poor reviews can sink a small business faster than anything.

On my afternoon dog walks, I tried to quiet my thoughts. I

didn't want the distress from yesterday to be a distraction. I also didn't want the negativity I'd felt toward Evan's new girlfriend to cloud anything, either. I needed to be serene, my mind undisturbed, to get the best possible reading. A hum of excitement filled me at the idea of discovering something about my future husband. If I was going to do this, I might as well do it right.

Then I wondered if Bertram would be able to read my mind. I hoped not. Suddenly, impure thoughts began popping into my head like dirty whack-a-moles. A flash of this, a glimpse of that. As fast as I tried to shoo them away, another one popped up. Would he be able to see this? I closed my eyes and rubbed my hands over my face, trying to disrupt this onslaught of mental images. What was wrong with me? I took a breath and calmed myself. He was a psychic, not a mind-reader. Those were probably different skills, right?

I'd written down the address last night and mapped it out online. It was approximately sixteen miles from my house, north of downtown, and a little bit east in an area I'd never visited. I'd sped past these neighborhoods on the tollway going to and from the airport but never stopped.

I showered and changed after my dog rounds, grabbed a quick sandwich, and fed Addie before leaving my house extra early. Despite rush hour traffic, I found myself making decent time. Just as I'd thought, Bertram's neighborhood was a little worn. I cruised the blocks slowly, taking in the ambiance. The houses here were tiny, the majority one-story with an overabundance of burglar bars. Several homeowners had taken additional security measures and had added tall, wrought iron fences with spiky points on top. If only they'd had working gates, it might have been beneficial, but of all the ones I passed, most of the gates were either off the track or appeared to be rusted in the open position.

I glanced at my dashboard clock. I was fifteen minutes early. According to the directions on my phone, my destination was ahead on the right. I rolled past an auto salvage yard and fixed my sights on the next house. My phone began bleating at me that I had arrived. As I continued on, it recalculated and directed me to take the next right. I couldn't find any street numbers, so I followed the Google map directions and circled the block. Again, my phone assured me I had reached my destination at the auto salvage yard.

I pulled onto a dirt driveway outside a corrugated metal fence and searched for a street number. Below a drooping string of barbed wire, giant red letters proclaimed this as Bubba's Auto Salvage. I must have written the address wrong, or maybe I'd entered it incorrectly on my app. Shifting into park, I peered at the screen where I'd entered the street address last night. Tires crunched on the drive beside me, and through my passenger side window, I saw Kip staring out at the salvage yard, his mouth drawn back in a horrified frown.

I exited my car and approached Kip, my cute flat-bottom sandals sliding a little on the dusty gravel. His window slid down silently.

"This can't be right," he said. "Bertram told me he was moving a few weeks ago, but in no way would he ever move to —" he looked wildly, side to side. "To somewhere like this. Let me call him. I'm sure there's a misunderstanding."

The salvage yard was sizeable for something smack dab in the middle of a residential neighborhood. Although, this wasn't conventional suburbia. I'd passed other commercial properties when I'd gone around the block. This is what happens with no zoning regulations, I thought. A red metal building bisected the fence in the middle, dirty steel doors closed and padlocked shut. A faded sign in the window said Open, although it looked like the sign had been there for decades. I moved towards the door.

"Bertram," I heard Kip say, sounding shrill. "Where are you? The address you gave me was wrong."

Through the dirty window in the door, I could make out towering shelves stacked with dusty metallic objects I couldn't identify and bins piled with additional metal chunks, also unidentifiable. The only thing I recognized with certainty was an enormous gumball machine inside the door. I wondered what year those oversized gumballs had rolled off their assembly line.

"You live in a *junkyard*?" I walked back towards Kip's car, feeling the need to wash my hands even though I hadn't touched anything. I regretted dressing up as much as I had. I should have worn the dog-walking clothes I'd had on earlier. Kip was mm-hmming into his phone, even as he unbuckled his seatbelt and stepped out of his car. He frowned again as he observed the dust poof in clouds under his shoe. "Okay, okay." He swiped at the screen and looked at me. "He's going to come around and let us in."

Despite the care I'd taken dressing, Kip—as always—outshone me. He sported tight salmon-colored pants, short at the ankle with a pair of conspicuously expensive leather boat shoes, and a tight white shirt topped with a lightweight, custom-fitted blazer. A fluttery pocket square that matched his pants rustled in the breeze against his chest.

"Wow," I said. "You look great."

"Thank you, darling. You look nice as well." That was probably the highest praise I would ever get from Kip Willetto, and I felt a flash of pride. He moved closer and gripped my upper arm, leaning into me for courage. "I had no idea Bertram was living somewhere like this," he whispered as if anyone else might over-hear. "Look at this place." We stood silently, taking it all in. The corrugated fence shielded most of the yard from view, but even from here, I could see tall metal scaffolding holding an array of hubcaps and what appeared to be side mirrors. A stack of tires rested against the fence and rose like a giant Jenga game, waiting for someone to knock it over. A metallic scent filled the air so strong I could taste it on the back of my tongue, intermixed with rubber and heavy lubricants. I leaned closer to Kip, endeavoring to catch his expensive, woodsy scent.

Within moments, we heard the screech of metal on metal.

"Hola! Kip and Kip's friend! Yoo-hoo! Over here!"

To the left of the building, a section of gate rolled back, and a bantam-weight, dark-haired man waved at us. Kip waved back and shouted, "Hola, amigo!" Then he looked at me, took a breath, and said, "Okay. This is fine. I'm sure it's not an indication of how your search for a man will go."

We moved in tandem towards Bertram, Kip still clutching my arm. His nostrils flared as we advanced toward the opening, and the metallic scent intensified. He let go of my arm long enough to return Bertram's embrace before turning to introduce me.

"Bertram Mendoza, this is Jessie Gallagher. Jessie Gallagher, this is Bertram Mendoza."

"No, Kip, no! Remember, we talked about this." Bertram stamped his foot against the packed dirt and huffed. "It's Bertram. No other name. I am Bertram." He turned and pulled the gate closed, slamming it against its base before sliding a hinge down and securing a lock. He turned back, looking on the verge of tears. "I said so, remember?"

Kip made a little clucking noise as we picked our way past two rusty forklifts and a pile of broken pallets toward a wooden staircase affixed to the back of the building. I searched for something polite to say to try and alter the mood.

"I'm certainly excited about my reading," I said as we made our way single file up the stairs. "Kip told me how talented you are."

Bertram glanced back, his face hopeful. "He did?"

"Oh, yes. I've never had a reading, and I'm a little nervous."

"Me too," he said as he pulled open a door at the top. "Please, come in."

I squeezed past him into a small, dark room that looked about what you'd expect to find over a salvage yard. An air conditioning unit turned to high speed blocked one of the two windows. It hummed loudly and dripped a line of condensation down the plywood wall beneath. In spite of its best efforts, the room was hot, and I could sense the hair near my temples coiling in the humidity. Against the far wall, hunched a lumpy sofa covered neatly with a handmade blanket in vibrant shades of green and orange. This appeared to be both a living area and a bedroom space. He had a tiny refrigerator and a hot plate, and through a partially opened door, I saw the edge of a porcelain toilet.

He'd set up a table in the middle of the room and covered it with a purple velvet cloth. Tiny cut-out hearts dotted the table like confetti at a child's birthday party. The smell of peppermint and lavender filled the room, and I spotted a diffuser on the floor beside an uncovered electrical outlet. Bertram stood watching me, his fingers plucking nervously at a wide leather bracelet that circled his left wrist.

"Please, you sit? I get ready," he said, gesturing towards two mismatched chairs on one side of the table. Kip and I arranged ourselves carefully while Bertram disappeared into the bathroom.

"I can't be held liable for anything that happens here today," whispered Kip into my ear. "I mean, he's done some readings for me. Okay, not readings exactly," he said. "He's told me some things that seemed true. For instance, he predicted one of the fabrics that I wanted to use for my latest pillow line would be a smash, and in fact, it was the one that launched my success in Japan."

I ran my finger along the velvet edge of the table covering and wondered how normal people met their matches. I'll bet not many turned to a psychic over the top of an auto parts salvage yard as their first step.

CHAPTER NINE

Bertram emerged from the bathroom wearing a black tunic and flowy black pants that seemed too big for him. Around his neck, he wore an assortment of crystal necklaces that overlapped on his chest, clicking slightly as the stones rubbed together. The hair on half of his head flared to the side where he'd apparently disrupted his coiffure when he'd changed. He brushed at it roughly, then picked up a thick white candle and set it on the table before settling himself in the chair across from us. He struck a match to light the candle, biting nervously at his lower lip.

In the dim light, the flame danced, changing the ambiance. Bertram blew out the match, pinching it to ensure it was out before setting the tip on one of the cut-out hearts. He looked up at me, his dark eyes gentle.

"Let us take a moment to center ourselves," he said quietly. From the nervous jiggle of his leg, I guessed he meant himself more than me. "I want so much to help you," he said, his voice soft, his accent fading as he recited what sounded like practiced phrases. He took a deep breath and closed his eyes. I followed his lead. Beside me, I could feel Kip fidgeting, and I reached out a hand and smacked at him without opening my eyes.

We sat silently for a couple of minutes, breathing and listening to the discordant whir of the air conditioner. At first, my mind flitted like a moth beating against a lampshade. I wondered if Bertram would tell me exactly where I would meet my husband and what he would be like. How long until I met him? Would he be cute? Funny? Smart? Then I flashed on Gabriella, looking at me over Evan's shoulder. That look on her face was so smug. Forget that. Focus on finding my own person. This wasn't about them; it was about me. And finally, my mind began to quiet until I was floating along on the drone of the air conditioner, my breathing syncing to Bertram's soft breaths.

"Good," he finally said, opening his eyes and smiling at me. I felt groggy in the heat, but I also felt calm. "Good," he repeated. "You relax now, and I reach out to your guides and see what they want to share with you." He closed his eyes again, and I wondered if I was supposed to be doing anything. I have guides? I tried to feel them, wondering how many I had and what they looked like. I felt a nervous giggle bubbling in my throat, and I didn't dare look over at Kip in case it ripped forth. I could almost feel my guides shaking their heads now, like see what we have to put up with?

"Hmm." Bertram's eyebrows drew together, creating perpendicular creases that zoomed up his forehead.

"What?" I asked. "Is it something bad?"

He opened his eyes and patted my hand across the table. "Shh. I try to understand what it is they show me."

"What? What are they showing you?"

He sighed. "You try to center again." I endeavored to recapture my calm feeling. "Okay, I see strong female energy around you. I see someone, how I say, bossy with black hair." My mind raced. A bossy woman.

"My old manager was bossy," I said. "Her hair wasn't black, though. Is she there? Is she trying to talk to me?" My old boss had been murdered last year, but they'd caught her killer, so what could she possibly want to talk to me about? Her dog? Henry was with Evan now, living the good life. "What does she want?"

Bertram looked up at me. "She is dead?"

"Yes, she was killed last year."

"No, I don' talk to the dead. This is not that kind of reading."

"Oh." I probably should have researched what I was getting into before I came.

"And this bossy energy has white hair. And is smart."

Frances had white hair. Well, grayish hair. "My grandmother?" Frances wasn't bossy. She was one of the least bossy people I knew.

"I thought you said black hair," said Kip.

"Black and white hair."

"So, gray?"

"No. Do you know anyone who looks like, hmm, what her name is? Cruella. Cruella, something from that dog movie?"

"No?" My mind raced, trying to find a black and white-haired female in my life. "Wait. My dog? My dog is black and white."

Bertram leaned back and closed his eyes. "This has energy, is smart and bossy? Black and white, and the guides say so smart, and they think is funny." His eyes popped open.

"Addie? My dog?"

"Yes! They say the dog is cause for much joy. Keep you balanced."

"See?" said Kip into my left ear. "I told you he is good."

I wasn't so sure. I'd fallen for the trick of nearly spoon-feeding Bertram the answer to that. I wouldn't fall for that trick again. Although he had picked up on the black-and-white part.

And Addie could be kind of bossy for a dog. Well, we'd see. He sank back in his chair and closed his eyes again.

"You want to know love, yes? This why we are here today." He took a deep breath, exhaling slowly. My heart rate ticked a little faster. This was it. I was about to find my husband. Bertram's head moved slowly to the side as if surveying something from behind his closed eyelids. "There is love for you," he said. "Many people love you."

My finger made a little hurry-up motion, and I slipped my hand under my leg, not wanting to be rude.

"But there is also, how do I say, um, fighting? No, not fighting, but feelings of fighting." He opened his eyes and waved his fingers, hoping to snatch the right word out of the air.

"Conflict? Pettiness? Peevishness? Disputes?" Kip was on a roll. Bertram looked overwhelmed at the selection.

Bertram looked at him, then back at me.

"Like a disturbance in your energy," Bertram finally said, ignoring Kip.

"Yes, I feel that," I said. Discovering Evan had a girlfriend was definitely a disturbance in my energy. "Which is why I want to find someone. To fix that disturbance." Although, maybe the disturbance was coming from Christine's death. Perhaps she'd been fighting with someone before being pushed down the stairs. I glanced at Kip. "Do you think this disturbance could be from Christine's death?"

He sucked in a breath and tapped nervously at his chin. "Oh, honey. Maybe." He turned to Bertram. "She found a dead body yesterday. Maybe this disturbance is the dead woman's spirit."

We stared at Bertram. He closed his eyes briefly as if checking. "No," he said. "I tol' you, I don' do dead. This is disturbance for living. Let's start again. You say you want to find a romance to fix disturbance in energy, but that won't fix. Let me try more." He took a deep breath. The candle flame flickered, emitting a small black puff like a miniature smoke signal. Maybe it was my guides trying a new method to get through. Kip perched rigidly on his chair, legs crossed and hands lined neatly on his knee. His eyes were fixed on Bertram intently, and I leaned forward as well. So far, I hadn't heard anything helpful.

Finally, Bertram frowned and shook his head slightly. "I don' understand this image." He sighed, then continued. "I don' know why they tell me you will meet a weak, how I say, donkey." His hands moved through the air as if outlining a miniature donkey.

Kip tittered before managing to stifle himself. I stared at Bertram. This was my reading? His cheeks flushed, and he looked as if he was seconds away from crawling under the velvet tablecloth.

"Sometimes it's," he paused, running a finger along his collarbone and tapping hard on the bony protrusion. "Hard to make pictures in my head fit words," he said. "And my words...I don' always have the right words."

"Oh, sweetie, you're doing fine," said Kip encouragingly. "Just keep going."

"I'm going to meet a weak donkey," I said, trying to sound as if this made perfect sense.

Bertram closed his eyes. "The kind that likes shiny things."

Kip and I glanced at each other.

"A weak donkey that likes shiny things?"

"Oh, I got it!" said Kip, bouncing in his seat. "You're going to meet a rich ass. And he's going to be weak."

Bertram and I stared at him. Bertram considered this. "Maybe," he said slowly.

"Maybe they're trying to tell you you're going to meet a man who's an ass that likes shiny things, so he's rich, but he's also weak, so maybe he's ancient." He shot to his feet and clapped his hands as if firing off the winning answer in a heated game of

Charades. "You're going to meet a rich old geezer who's horrible, but he'll put you in a love nest before kicking off. You'll never have to worry again!"

"I guess." I was getting more depressed by the minute. "But he didn't say old—he said weak."

"Potato potahto," said Kip, sitting back down and refolding his hands. "Do you have any more insights, Bertram? I think she's getting more disturbance in her energy."

Bertram's breathing was no longer calm and peaceful. In fact, he seemed on the verge of hyperventilating.

"Necesitó un momento," he said. "Por favor, I need...away." He stumbled from his chair and tripped on his overlong pants before reaching the bathroom and shutting the door with a bang.

"Well, this is great," I said, turning on Kip. "I thought you said he was good at this. And you said he was gentle or something. All he's said is I'm going to meet a weak donkey."

"And he said you have a bossy dog."

"She's not that bossy, and that in no way helps me."

"He was just getting oriented with that," Kip said, pulling out his pocket square and twirling it through his fingers.

"Maybe we should go," I said.

Before I could hop out of my chair, the bathroom door opened, and Bertram reemerged, the hair around his face wet as if he'd stuck his head under the faucet and patted his face dry. "I am sorry," he said. "I please ask you, let me try again. This usually goes easier." He hesitated, waiting for me to say yes or no.

"Of course," I said. Surely, if I had guides out there, they could help me a little more. Kip sat back, looking as expectant as a small child at a magic show. Easy for him to be amused.

Bertram rearranged himself on his chair, fingers running

across his crystal necklaces before alighting on a rough pink triangle. He stroked the stone and closed his eyes again.

"Your guides, they say, that one, the one we talk about, he is not the one for you."

"Good thing," muttered Kip. "Honey, you're too young and cute to be saddled with a geezer."

The tension in my stomach unclenched a fraction.

"They say don' rush. They want you to find peace inside."

The tension clenched again. I didn't want to wait. I wanted to find someone. It's a two-by-two world made for couples. I huffed a little louder than I intended, and Bertram opened his eyes, warm, brown, and empathetic.

"Your lover, he is out there," he said. "But your, how I say, vibration? Is vibrating wrong." He reached across the table and took my hand. "Let me try to tell you. Is like you want a husband, yes?"

"Well, sure. That's pretty much why I'm here."

"So, the way you vibrate now is—" With his free hand, he waved at the air again.

"Obsessive? Frantic? Desperate?" Kip-the-thesaurus was back at work.

"Maybe say needy," said Bertram. "So you send needy out, and you get needy seeking you. Oh, you do not want needy seeking you." He shook his head solemnly as if portending great misfortune from my current vibration. "Your guides like your happy self. This," he waved a hand again. "They say this is new? Not a good new. So we try to balance you back to happy."

He let go of my hand and walked to a box on the counter. He leaned over, rummaging through the contents before plucking two things out and returning. He first proffered a rough pink stone similar to the one around his neck.

"This is rose quartz," he said, pressing it into my palm. "Is for love. All love. Romantic love. Self-love. You love you, then your lover is attracted." He looked at the doubt on my face. "What's meant for you will find you." He gripped my hand and folded my fingers around the stone, squeezing gently. "Trust your guides."

I felt the peace of his words wrapping around me. His calmness and confidence exuded through his hands, and something inside me loosened slightly. Then, he broke the calm by handing me a black stone dangling from a cord.

"This is black tourmaline." He sounded out the word very carefully. "For protection."

I felt my eyes widen. "Protection from what?"

He closed his eyes. "I don' know, exactly. There is something that is not good energy."

"You should definitely wear it," said Kip. "Between the strumpet throwing people down the stairs and a shiny-loving weak donkey coming your way, you need some help."

I slipped the cord over my head, feeling the cool stone drop onto my chest. Unlike the loose pink stone, this one was smooth and shiny.

Bertram beamed at me. "Yes. That is better." He stood with his hands clasped in front of his chest, smiling as if he'd solved all my problems.

I rubbed the pink quartz between my fingers, hoping the love feeling would kick in. Mostly, what I was feeling was disappointment that my reading appeared to be over and I hadn't learned anything helpful at all. I finally had to awkwardly ask what I owed him since we'd not discussed it beforehand. An array of expressions flitted across Bertram's face as if he were replaying the visit in his head before declaring he didn't think he should charge me. Oddly, that made me feel even worse, as if what he'd seen and conveyed was so dismal it wasn't worth charging for. I finally convinced him to let me pay for the stones, and then I threw a tip on top of that.

"Let me know what happens," he said as we traipsed down the back stairs.

We'd reached the gate when Bertram said, "Oh, I forgot to give you the words! This will help." He turned and headed back towards the stairs. "Wait. Wait here. I just be a minute."

Kip and I stood silently as I gazed around at the piles of auto-junk baking in the early evening sun. He was examining his nails, frowning at a perceived imperfection on the cuticle of his ring finger. I wondered what kind of words I was about to get. My hopes were not exceptionally high at this point that any Bertram words were going to help.

A hot breeze blew across the yard, and the smell of metal and lubricating products mixed with the dust, working its way up my nose. If Bertram hadn't forgotten to unlock the gate for us, I'd already be in my car heading home.

"Where is he?" I asked. I yanked at the lock as if that would miraculously open it.

Kip pulled a pair of sunglasses from a breast pocket and slid them on. "I don't know," he said. "Look at what this is doing to my shoes." He leaned forward and waved his pocket square over the dust-coated tops.

Finally, we heard Bertram clattering down the stairs. "Here for you. Here, Miss." He waved a white square of paper and trotted towards us, kicking up even more dust. Kip tutted and moved farther away.

I took the paper from Bertram, an unlined index card with neatly printed words in black ink centered across the middle. "Together reach divine love," I read. "What's this?"

"These—they are switch words," he said, looking pleased with himself. "They, how I say, change your energy. These words bring you love."

"Really?" I read them over again. "And what am I supposed to do with them?"

"You say them." He was smiling. "You say them many times to attract your love. It changes your energy, and you attract the love."

So I had a pink stone and words to attract my lover and a black stone to protect me from some unknown negative thing. I felt like I was being pranked, but who knows—maybe it would help. It was more than I had this morning.

Although driving home, I still felt somewhat deflated.

CHAPTER TEN

I felt so out of sorts by Tuesday that I thought it must be nearly Friday. I'd tried saying my switch words on and off, but felt ridiculous, especially when my neighbor, Larry, overheard me reciting them as I dragged the garbage out that morning.

"Hey, girl next door," Larry said as I turned around. I hadn't heard him come up behind me. "What are you saying? Are you into Gregorian chanting now? I have to say it's cuter than I would have thought."

He was dressed for work and snazzier than usual. "Hey, Larry." His shirt was tucked in, his pants were zipped and secured with a belt, he was wearing shoes, and he wasn't scratching at any body parts. I took a good look at him. He was better looking than I'd thought. His round face was newly washed pink, and his hair was neatly parted and combed to the side.

"What's on your agenda today, my fine neighbor?" he asked. He dropped a black plastic garbage bag at the curb beside mine and stepped back, tilting his head as if awaiting a fascinating answer.

"Just the usual," I said. I squinted at him again. "You look different."

"I'm getting ready to head to the office." He smiled at me, and I found myself smiling back. I wasn't sure how to take Larry when he wasn't being disgusting. "Well, you have a wonderful day," he said, turning back toward his door. He gave me a little wave before heading inside.

I tamped down an odd little flutter. What had that been?

Evan called while I was baking and, to my surprise, asked if I wanted to meet him and Gabriella later for dinner and drinks. I took it as a good sign that he was trying to make room for both of us. He said they were going to a fish taco place he and I frequent, and we agreed to meet there around six.

During my dog-walking rounds, I had a stern conversation with myself. I needed to give Gabriella a chance. I didn't know anything about her, and I'd only seen her for hardly a minute when I met her at the park. Maybe my initial impression had been wrong. She was adorable and seemed to like Evan, so what was wrong with that?

I arrived at the restaurant a few minutes early. I didn't see Evan's Jeep in the lot, but they could be in Gabriella's car. The patio was full, so I headed inside and scanned the tables. There were only six tables inside, all tall café style with rickety stools that wobbled on the uneven tiles. No sign of Evan and Gabriella, and there was only one empty table in the far corner. It wasn't ideal since it was smashed up in a dead-end beside the bar, but it would have to work since it was the only one open. There were only two seats, so I smiled sweetly at the three guys closest and asked if I could take their extra chair. I was arranging the seats, deciding how to place them, when Evan and Gabriella walked in.

Evan beelined over, with Gabriella lagging behind.

"Oh, sweet! I was afraid we wouldn't get a table," Evan said, pulling out one of the stools and sliding on. "Have you ordered yet?" he asked.

"No, I just got here."

Gabriella edged closer to Evan and looked at the table. "Bae, this is tight," she said, glancing my way and giving me a quick smile.

"Yeah, but we're lucky we got a table," said Evan, pulling the extra stool out and patting it for her.

She puffed out her lip and gave it a tiny bite. "But I'm stuck staring at nothing," she said. She glanced at me indirectly, her gaze raking over my outfit. I'd thought I looked cute, but next to her, I was overdressed in my coordinating skirt and top. I fiddled nervously with my chunky necklace. I should have worn the black protection stone. How was she making me feel so old when I wasn't? Gabriella was wearing a thin cotton mini dress, and as far as I could tell, no undergarments. Her flip-flops slapped on the floor, and she carried a purse too small to even hold a credit card.

I squeezed around the table and offered to take the offending chair so she wouldn't be stuck staring at nothing, or more accurately, me. I angled the stool so that I could still look out at the restaurant, and Evan wedged himself into the tight space between the table and the bar. Gabriella slid in beside Evan.

"Gabriella, I'm sorry about your aunt," I said.

She made a little moue, trying to convey sadness but somehow falling short of the actual emotion. "Thanks," she said, reaching for Evan's hand, which rested on the table. "It's been, like, so hard." She entwined her fingers with his and lowered her gaze. "The only good thing's been that my friends feel so bad for me. They're all giving me really nice gifts to make me feel better." She leaned closer to Evan and looked directly into his eyes. I found it extraordinary that he managed to keep his eyes raised to that level, with her dress falling open the way it was. I was concerned we'd be kicked out before we could even order.

"Did I tell you about the cute bracelet my friend Mia gave me?" she asked him.

"Yeah," he said, his head swiveling around to check out the order line on the other side of the bar. "So what do you want?" he asked her. "There's not a line right now."

She leaned back, irritation flickering across her face before disappearing so fast I thought maybe I hadn't seen it. "Whatever you're getting, I'll have the same," she said.

"Jess? The regular?"

"Yeah, perfect." I reached for my wallet, but Evan waved me away, disentangled his hand from Gabriella, and trotted around to the far side of the bar.

"It's hard to get his attention when he's hungry," I said, leaning forward conversationally. She flicked a look at me before tapping a finger against her phone screen to turn it on. I resisted the urge to pull out my own phone, instead looking around the small space. It had been a while since Evan and I had been here, but it never changed. It was louder tonight than usual, but it was prime time. Evan and I usually came at odd hours whenever one or the other got a craving for a fried fish taco. There was something about the crispy cut cabbage and their special sauce rolled in a corn tortilla with fresh cilantro and crispy fish—my stomach began to growl. Evan was at the side bar, gathering chips and salsa. I wished he would hurry. This was like being at a lousy party alone.

"Have you been here before?" I asked Gabriella.

"Mm." She tapped at her phone with one hand while twirling a thick strand of hair with the other. Evan pushed through the crowd, balancing two plastic baskets piled high with fried chips and overflowing salsa containers. He slid into his seat, then swiveled around to retrieve the three beers the bartender had pushed his way.

"All set!" he said, distributing the beers and pushing one basket of chips my way.

"So, how'd you guys meet anyway?" I asked.

They looked at each other in the annoying way that new couples do. Gabriella scooted closer to Evan and began running her finger back and forth along her lower lip. His eyes followed her finger as if being hypnotized.

"I don't want her to judge me," she told him.

My mind immediately began to race through possibilities. Exotic dancer? I didn't think Evan frequented the gentlemen's clubs as a rule, but I clearly didn't know many things about him. Massage therapist of the illicit rubdown kind? Drug mule?

"She's not going to judge you," Evan said. "There's nothing to judge." He turned to me. "She works at a cupcake place."

"A cupcake place? Why would you think I'd judge something like that?" I experienced a slight letdown.

"Well, it's not all high-level or anything," she said, turning her doe eyes on me. "Like, Evan told me that you used to work with him, and now you have your own business and all. I'm planning to start my own decorating business, but I haven't gotten a break on that yet." She turned back to Evan and smiled. "But I am close to getting my first client."

Evan kept his eyes riveted on the chips. "Anyway, this place is in the food court at work, which is how I met her," he said.

"I'm only working there because my mom made me get a job," Gabriella said. "She got all bitchy about my car insurance and phone. I don't know what the big deal is." She rolled her eyes. "She's so ridiculous anymore. I swear to God, as soon as I save up a little money or find a roommate, I'm moving out." She looked at Evan again, tilting her head down while gazing up from under her lashes.

A ripple of unease churned in my stomach like the incipient rumblings of food poisoning. "So, you met at the cupcake place," I looked at Evan. "And you asked her out, and as they say, the rest is history?" I squinted at him. Evan was a lot of things, but being assertive in asking women out was not something I'd ever seen.

"Well, they had this big grand opening. You know, giving out free samples, stuff like that. And naturally, I went to try the cupcakes. They were free!" Gabriella tilted her head and studied Evan as if wondering how he would tell the story. "Gabriella was there, and she was really cute in her little apron—obviously." He smiled at her. "And I kept going back because, Jess, those cupcakes are amazing!" This part sounded like the Evan I knew. "And then last week, or whenever it was," he trailed off with the dazed look of an accident victim who couldn't quite understand what had happened and was relying on the kindness of witnesses to fill in the blanks. "We ended up going out."

Gabriella edged slightly away, pulling one spaghetti strap into place. "You only kept coming back because the cupcakes are amazing?"

"No, that's not what I meant," he said. "I mean, they are, but that's not the only reason."

Behind him, the bartender leaned across the bar and gave him a poke in the shoulder. "Dude, here's your order." He set three plastic baskets on the bar, and Evan turned, seemingly thankful for the distraction.

"Great! Here we go. One for everyone." Evan slid a basket to each of us, and he and I immediately went to work unwrapping the foil and diving in. The tacos were every bit as good as I remembered.

"Anyway, Evan kept coming around," Gabriella said, picking

up the story. "And I thought he was super sweet. Remember how you brought me that breakfast taco when I was all hung over that morning? It was so cute." She rubbed a hand up and down his bicep. Evan mumbled something behind a mouthful of food. "And then my favorite band was in town. He said he'd love to go, and we've been together ever since." She ignored her tacos, reaching instead to pick out a chip from their shared basket. She crumbled it into bits, dropping the pieces back into the basket as she spoke. "It's super crazy how much we have in common. And then I found out he's got a house that needs all this work, and it was like fate, you know?" She placed a proprietary hand on his arm and smiled sweetly at me.

"Yes, fate's funny that way," I said. I believed I was starting to get a clearer picture, but I wasn't sure what to do about it.

Gabriella took another chip, dipped it into the salsa, and ate it.

"I'm starting to think that Aunt Christine dying this way is fate, too," she said. My eyes flew to Evan, but he was staring at his food and chewing as placidly as a cow in a field. Gabriella stirred a finger around the basket and pulled a broken chip from the bottom of the pile. "My dad said she was loaded, so we'll probably get a bunch of money. We totally *should*. We're family."

I was about to say something when Evan kicked me under the table. I stared at him, and he gave an almost imperceptible head shake.

"Although she was kind of a bitch, so I don't know," Gabriella continued, unaware of our exchange. "My mom gets mad when my dad says that."

"Was Christine your mom's sister?" I asked. I could see why she'd get mad.

"No. She was my dad's sister. But she and my Aunt Penny were both awful to him when they were growing up. We don't see much of them. Well, sometimes, but not often. It's not like either one of them has ever been that nice to me. I mean, my dad works super hard, and it's not like we have a lot of money. Both of them have way more than we do, and they don't share. Like, what's up with that?"

She looked from me to Evan as if expecting an answer. "Family," Evan muttered.

"Right?" She picked up another chip and crumbled it over her taco basket. "I hope I get her jewelry. She had some really nice jewelry that my uncle gave her before they divorced. Like, *really* nice stuff. Penny should definitely not get that. She's a nurse, and she dresses ugly. I'd look good in rubies, don't you think?" I thought she was talking to Evan, but she was looking at me. With her coloring, she would look good in rubies.

"Definitely," I said. She rewarded me with a full-watt smile and tilted her head.

"You'd look good in sapphires, I think. Don't you think, Evan? Wouldn't she look good in sapphires?"

He looked at me critically as if taking the question seriously. "I guess," he said. "Which color are those again?" As a matter of fact, I did have some lovely sapphire jewelry my parents had given me, although I didn't have many occasions to wear it these days.

Gabriella turned to Evan and touched his cheek affectionately. "Blue, silly. You—you would look good in leather." Evan looked vaguely alarmed and reached for his nearly empty beer glass.

"I don't know about that."

"A leather necklace," she clarified. "With a silver pendant of some kind. We should go shopping this weekend. I know just the place we could find you one." She turned back to me. "I don't know why Aunt Christine didn't wear her nice pieces more often. She always wore this cheap stuff. I remember her letting me see all the nice things when I was younger. We'd dress up. It was fun. So hopefully, I'll at least get that."

She stopped talking and took a sip of her beer. I wasn't sure what to be more concerned about—her utter lack of emotion around the death of her aunt or the fact she was ingratiating herself with Evan in ways he didn't even see.

CHAPTER ELEVEN

I was home early, declining Evan's invitation to join them. Join them for what was still up in the air as he was arguing for an evening in, and she was going full-court press to hit a couple of clubs. Gabriella mentioned that she hadn't been to work all week due to the emotional trauma of her aunt's death. In the next breath, she said she was bored and wanted to go out and burn off some energy.

They were still squabbling as we made our way to the parking lot. Evan mentioned that he had to be at work early for a meeting, and she countered that she had to be at work too, but that wasn't going to stop her from living her life.

I was glad to get home to Addie.

I hadn't been home long when my phone. I didn't recognize the number.

"Hello?"

"Yeah, hi. Is this Jessie?"

"Yes?"

"Yeah, this is Chaz. My mom gave me your number? And said you wanted to go out?"

I'd forgotten all about Chaz. As much as I'd been in a hurry to find someone when I called my mom, I now felt that I'd rather sit alone on my couch forever before going out on a blind date. He sounded as excited as I felt.

"Hi, Chaz. Yes, um, my mom said you'd recently moved here and thought you might want someone to show you around?"

He breathed loudly into the phone. A loud breather.

"I've been here a while. I basically know my way around."

We sat in silence while I listened to Addie's tags tink against her water bowl in the kitchen.

"Okay, well…" I finally said, not sure how to get out of this gracefully.

"Well," he sighed. "Maybe we could get together for some drinks or something," he offered. "Or dinner? Would Thursday night work? Say five-thirty?"

"Okay," I said. As much as I wanted to say no, I probably wasn't going to find anyone while sitting on my couch. But who has dinner at five-thirty? He suggested a Mexican restaurant not far from the Galleria, which I agreed to mainly because it seemed a good idea to meet him somewhere else and not have to deal with the awkwardness of returning to my house with whatever expectations that conveyed.

After we hung up, I slumped against the couch. I considered texting back and canceling. I was sure he wouldn't care, but then I thought about the fact that I didn't have many opportunities to meet guys anymore. It was one thing when I was working and surrounded by people all the time. Not that I'd met anyone then, either. But these days, I spend most of my time alone or with dogs. I had virtually no chance of meeting someone if I didn't step outside my routine.

I paced around the house, antsy and out of sorts. I wanted to talk to someone. I wanted to talk to Evan, but obviously, that was out. Instead, I called Kip.

"Hey, girlfriend!" he said when he picked up. "How's the manhunt?"

"If you must know, I accepted a date for Thursday night."

"That's wonderful!" he gushed. "But remember, he's probably the weak ass Bertram told you about, and this won't be going anywhere."

"Hey, are you at home? Can you look out and tell me if Evan's car is there?"

"Oh, sweetie, are you having jealousy issues? I saw the strumpet's car there earlier." There was a pause. "No, her jalopy is there, but his vehicle is not."

She must have won the debate. "Do you think it's weird that she's not upset by her aunt's death?"

"Did you honestly think she would be? Honey, I knew that girl was bad news. I knew as soon as I saw her. I told you as much. She has a taker vibe. I've seen them before." I wasn't entirely sure what he was talking about, yet it sounded right. "And if you cross a taker—well, it's better if you don't. Just skip town and don't leave a forwarding address."

"It sounds like you have experience."

"You have no idea. Maybe the aunt crossed her, and that's why she's dead."

"Gabriella did say she wants her aunt's jewelry."

"Bingo! There it is. Once a taker, always a taker; don't even think about trying to thwart them."

"Now she wants to decorate Evan's house and maybe move in."

"Oh, she's good. Next thing you know, your friend will be down the stairs too." He paused. "Although," he said slowly, "I'm not sure I want someone like her living so close to me."

"I don't think there's much we can do about it," I said.

"It's like you don't know me at all," he said. "There's plenty we can do. We just need the right information. We must study this girl in her natural habitat," Kip continued. "Do we know where she lives? Works? Hangs out?"

"She works at a cupcake place downtown."

There was a moment of silence. "A cupcake place. I had her pegged as a dancer or maybe a nail stylist. This is better. I didn't relish the thought of going into one of those topless places, although I could use a nice manicure. Nevertheless, cupcake place it is, then. We'll start with her coworkers. Coworkers like to dish on unpleasant people. I'm sure you could find out plenty from them."

"I can't show up there; she knows me." I also wasn't sure what exactly we could hope to find out from her coworkers, but maybe Kip was right. Maybe I did need to find out as much as possible, and if she was harmless, then I could leave Evan to it. And if she was a fortune-seeking killer, better we find out now.

"We'll work that out," he assured me. "I'm quite good at getting people to spill the tea. And if she's there, I'm sure I can engage her just as well. You can sit back and take notes."

I wasn't sure this idea made a ton of sense. Okay, I knew it didn't, but it made me feel like I was doing something. Before I knew it, I'd agreed to meet Kip downtown tomorrow after my dog-walking rounds. If I started my schedule a little earlier, I should be able to be there by three-thirty. Good, bad, or otherwise, we were going to learn a little more about Gabriella Goodman.

CHAPTER TWELVE

I arrived downtown shortly after three the following afternoon. We'd agreed to meet in the lobby of the building adjacent to Evan's to reduce the chance of running into him if he was wandering around. Although, now that I was standing here, I realized yet another flaw of this plan—what if Evan was actually at the cupcake place? He'd mentioned how busy he was at work, but my luck, he'd be taking a break to visit Gabriella when we showed up. Well, I had to hope he wasn't.

I'd rushed down here so I wouldn't be late and hadn't even thought about changing. Now, as all the business casual wear paraded past me, I felt out of place in my baggy shorts and clunky running shoes. I pulled out my phone and pretended to be engrossed by something on the screen while my eyes darted to and fro, watching for Kip and keeping an eye out for Evan.

When Kip finally did arrive, I nearly missed him.

"What is this?" I asked, looking him up and down. "You look—"

He jutted out his chin and put one hand on his hip. "I look perfect," he said. "What is *that* you've got on? Are you *trying* to stick out?"

I'd never seen Kip appear anything less than photoshoot-ready. But today, this Kip-the-office-worker looked entirely different. From the way he'd parted his hair and combed it unbecomingly flat to the stubble on his cheeks. Somehow, even his skin looked pastier, as if he never left his cubicle during daylight hours. He wore a wrinkled button-down shirt with a narrow, straight-edge necktie. Khaki pants, at least a size too large, hung off his thin hips. But his shoes clenched it. Large and brown with black rubber soles and droopy laces, they were far from his customary footwear.

"You had these clothes in your closet?" This looked more like what Evan would wear.

"Girl, I would not be caught dead with these clothes in my closet. I borrowed them from someone I know." He lifted his arm, pushed back his cuff, and glanced at a black plastic watch. "Shall we get this show on the road?"

"I'm not sure how we're going to do this," I said. "Gabriella knows me. And I'm not even sure what we're hoping to find out."

"We are here to observe and find out whatever we can. She doesn't know who I am, so I am the perfect one to initiate a conversation with her. You have no idea how good I am at getting people to open up to me."

We walked across the skywalk between office buildings and crossed the lobby of the building I'd spent so many years in. We headed for the down escalator, my senses triggering memories I didn't realize I had, from the way the mid-afternoon sun streamed through the side windows and fell across the marble floor to the mixed scents wafting up from the food court. Even the way voices echoed past the security desk, all these things flooded back, making me feel I'd never left.

For a split second, I forgot I was standing next to Kip and turned, expecting to see Evan's profile. We'd been carried side by side down this escalator countless times—to lunch, coffee breaks, lottery ticket runs, walks in the tunnels, shopping for greeting cards, and an occasion cookie break. As much as I'd hated my job, I still missed some aspects. Now Evan had moved on to cupcake breaks with Gabriella. With that in mind, I scanned the open expanse as we drifted to the lower level. Being as late in the afternoon as it was, there weren't many people around. A couple of men slumped at empty tables, scrolling on their phones. Two workers with rolling buckets and tall yellow caution cones slopped the floor with oversized mops. A cluster of women in skirts and sneakers huffed past the tables and headed down one of the corridors leading to the next section of the tunnel. I wondered which route they were taking, remembering all the times Evan and I ventured down the various offshoots. If I recalled correctly, there were nearly six miles of tunnels down here, looping between all the major buildings.

Kip's nose wrinkled. "What is that smell?"

"What smell?" I knew what he was talking about. There was a mix that was unique to the tunnels. Of course, the food court smells—some better than others, but also various cleaning solvents and a mustiness that no cleaner could touch. Having an underground tunnel system in flood-prone Houston carried its risks.

Across the way, I saw the cupcake shop. A black and white polka dot awning hung above a wide glass counter, with a bright red sign above screaming 'Chonk Cupcakes!' The trays appeared almost empty, and an employee in a black and white polka dot apron was emptying what was left into a large plastic container. A second employee leaned over the glass, talking to a silver-haired man in a crisp blue suit. It was Gabriella.

We'd reached the bottom of the escalator, and I raced to hide behind a grove of corn plants that dotted the eating area. Kip strolled unhurriedly along behind me.

"Would you please calm down," he said, catching up to me.

"You look suspicious enough that if I didn't know you, I would call the mall police. Wait here and try not to get hauled away."

He pulled his phone out and ambled toward Chonk, stopping periodically as if mesmerized by what he was reading. He zig-zagged his way closer to the counter, still stopping and starting as if completely unaware of his surroundings. I slunk closer myself, quick-stepping from column to column. Judging by the looks the floor-moppers gave me, I still looked suspicious. Taking a cue from Kip, I pulled my phone from my purse and hunched over the screen, letting my hair fall over my face. I couldn't stay behind a pillar and wait for Kip to tell me his version of what happened—I wanted to watch for myself.

The man in the suit had his back to me, but even from here, I knew expensive apparel when I saw it. This guy oozed money. He leaned forward on the counter, brushing a strand of hair behind Gabriella's ear while she giggled. And I'd thought Evan was too old for her. This man had to be thirty years her senior— at least. Her eyes did a quick sweep of the food court, falling for a moment on Kip before returning to the man. Kip was less than ten feet away, seemingly engrossed in his phone. Next to the well-dressed executive, Kip looked like the office drone he was impersonating—clearly not good enough to draw her attention away.

Her coworker rolled her eyes and bumped Gabriella out of the way so she could pack up the remaining cupcakes. Gabriella took the opportunity to come out from behind the counter, slip her apron straps over her head, and shake her hair loose, flipping the heavy strands back over her shoulder while observing the effect she was having on her target audience. Too bad Evan wasn't around. As I watched, the man pulled a card from his breast pocket and handed it to her. She took it, stared at it long enough to make me think she was a slow reader, and then tucked it down the front of her shirt between her breasts.

Kip snorted and coughed; then, as the couple turned to stare at him, he looked up as if suddenly aware of his surroundings before patting himself on the chest, murmuring, "Sorry, sorry. Tickle."

Why hadn't I thought to take a picture? The man leaned forward and cupped a hand on Gabriella's face while leaning in and whispering something in her ear. She grabbed his hand and rubbed a thumb across it before ducking away laughing. He watched her wiggle her way through a door in the back of the shop before adjusting his trousers, and with a final look, he disappeared around the bend of the tunnel.

Well, well, well. While I wasn't surprised, I also wasn't sure how to break this to Evan. I couldn't see any way of bringing this up without it boomeranging back and exploding in my face. This wasn't my business. And yet, here I was, hiding behind a pillar in the downtown tunnel, spying on Evan's girlfriend. Not my business. Didn't want to see my friend get hurt. Still, not my business. I could go around this circle for days.

I peered around the pillar to see Kip at the counter talking to Gabriella's coworker. The coworker glanced over her shoulder toward the back of the shop before leaning across the glass, closer to Kip. They were so close their faces nearly touched. When Gabriella sailed through the door, the coworker leaped back so fast it looked like she'd been electrified. Gabriella didn't even acknowledge them; she tossed her head and strode toward the escalators. Within seconds, the coworker was back to unloading on Kip, no longer quiet. I could hear her voice but not the words. Her arms gesticulated, and she appeared to be strangling the air at one point. Good move on Kip's part. There's nothing like a coworker who doesn't like you to sell you out.

By the time Kip joined me, I'd parked myself on a metal chair at one of the tables. He plunked a white box in front of me with a handful of napkins and a plastic fork.

"Enjoy," he said. "They look lovely and smell divine, but do you know what sugar does to your complexion?"

I pulled the container toward me.

"Wow, look at this," I said, lifting the lid and staring into the box. The sweet smell of sugar, almonds, and chocolate wafted up, igniting my salivary glands almost painfully. Two hunks of cake pressed side by side, not your standard cupcakes, more like triangular chunks of cushioning supporting a soaring layer of frosting that cascaded down all three sides. It was like a work of art touching multiple senses. "Are you sure you don't want one?" I asked. "I can't eat all this."

"No, you go ahead." He pulled out a chair next to me, took one of the napkins, and dusted off the seat with it before sinking onto the edge.

I debated which one to eat and which to save for later. One was chocolate with raspberry ganache; the other was a white fluffy dream covered with toasted almond crumbs.

"It seems that your friend's little friend is not exactly beloved by her coworker," said Kip. "However, she is beloved by many of the men who frequent...what is this called? The food cellar." He started to lean forward, then recoiled before his arms touched the table. "I get the impression your friend is not her only paramour."

I sighed, placed the fork in the box, and closed the lid. How could I enjoy something so delicious when I was about to hear something that would inevitably hurt Evan?

"Yeah, I noticed that older guy. He was all over her."

"I heard him tell her that a pretty girl like her should have no trouble making money. Maybe he's a pimp looking to expand his stable."

"Kip, that's terrible! And he didn't look like a pimp. He looked like a lawyer or a banker or something."

"Pimps come in all shapes and outfits," he said as if he knew this for a fact. "Donnette said the trollop doesn't work; she spends her time trolling for a sugar daddy. Maybe that good-looking, silver-haired man in the tailored suit wasn't a pimp. Maybe he's looking for a little direct action."

"Evan's not exactly a sugar daddy, so I'm not sure where he fits in if that's what she's looking for."

"Honey, when you're a teeny-bopper punching a timecard at a place called Chonk, any man in non-polyester pants would look like a sugar daddy. Maybe she snapped your friend up when she thought that was as good as she could get."

Good point. I reopened the box and forked a corner off the chocolate hunk of cake. The pillowy softness melted against my tongue, a delectable mix of dark chocolate, sweet raspberry, and enough butter to make my eyes roll back in their sockets. "Oh, sweet heaven," I said. "This is incredible."

"You look like you're having a sexual experience," said Kip. "You're embarrassing me."

I opened my eyes. "I just said it's incredible."

"Yes, but it's the look on your face. I hope you don't look like that when you're in the throes of passion with men. I'm not sure it looks like what you think it looks like. Maybe you should practice your sexy face in the mirror before your next date."

I put the fork back in the box and closed the lid again. I'd never even thought about my sexy face. Kip was furnishing me with a whole new collection of insecurities. As much as I didn't want to admit it, I knew I would be attempting to recreate my sexy face in front of a mirror in the near future.

"What else did you find out?" I asked.

"Well, according to Donnette, Gabriella comes in late, leaves early, and flirts like a nymphette with every halfway presentable man that comes within twenty feet. And she chews like a cow."

"How does she keep her job?"

"Apparently, she's really good with the baking, and some of

the more popular concoctions have been hers. The owner loves her creativity. I'm guessing Donnette has all the creativity of a potato." He leaned forward and lifted the box lid. "That does smell delightful."

"Have some."

He picked up my fork and swiped at a cupcake, lifting a minuscule bit of white frosting before licking it daintily off the end of the tong. He moaned a low sound, then scooped up a hefty chunk, shoved it in his mouth, closed his lips around it, and pulled it slowly off the end of the fork. "Oh, God." His eyes closed, and one hand flew to his chest as he moaned louder.

"Stop it. You're embarrassing me," I said.

He waved the fork at me and pulled the box closer. "Whatever. Anyhoo, my friend Donnette seems to think Gabriella is a skanky little psychopath." He took another bite, seemingly unconcerned that Evan was dating a skanky little psychopath. Frankly, his words chilled me. Skanky is one thing; psychopath is another. If she really was a psychopath, she would have had no qualms about pushing Christine down the stairs.

"Do you really think she's a psychopath? Or was she saying that because she doesn't like her?"

"I don't think most people like psychopaths. Well, once they realize they are a psychopath. Supposedly, most are very charming people. Do you think this girl is charming?"

"She's quite attractive."

"Attractive is not the same as charming."

"Okay, so not really."

"Well, there you go. She's probably not, then. Although I still don't want her as a neighbor."

CHAPTER THIRTEEN

"Probably not" did not give me much comfort. I spent the rest of the evening trying to decide what I should do—if anything. No matter how I looked at it, I couldn't see a way to warn Evan about Gabriella without him turning on the messenger. Not to mention, he would totally freak out if he knew Kip and I had been spying on his girlfriend. It seemed like I would have to let him figure this out on his own.

Unless, of course, Gabriella had, in fact, been involved with Christine's death. That was a different situation entirely, but I could not prove that either. I needed to stop obsessing over this and get back to my life. My business wasn't going to run itself, and I had my date with Chaz to think about.

I spent all day Thursday trying to get excited about my date. I did. But the closer it got, the more I wished I could stay home. The parking lot at the restaurant was snarled with cars, crowds, and aggression. I had a combo adrenaline rush and road rage experience before finally finding a tiny parking place at the far side of the lot. I could only hope the truck driver who'd blasted his horn and flipped me the bird wasn't Chaz.

When I pushed my way into the restaurant and through the

throng of bodies jammed around the hostess stand, I could feel an unpleasant slick of perspiration dripping from all my previously cleaned parts. Chaz hadn't indicated if he would get a table or wait for me at the bar, nor did I have any idea what he looked like. The two hostesses ignored me as I tried to get their attention, so I finally gave up and shoved my way toward the bar. A giant sign hanging from the ceiling indicated that Thursdays were two-for-one margaritas and free quesadillas until six p.m. I wondered if that was why Chaz picked this place and suggested we meet so early. This was really shaping up.

"Hey, honey, you looking for somebody?" A rotund man in a plaid shirt, faded jeans, and a ratty baseball cap pressed against me, placing a hand on my right hip.

I twisted sideways, using my purse to knock away his hand. "I'm waiting for someone."

"Oh, feisty. Well, I'm *someone*." He leered at me and reached under his overhanging belly to tug at the waist of his jeans. His teeth were yellow, and his cheek bulged with a wad of chewing tobacco. He raised a plastic cup and spat a stream of brown liquid into it. I gagged at the smell and turned away, bumping into someone else.

It was another guy, this one taller, recently bathed, and no dip in his cheek. I pushed farther around him and away from the dipper. The plaid guy muttered something but walked back to his barstool, where he and a couple of lookalikes started punching at each other and guffawing. I took another look around the crowd.

"Are you Jessie Gallagher?" The clean guy stared down the length of his nose, looking me over.

"Chaz?"

He hesitated, and I halfway expected him to say no. "Yeah, hey, nice to meet you," he finally said. We stood awkwardly as people jostled us closer together. He towered over me, and I estimated he was at least six two, if not taller. The hollow of his neck was level with my eyes, and directly below, I could see the smooth, hairless rise of his pecs. It's not that I was trying to check out his pecs, but with the top three buttons of his shirt undone and the edges pulled open, one couldn't help but be treated to the show. I tipped my head back to look up at his face, taking in the high cheekbones and straight-edged jawline. There was something about his perfect angles that made it seem he'd been cast in a precision mold and carefully extracted to maintain the edges. His hair was brown with golden highlights, and I wondered if that was natural or chemically enhanced. If I had to guess, I'd say there were chemicals involved. Excellent cut, though. He raised his face skyward and shook his head as if channeling his inner rock star in a cheesy music video. I nearly laughed out loud, although the humor was offset by a sinking feeling.

"I've got a reservation, but how about I get us a couple of drinks before we sit down?" He turned and went to the bar before I could answer. I took the time to try to get myself into a better frame of mind. Forget the Neanderthal at the bar. Forget the fact it was a thousand degrees in here, and sweat trickled freely down my chest. Never mind that Chaz was getting me a drink without even wanting to know what kind of drink I preferred. He was cute. He was clean. He wasn't dipping chaw or hoisting at his pants. Seemed like my standards were reasonable.

It took him several minutes to return. I'd lost sight of him in the crowd, and for a minute, I was afraid he'd bailed on me, but he finally reappeared holding two tall margaritas, dripping salt and condensation.

"Here you go," he said, handing me a glass. I took a small taste, wishing he'd bothered to ask me what I wanted. I didn't handle tequila well, and I'd recently seen a frightening show about how easy it was to spike a woman's drink if she wasn't observant. Not that Chaz seemed like the kind of guy to spike a woman's drink, but still. Also, it reinforced the idea that he was frugal at best because this was evidently part of the two-for-one deal. He took several gulps, throwing his head back with each swallow as if participating in a frat-house initiation. Apparently, his wasn't spiked. "Is yours okay?" he asked.

I took another small sip. "Yes, it's good." For a drink I didn't want, it wasn't bad.

"Awesome. Let me see about our table. Do you want to wait here? And do you want me to get another drink to have with dinner?" He was off again before I could answer. I debated making a run for the door, but since I was here, I might as well see how it went.

He was gone even longer this time. Fortunately, as six o'clock approached, the two-for-one crowd began to thin out. I finally spotted him at the bar, cozied up beside a cute little blond girl in a halter top. He flicked at a strap near her neck while she giggled and swatted at him playfully. I was looking for somewhere to set my drink down when he looked up and caught my eye. He had the grace to look embarrassed, and he quickly grabbed two more margaritas and headed back toward me.

"You ready to sit down?" he asked, still holding both drinks. We walked over to the hostess, who grabbed two plastic menus and led us to a table in the dining room just a short distance from the bar. Chaz quickly scooted around the table's far side and slid into a seat, forcing me to take the one across. I glanced over my shoulder. Yep, he had an unobstructed view of the bar and the cute little blonde who looked slightly put out when she saw me.

Chaz plunked the glasses down on the table, keeping one and pushing the other a few millimeters toward me. I'd hardly made any progress on my first one, so he was probably beginning to doubt that I'd slam them back and turn into an instant party girl. A waiter appeared with a basket of chips, salsa, and two iced waters and asked if we'd like an appetizer while we looked over the menu. Chaz ordered guacamole, once again forgetting I might have an opinion.

I picked up a chip and dragged it through the warm homemade salsa. The taste of tomato, cilantro, and fresh jalapeños filled my mouth with spicy comfort. Chaz faded away briefly, and I had a second of joy. I opened my eyes to catch his eyes darting away from my face and over my shoulder.

"So, Chaz," I said. "What do you do?"

"I'm in an investment banking program," he said. He took a chip, scooped up an oversized glob of salsa, and maneuvered it into his mouth. "It's pretty prestigious. They only take guys they know they can groom for top positions." He pulled his shoulders back and raised his chin, the epitome of smugness.

"That sounds great," I said flatly. His eyes flitted past me again. I'll bet the little blonde would be impressed. He made a great effort to focus on me.

"And, what do you do?" he asked.

"I used to be an oil and gas analyst," I said. "But I left there and started my own business."

He dragged his attention back from the bar to me. "Oh, uh-huh." Back to the bar.

"Yeah, I started a gourmet dog biscuit company. It's pretty cool, as a matter of fact. I'm doing okay, but it's hard to balance. You know? For instance, I need more hands to make more biscuits to expand where I sell, but I'm not selling enough to hire anyone, and I'd need to rent space in a commercial kitchen to ramp up. So, I'm still trying to figure it out."

I could tell I'd lost him as soon as I started talking. The waiter returned with the guacamole, setting it between us with a flourish. "Are you ready to order?"

"No, we need a couple more minutes," I said. Chaz was gazing past me, a smile playing across his lips, and I had to physically restrain myself from turning around to look. The waiter moved off. "Have you been here before?" I asked. "The salsa's good. Really fresh. And everything smells good." It was like rambling in an empty theater.

"Would you excuse me?" Chaz asked, shoving his chair back. "I need to go to the restroom."

This time, I did turn around. I'd expected to see Chaz back with the blonde, but surprisingly, he'd passed her and made his way down the hall toward the restrooms. I turned back in my chair and tried the guacamole. It was every bit as tasty as the salsa. I'd worked through about a quarter of the basket of chips, a good portion of the guacamole, and more than half the salsa when I started to wonder what was taking him so long. Twisting around, I scanned the crowd at the bar. No sign of Chaz, and the blonde girl was gone.

CHAPTER FOURTEEN

I couldn't believe it. Okay, it's not that I couldn't believe it, I could believe it—but still. My first date in however long, and the guy literally walked out in the middle. No, not even the middle. I sagged in my chair and drank my now watery margarita. I sure wished Evan was here. Based on what I'd sampled, the food was great, and he and I would have had a good time. But no. I was sitting by myself while crowds swirled around me. I considered ordering myself dinner but decided that felt too pathetic. I was fishing around my purse for my wallet when I felt someone hovering.

"Hey, I'm sorry to intrude. Um, my father and I couldn't help but notice what," he paused. "Happened here." I sighed, nearly too embarrassed to look up. This guy looked familiar, but I couldn't place his face.

"Yeah," I said, wondering how much the guacamole was. The waiter passed between tables and saw me with my wallet. I made the universal gesture for check. He nodded and headed in the other direction, presumably to close out my ticket. Then I hesitated, wondering if Chaz *was* in the bathroom. Maybe he'd been taken ill or something. "I'm not exactly sure what's going on. I'm not sure if maybe my date is still in the restroom."

"Oh, no," he said. "He left with that blonde girl. We watched him go."

"Well, that's embarrassing," I said. "Not my finest moment."

"Clearly, this isn't your fault!" he said. "That guy seemed like a jerk. We spotted it a mile away. Anyway, we were wondering —" He turned to the adjacent table and pointed to an older man who smiled at me. "My father and I. We were wondering if you wanted to eat with us. We just ordered. I'm sure you could order, and it would all come out together."

I waffled. Part of me wanted to go home, lie on the couch, sulk with Addie, and decompress on stupid television. The other part reminded me that I needed to get out of my comfort zone if I ever wanted to get a life.

"That's really nice of you," I said. I squinted, trying to place his face. I felt like I'd literally just seen him. "Why do I know you?" He smiled, clutching his napkin, and I suddenly remembered the nervous fingers. "Oh, you're the document guy from Sunday morning." It was the courier that had been delivering Christine's documents.

"Right, Martin Amos," he said. "That's my dad, Jerry. We'd love it if you could join us."

The waiter returned with a vinyl check register. I peeked at the ticket and laid a bill inside, covering the guacamole and a nice tip.

"She's going to join us over there," said Martin to the waiter. "Could you maybe hold up our order until she has a chance to decide what she'd like so it all comes out together?" The waiter smiled at me and assured Martin he would handle it.

I gathered my things together and moved one table over. Martin's dad beamed at me while I got settled. I could see the resemblance between the men, although the father was smaller and leaner than his son. He wore a short-sleeved plaid shirt, neatly ironed and buttoned almost to the top. After the Chaz show, I realized how much I appreciated men who buttoned their shirts. Martin was also fully buttoned, still in a dress shirt and tie, probably direct from the office.

"We're so glad you joined us," Mr. Amos said, half rising and extending a hand. "I'm Jerry Amos, and this is my son, Marty." He clutched my hand in both of his, squeezing gently. I introduced myself.

"I appreciate this," I said. "To be honest, I'm pretty embarrassed."

"Nothing for you to be embarrassed about, my dear," said Jerry. "It's a lucky day indeed for the Amos men."

I saw the waiter approaching from the corner of my eye, so I gave the menu a quick speed read before ordering. I heard my phone buzz in my purse but ignored it, not wanting to be rude.

"So, how'd it go with your boss?" I asked Martin.

Jerry looked from me to Martin. "You two know each other?"

"Not exactly," I said. "We saw each other Sunday morning. It was a random thing."

Martin started running a finger up and down the condensation on his beer glass. Casting a quick glance at his father, he said, "I was going to tell you what happened. I was supposed to deliver some signed documents to one of our clients last weekend." He closed his eyes and took a breath. "But, well, it seems she died."

His father's shoulders sagged, and he reached out for his son. "Oh, Marty, I'm so sorry. I knew something was bothering you. But when you're in estate planning, you have to be prepared for that."

My phone buzzed again.

"But Dad, that's just it. Our client wasn't old. Well, not old old. I think she was in her fifties." Jerry frowned and quirked an eyebrow at his son. "Did you find anything else out? Did the police tell you anything?" Martin asked, turning to me.

"No. It sounds like they're investigating," I said. "Seems she fell down the stairs."

There was a moment of silence.

"That's tragic," Jerry finally said.

Another silence fell, and I wished I'd gone home. My phone buzzed again, and I worried that maybe there was an emergency. I excused myself, took my purse, and headed for the ladies' room.

Two texts from Evan: *Gabriella is mad because I didn't take off work to go to her aunt's funeral with her.*

Two minutes later: *Are you there? I don't think that was wrong, but you're better with girl things. Am I wrong?*

Well, good. Maybe she'd get angry enough that she'd drop him. I fired off a quick response. *You barely know her, and you have a lot going on at work. Not wrong.*

I fluffed my hair and put on some lipstick. Maybe Chaz walking out was the universe's way of setting me up with the right person. He was an ass, and he was attracted to shiny blonder things than me. So there, maybe I got the bad one out of the way. Martin seemed pretty nice.

When I returned to the table, they'd moved on to lighter topics. Martin's dad was patently proud of his son and relished the opportunity to share. He talked about how there hadn't been enough money to send Martin to a prestigious university, so he'd made the most of community college for a couple of years before transferring to Sam Houston State for his undergraduate degree. Martin kept trying to change the subject, but Jerry was not to be deterred. He wanted me to be impressed by his son, and I found his efforts endearing.

Jerry visibly puffed up talking about Martin's studies at law school. Our food had arrived, and I was thankful that the burden of conversation wasn't on me. Martin had moved back home and worked while attending law school, and I wondered briefly about a Mrs. Amos. Jerry finally became aware of the food steaming under his face and shook himself gently.

"Enough about us," he said, picking up his fork. "Tell us a little about you."

I noticed his use of 'us' only included Martin, but I guessed that was how a proud dad sounded. I skimmed over most of my life. What should you talk about when someone asks such a broad question outside of a job interview? Between bites of food, I did a quick run-through of my years as an analyst and my current foray as a self-employed entrepreneur.

Eventually, we ended up circling back around to Christine. I don't know how we did, but we did.

"How did you know Christine?" Martin asked.

"I met her last week at this Bark at the Park Festival," I said. "My friend is going out with her niece, and they introduced me. Her work was amazing." I looked at Mr. Amos. "She was an artist. She mostly did pet paintings, from what I could tell." I looked back at Martin. "Did you know her well?"

He pushed his fork to the center of his empty plate. "I'd met her a few times. We were doing some estate work for her. Obviously, there's attorney-client privilege, so I can't discuss it."

"Does your firm usually hand-deliver documents?" I asked. I didn't know anything about estate planning.

"Sometimes. Actually, most of the time. We're a niche firm. We primarily work with wealthy clientele, and they tend to like the personal touch."

Jerry squared his shoulders and lifted his chin, once again nearly bursting with pride.

Christine said she'd been divorced for around two years, so either she was just getting around to *making* a will, or she'd been making changes *to* her will. I wondered who was going to bene-fit, or maybe who was going to suddenly not benefit.

"I know you can't fully talk about it," I said. "But, wouldn't you guys know if there was a reason for someone to try to..." I hesitated. I didn't want to say it. Mr. Amos stared at me, a pleasant smile still gracing his face, unaware my thoughts had taken such a dark turn. "Well, as estate lawyers, you'd know who she was planning to leave her money to, if she was making any changes, and if someone had a reason not to want those changes made..." I trailed off as Mr. Amos's mouth made a sudden Oh.

He swiveled to Martin. "Oh, do you think someone might have..." he trailed off as well, too charitable to believe anyone could do something like that.

Martin's skin turned pinkish as we both stared at him.

"Was this a new document? Or was she making changes?" I wanted to ask specifics, like whether Gabriella had a reason to shove Christine down the stairs, but I knew I was pushing well past the bounds of civility even with my current inquiry.

Jerry and I continued to stare at him as he squirmed uncom-fortably. "Okay, I shouldn't even tell you this, but yeah. She'd made some changes to her estate. In the overall scheme of things, it wasn't a huge deal." Jerry rolled his hand as if trying to pull more information from his son. Martin stopped.

"So you were delivering the final *signed* documents?" I asked. "Or was this pre-signature?"

Martin sighed. "I was delivering copies of previously signed documents. One of my associates and I went over Friday to review the changes she'd wanted, make sure they accurately reflected her wishes, and get her signature. Once we have signed documents, one of the partners reviews them, and then we deliver a copy so our client has it for their personal records. I was supposed to deliver the copies on Saturday, but when I went by, no one was home. I knew my boss would be pissed if she didn't get them over the weekend, so I went back Sunday morning."

He closed his mouth and turned an imaginary key, letting us know he wouldn't give out any more information. Could Gabriella have known Christine was making changes? It seemed doubtful. This was all murder mystery speculation, not the real-world likelihood that Christine had slipped and died in a tragic accident.

Jerry leaned back in his chair, creases marring his forehead as he stared mindlessly at his plate. "You don't think her accident had anything to do with her will, do you? Maybe the new beneficiary got a little carried away?" He looked up at Martin.

Martin snorted. "I don't think they even know they're a beneficiary at this point."

They, I thought. Was he being tricky with pronouns? Or was it multiple people?

"How long does it usually take to notify the beneficiaries?" I asked. A waiter approached the table and asked if we wanted to see the dessert menu. Considering how much food the three of us had consumed, I wasn't surprised when everyone demurred. The waiter presented the check, and there was a small flurry as we each reached for it. Martin snatched the vinyl holder and held it aloft, out of reach for his father and me. I rummaged through my purse and extracted a credit card from my wallet.

"Here. This is for my share," I said, holding it out.

"Marty, let me have that," said Jerry. "This is on me."

The waiter faded away as Martin pulled the check close to his chest and peered inside the fold. "I've got it," he said, pulling out his wallet and slipping a card into the plastic slot.

"Son, let me do this. I've enjoyed my tremendously."

I waved my card again. "Look, let's have the waiter split it three ways," I said. "I don't feel right having either of you paying for my meal." They turned matching brown eyes on me.

"No."

"Absolutely not."

Finally, Mr. Amos took a breath and smiled. "Thank you, Marty." He turned to me. "Please, let my son treat. Your company has been a delight for both of us."

I wanted to protest but didn't want to seem impolite, so I smiled instead. "Well, I certainly appreciate you guys coming to my rescue tonight. You turned an embarrassing and terrible evening into something enjoyable, and I can't thank you enough."

The mood brightened again, and I gushed over how great the food had been and what a lovely time I'd had. They insisted on walking me to my car even though it was still fully light out. The traffic jam in the parking lot was gone, although most spots were taken. Martin asked me for my phone number, and while I wasn't entirely sure I wanted to give it to him, seeing his father's hopeful eyes fixed on me made me feel it would be rude to refuse. And who knew? Maybe Martin was the "One," and this whole thing could be one of the funny stories we told our grand-kids someday. It didn't feel likely, but stranger things have happened.

CHAPTER FIFTEEN

I visited all my biscuit distributors Friday morning, as I do every week. The transactional part of my business is conducted primarily online, but the one-on-one feedback helps me develop my baking plans. If one flavor sells particularly well or customers have provided positive feedback, I increase my baking accordingly. Conversely, if something's not selling well, I can cut back. It's not rocket science, but my years as an analyst still have me building spreadsheets to track my flavor trends. The only thing I know for sure is that dog preferences seem to be statistically unreliable.

At my last stop, I noticed a new display next to the side of the counter and went to check it out.

"What's this?" I asked the owner, picking up a small box.

"I just got that in," she said. "It's CBD oil for dogs. It can help with so many issues, like health and anxiety, you know. Like the same for people."

I immediately thought of Lucille. I launched into Lucille's story while the owner stood rapt.

"That poor baby!" she cried. Coming around the counter,

she rummaged through the different boxes before holding one up. "This. You need to start her on this one. It can help with anxiety and should help her process the trauma. We also have CBD treats, but I think the oil would be better for a dog that's been through so much."

I turned the box over in my hand, reading the tiny print. "Do you think? I've never seen a dog this distraught. If it could help, it would be wonderful."

"We've gotten excellent feedback," she said. "Please, take that and give it to her new owner, on me. I had a dear friend who went through a traumatic event," she said. "Human, not canine, but CBD oil was one of the things that indisputably helped her recover her equilibrium."

"I'd be happy to pay for this."

She waved me away. "Let's consider it a small good deed to apply to my karmic balance."

"I have another friend who has a crazy cat. Could this help settle him down?" I thought of the unearthly yowling I'd heard from Kip's cat the few times I'd been to his house. I'd never even been allowed in, and frankly, I was glad. Judging from the sound, it seemed Frenzy would take your face off before you entered the door. "I could buy one for him and let you clear your karmic balance on Lucille."

She pulled a pair of readers on a cord from the depths of her shirt and put them on, peering at the next shelf down. She snagged a bag of treats, read the back of the package, and straightened up. "This would probably help—infused cat treats. You've got a better chance with these. I don't think too many cats will voluntarily have someone put drops in their mouths." I hadn't even thought of that.

I paid for the cat treats before restocking the Barker Street Bones packages. I was thrilled to see how well they'd been selling. I was also excited about having something to help Lucille, and I texted Penny when I reached my car. She responded immediately that she'd be at her sister's later in the afternoon and was willing to try anything. That didn't sound good.

I flew through my afternoon walks. The dogs, always well-rested by Friday, acted like office interns minutes away from happy hour. I was worn out when I deposited the last one at home with a biscuit.

Christine's street was quiet as I pulled to the curb and parked in the dappled shade of the big oak tree. A car was in the driveway, and Penny stood holding the front door open as I approached.

"I'm so glad you're here," she said, opening the door wider. I followed her into the cool, dim hallway, averting my eyes from where Christine's body had lain. As we moved into the bright light of the kitchen, I saw how haggard she looked. Her face had the pallid cast of week-old tuna salad, and her eyelids puffed like dough, nearly overlapping her eyelashes. She wore an oversized shirt that looked like it had been plucked from the laundry basket and a pair of gym shorts that I assumed were her husband's. Gabriella would undoubtedly have some opinions about this. She hitched at the waistband and glanced down at herself.

"I apologize for how I look. I was starting to go through some things," she said. "There's so much to be done." Stacks of papers and crumbled tissues littered the table and countertops. I looked around for Lucille, concerned that she hadn't even come to check out a stranger's arrival. Penny sighed. "She's back here. She went straight to the couch and hasn't moved since we got here." She led me to a cozy, enclosed sun porch off the back of the house with a view of the backyard and a small studio beyond.

Lucille had curled her big body into a tight circle at the end of a worn leather couch. She didn't even look up as we entered.

"Aww, baby," I said softly, walking toward her. She still didn't move. Her eyes were red, but it was hard to distinguish between the normal bloodhound appearance and anguish. Probably a combination of both. I sank down on the floor and reached out a hand for her to sniff. She ignored it. "Wow."

"I know," said Penny, moving to the couch. She sank gently onto the cushion beside Lucille and touched her softly on the neck. One ear twitched, but she didn't try to move away.

"How's she been doing?" I asked.

"This is pretty much it," she said.

"Is she eating?"

"Some. And she drinks some. And she does her business. I don't know, never having been around dogs, what's normal."

I reached out and ran my fingers across the wrinkles on Lucille's head. "This isn't entirely normal," I said.

"That's what we thought," she said. "This is actually better than she's been at our house. There, she goes behind furniture and hides in corners. We can't get her to come out for anything."

"It's just going to take time," I said.

"Christine's funeral was yesterday. I'm afraid I'm such a blubbery mess that I'm making it worse for Lucille." Right on cue, her nose reddened, and tears slid down her cheeks. She fumbled for a tissue. "And if getting through the funeral wasn't hard enough, that detective called me. They're still investigating. They were asking me if anyone would want to hurt her, if I knew of anyone with any grudges against her, that kind of thing." She pressed the tissue under her nose. "They wouldn't tell me much, but I got the feeling there was something about how she fell or landed that didn't sit right with them."

I felt a flutter and tried to think back to what I'd seen that morning—a crimson puddle on marble, hair fanned out in bloody strands, a colorful scarf, one shoe on the floor, one caught in the hem of a flowy teal dress, and a dog toy nearby. Mostly, what stuck with me were the sounds Lucille had made. I was still trying to erase those from my memory.

"She could have lost her balance," I said. "I wonder what their thinking is." I stopped myself before jumping thoughtlessly into speculation.

"They asked if Lucille was a jumper. I guess they're considering maybe she could have gotten excited at the top of the stairs and jumped at Christine as she came up." My heart lurched at the thought that Lucille could be responsible. "But Lucille doesn't jump. She's the calmest thing, even before—I can't see that happening."

My mind began to whir with possibilities. Christine walking up the stairs and tripping on a dog toy in the dark—clutching at the banister as her heel caught in her dress, toppling backward. It seemed possible. Christine going up the stairs as Lucille raced past, bumping her with her big body. It could have happened, although judging from what Penny said, unlikely. Christine walking up the stairs, a shadowy figure at the top reaching out to give her a shove. Goosebumps broke out on my arms, and my heart started to hammer.

"Besides Lucille, do they have any ideas?"

"I believe her ex and his new wife were cleared. They were at the fundraiser with Christine, and then long after she left. There were hundreds of witnesses. They said she left early because she didn't feel well."

"If she was sick, maybe she got dizzy on her way upstairs."

Penny hmphed. "If anything, I think seeing Michael there with his new wife made her sick. She stayed through dinner and covered her obligations to the foundation. Knowing Christine, she wanted to forgo the bullshit and get home to Lucille."

Her cell phone rang from the counter, and she pushed up

from the couch, grunting with the effort. She reached it on the third ring.

"Hi, Wayne." Her tone was flat and even. She paced in a small circle as she listened to the caller, her head down, staring at the kitchen floor. "No. We only buried her yesterday. I told you this would take time." I bent toward Lucille, feigning deafness while my ears strained to hear both sides of the conversation. I wondered if this was Gabriella's father.

"No. Do not come over here. I am working with the attorneys to settle the estate, but it takes time." I could hear the strident tones of male squawking coming through the speaker, but I couldn't make out any words.

"No! I don't care what Gabriella wants. Everything is going to be distributed the way Christine wanted. I have no say in that. You have no say in that. We are doing what Christine wanted." Her voice rose, and Lucille lifted her head to watch, her ears pinching back against her head, her tongue flicking out and licking her lips in nervous darts.

"Wayne. Wayne! No. No. Okay, fine, you want to talk to the attorneys, knock yourself out. They're going to tell you the same thing. Fine!" She disconnected and smacked the phone down hard on the counter. Lucille jumped.

Penny clenched her jaws so tightly I could see the hinges grinding in ways dentists warn you about. "Sorry about that," she said. "That was my brother." She moved back to the couch and plunked onto the cushion. Lucille raised her nose and sniffed Penny's chin before scooting closer to lean against her. "He is such a shit." She reached for Lucille. "It's probably our parents' fault. They only ever wanted a boy. Christine and I were disappointments from the get-go because, as you can see, we were girls. But when Wayne arrived, you'd have thought the second coming was here. He could do no wrong, and everything Wayne wanted, Wayne got. He was like a little king."

Apparently, Gabriella took after her father.

"Wayne's probably the reason Christine and I never had kids," Penny said. The anger seemed to give her strength, wiping away her grief like a tidal surge clearing the beach of debris. She pulled another tissue from her pocket and blew her nose in a series of wet honks. "Anyway, one of the attorneys handling Christine's affairs called me. I knew she'd named me the executor of her will after her divorce, but they said she'd added a codicil recently that they wanted me to be aware of before we started doing anything with her belongings." She started to tuck the sodden tissue in her pocket, then thought better of it and dropped the crumpled mess on the cushion beside her. "It seems she'd been thinking about how much her ex hated dogs and how much she loved this one, so she recently changed her will to stipulate that all the jewelry he'd ever given her should be sold and the proceeds given to the rescue that brought her together with Lucille."

"Seriously?" I laughed. "That's awesome." Too bad for Gabriella.

"Isn't it, though? I can't wait to tell him. She even had everything appraised and documented so there wouldn't be any confusion. Only, here's the problem," she said. "I can't find it."

We stared at each other. "You can't find what? The jewelry? Maybe if it's worth that much, she put it in a safety deposit box."

"Maybe, but this was all done last week. The lawyers handled the appraisal for her, and she picked everything back up last week. I found the appraisal documents upstairs in the side compartment of her jewelry cabinet. But no jewelry." She got up from the couch again and went to the kitchen table, running her fingers over the piles of paper. "I've collected all her banking information. I guess there could be something I'm missing, but I haven't seen anything about a safety deposit box.

Anyway, here." She walked back and handed me a glossy brochure.

It looked like a catalog for an upscale jeweler. The collection was extensive—fat sapphire necklaces set in glossy white gold, ruby chokers in varying lengths, rows of tennis bracelets glittering with both white and black diamonds, as well as numerous earrings and rings representing most of the expensive gemstones one could buy. It seemed like Christine's husband had loved her at some point. Or maybe he just liked buying lavish gifts. The listing appeared to be arranged from most valuable to least. Although, as I looked at the last page, the least expensive earrings were appraised at three thousand dollars. All pieces were beautifully photographed on black velvet, described in detail, and assigned an estimated value. The collection must be worth at least a couple hundred thousand dollars. At least.

"Wow." I rued the fact that I wasn't good at doing math in my head.

She flipped a few pages before tapping at an image. "I found one of these earrings on the floor upstairs." The picture she pointed to indicated a distinct pair of earrings, shaped like flowers and bursting with emeralds and yellow diamonds—appraised at nearly nine thousand dollars.

"Wow," I said again. "They're beautiful."

"Yeah. I never saw her wear any of this, but if she was going to, I think she would have loved these earrings." She stepped back. "So why would one of those be discarded on the floor upstairs? They're obviously expensive. Christine wasn't careless like that. So, where's the other one? And where's the rest of this?"

I handed the brochure back. The codicil must have been what Martin had been delivering, and this was undoubtedly the jewelry Gabriella had been talking about—the jewelry she was hoping to get. I was genuinely starting to wonder where she'd been last Saturday night. How could I ask Evan this without getting him all twisted up and defensive on her behalf?

"So, I mentioned that I met Christine at a festival where she was showing her work," I said slowly. "A friend of mine invited me. When he saw Christine's work, he knew I would love it." She looked at me as if wondering where this was going. "He was there with Gabriella. They just started going out."

Penny rolled her eyes. "Good luck to him," she said. Then she looked embarrassed. "I'm sorry. That sounds terrible. She is my niece, and I suppose I love her. Or I should. But she's exactly like her father in female form." She rolled her shoulders a couple of times as if releasing tension. "They're like those pigs in Europe," she said, stretching her neck from side to side. I heard a crack. I had no idea what she was talking about. "You know, the truffle pigs. Or maybe they're hogs. I'm not sure I know what the difference is. Anyway, they're out there rooting around, trampling over everything just to find some valuable fungus blobs."

I'm sure Gabriella would love hearing herself compared to a truffle hog. "I don't think they use pigs anymore," I said as if this was relevant. "I think they use dogs now. I saw a show about it a couple of years ago. The hounds don't eat the truffles like the hogs do. It was actually really interesting."

"Either way," she said. "Hounds, hogs—just digging around for goodies. Same result."

As much as I wanted to prompt Penny into giving me the scoop on Gabriella, I'd seen this trap before. You think you're on the same page with someone and say something snide when suddenly the blood bond kicks in, and they get angry that you attacked a relative. "I met Gabriella and my friend for dinner earlier this week. She talked about how she and Christine used to play dress up with her jewelry when she was younger."

"Was she now? I guess she thinks that entitles her to it. Yes, she and Wayne made it clear at the funeral yesterday that they think they will be getting—well, they have expectations." Penny moved to the table and stared down at the mess. "I hate this." The grief that had subsided was making a comeback.

"I know this is none of my business, but do they have a key?"

She looked directly into my eyes. "No. There was no way Christine would have given either of them a key." She sighed. "Believe me, when the detective was asking me questions, I can't say I didn't think of Wayne. But honestly, he's too lazy to kill anyone. But now that she's gone, he has found some energy to suddenly care about the money."

I noticed she didn't say anything about Gabriella.

"Penny? What happens if you can't find the jewelry?"

She leaned heavily against the counter. "I don't know. It was unquestionably important to Christine to give this money to the dog rescue, but it seems like it was just as important that the money comes from her ex-husband via this jewelry." She attempted a smile. "It really is the perfect *up yours*, don't you think?"

"It really is."

"I know the value, so I could always take it out of the rest of the assets, but somehow it doesn't have the same impact." She straightened up. "So then, I keep looking. I've checked most of the house, and I'm finishing up Christine's bedroom, but if you have a little time, would you mind taking a quick look through her studio? I poked my head in there the other day, but it's the one spot so full of Christine's spirit—I want to set aside time to go sit—not root around." Penny pulled a key from a hook by the door and handed it to me. "If we can't find them, I'll need to call that detective back to let him know about this wrinkle, and I just want to get it over with."

I did want to see the studio. There's something about creative spaces that appeal to me. "I'll try not to disturb anything." I walked to the backdoor, and Lucille surprised us by dragging herself off the couch and lumbering to the door with me. "Looks like she wants to go with me. Is that okay?"

"It's the first interest she's shown in anything, so sure."

I opened the door, and Lucille loped across the yard toward the studio door, her tail waving in slow arcs as she moved. I hoped it wouldn't break her heart all over again when she went in and realized Christine wasn't there either.

CHAPTER SIXTEEN

The studio was adorable. It was a small, stand-alone structure with white-washed shingles, large windows, and a colorful row of pots arranged attractively along the front. It looked like it belonged more on a windswept hill in Maine than in a Houston backyard. The door was painted a soft lemon, and I pushed the key into the lock as Lucille danced beside me, shoving her nose to the opening as if to hurry me along.

I'd barely opened the door when she shoved her big body through the gap and galloped across the tile floor to a saggy couch, where I was surprised to see a man lying. He looked as surprised to see us as I was to see him, and he barely had a moment to brace himself before Lucille launched at him and landed her upper half squarely onto his abdomen.

He expelled a whoosh of air as the bulky dog pushed up and pinned him back against the cushions. It was hard to see past Lucille as she straddled him, shoving her nose against his face and neck as he twisted to escape the assault. Her tail swayed in droopy arcs, and her giant paws slipped on the leather. He finally managed to slide out from under her, shifting sideways and pushing halfway up into a sitting position. A pair of glasses hung askew on his face, and a clunky set of headphones had dislodged from his ears, strangling him as Lucille's leg caught in the cord. It was the neighbor.

He adjusted his glasses, pulled off the headphones, and peered at me as if trying to place me.

"Hi," I said.

He swung his legs to the floor and wrestled Lucille to the cushion next to him, wrapping his arms around her and rubbing one hand roughly up and down her chest.

"Hi," he said, looking away. "I'm sorry. I didn't realize anyone was coming." His face looked pale, purplish crescents circled beneath his eyes, and puffy red eyelids indicated that I'd interrupted him having a good cry alone in Christine's studio.

"I'm sorry," I said. "I didn't mean to intrude. Christine's sister is inside, and she wanted me to come out here and take a look around." I stopped myself, unsure if I should mention the missing jewelry.

"I'm David Pierce," he said, trying vainly to push himself up from the low-slung sofa. "I live next door."

"No, please, don't get up," I said. "That's the most life I've seen in Lucille since, well, I've only seen her distraught. So, please, don't get up. I'm Jessie Gallagher. I was here Sunday."

He bent his head to allow Lucille's big, wet tongue to slap against his face. Soft music drifted from the headphones, and he leaned over and hit a button on his phone.

"That's right," he said. "You were outside with Lucille."

"Yes," I said, glancing around the room. This was an artist's dream. It was light and airy and a riot of joyous colors. On one side, big windows overlooked the backyard, and on the other, French doors led to a small patio with a cozy grouping of chairs around a small metal fire pit. Saltillo tiles covered the floor in uneven squares of rust with multicolor rag rugs laid down strategically where Lucille might like to rest. Canvases were stacked and strewn in haphazard piles, some completed and others blank. Brushes of assorted sizes and tubes of paint in varying stages of depletion littered most surfaces, as well as palettes covered with dried blobs of color. Alongside a wide table, a covered easel held a large canvas, and I had to stop myself from taking a peek under the cloth. This was probably one of the last things Christine had been working on. "This is a beautiful space," I said, glancing back at David. He'd managed to compose his features, and only a discreet sniffling and a pink-rimmed nose remained of his tears.

"You're probably wondering what I'm doing here," he said, not looking at me.

"No, no. I'm sorry to intrude. I didn't realize anyone was here."

"Nor did I," he said with a sad smile. Lucille rolled onto her back and wedged herself along the back cushions, the flaps of her lips hanging loose, a look of peace settling on her face.

"It's great to see her relax," I said. "Christine's sister has been so worried about her."

He ran his hand up and down her belly, and she let out a sound that was half groan, half sigh. "Christine was her person," he said. "I've wondered how she would cope."

"Apparently not well," I said. "Although she's obviously comfortable with you."

"I used to come over here sometimes when Christine was working." His gaze moved to the covered canvas, and I could tell he was seeing more than the here and now. "She was wonderful. Such a talent. And one of the warmest people I've ever known. I would sit right here with Lucille and watch her work."

A silence fell, and I stared out the window, feeling like I needed to extricate myself and leave him to his grief. Perhaps Penny could search through the studio later. I heard a small, stifled breath and realized he'd begun crying again. I glanced over in time to see Lucille, still on her back, waving a paw at his face. She connected with his cheek, and he jerked back, his hand reaching up and touching the scratch.

"Ouch." He leaned closer to her and nuzzled the side of her face to show no hurt feelings.

"Are you okay?" I asked.

"I'm fine," he said, his hands rubbing along the folds of her neck. "She's still so young. She meant no harm."

His cheek reddened along the edges of the double cut made by Lucille's long nails. "I'm sure if you put something on it, it'll heal in no time."

"Even no time won't be fast enough," he said. He looked up at me, his gray eyes direct. "I'm not sure how my wife will feel about this. She doesn't know I come over here."

"Oh." We locked eyes again, and my heart fluttered a little. I wondered if Christine had found him attractive. Judging from his grief, he'd seen something in her. I had to admit, there was something appealing about him, never mind that he was older than my father.

"Maybe she won't notice," he said.

"Maybe," I said doubtfully. "Well, I better get back inside. Penny's probably wondering what happened to us."

David pushed Lucille gently off his lap and pulled himself to his feet. "Yes, I better be going too." He adjusted his glasses and tapped at the frames, suddenly uneasy. "I want you to know I'm not touching anything in here. I would never—"

"Oh, no, please," I said, holding up a hand. "I never thought..."

I called to Lucille, but it was as if her sorrow had returned, blotting out the small moment of joy she'd had here with David Pierce. Ultimately, it took both of us to lift her to her feet. The first few efforts she resisted by letting her legs go limp and sinking back down. She made it clear she had no intention of going with me, and it wasn't until David coaxed her out the studio door and crossed halfway across the yard with us that we got her moving in the right direction. Before we reached the back door, he veered away toward the gate and gave a sad little wave as he disappeared.

Penny wasn't in the kitchen, and Lucille slumped back into the sunroom, resuming her place on the couch.

"Penny?" I called.

"In here," she yelled, her voice reaching me from a formal living room off the front foyer. "Did you find anything in the studio?" she asked.

I told her about finding David Pierce and Lucille's reaction to seeing him. She stepped down from the small stool she'd been standing on and turned to face me.

"I'm not sure what to make of that," she said. Her hair was sticking out in wild strands, and dirt streaked the front of her shirt. She ran a hand through her hair, adding to the bird's nest look. "Now I'm not sure what to do about Lucille. It's not like Bill and I are strangers to her. She knows us, but she's never spent enough time with us to entirely bond. If she loves the neighbor so much, should I consider letting him have her?" Her nose turned red, and I feared this could be her breaking point.

"No." I shook my head. "He never suggested anything like that, and in fact, the first time I saw him, he mentioned his wife had cats and a crystal collection or something. I get the sense she doesn't like dogs. *And* I think Lucille needs you. It's just going to take some time." Not to mention, Penny looked like she needed Lucille. "She's spent more time with this neighbor than with you, so she's comfortable with him. But she will bond with you. I promise. She's sweet and young, but she's been through something traumatic, and healing from that can't be rushed."

She took a deep breath. "I met the neighbor," she said. "He was here that day, you know, and he was at the service."

"He seems very nice."

"I don't know much about Christine's personal life," she said slowly. "Of course, I knew about the divorce and what happened with that mess. But lately, she only talked about Lucille, her art, and her business."

"David said he would come over and watch her work and sit with Lucille. It sounds like they were good friends."

She took a breath and stood back up. "Well, I'm glad she had someone to talk to. I know how rough her divorce was, and she seemed reluctant to talk to discuss it. Maybe she had someone to help her through it. He certainly seems like a nice man."

"I didn't get a chance to look through the studio, though," I said. "I didn't want to mention the missing jewelry to him, and I didn't want him to wonder why I was poking around. Do you want me to go look now? He's gone home."

"We'll both go. I can spend some time by myself in there later."

As we went out the back door, Penny veered right and lifted a small painted flower pot. "Christine always put a spare key under a flower pot. Usually a painted one." Putting that one back down, she began lifting every flower pot on the back patio. "Nope."

"Could someone have found the key and gotten in that way? I'm sure the detective told you the front door was unlocked when we found her."

"That's what I was wondering. I'd told her a thousand times it's a terrible idea to leave a key out, but once she got Lucille, I think she let her guard down."

"You'd think Lucille would have deterred a burglar."

Penny reached the last pot, lifted it, and set it back down. "No key. So either she stopped hiding keys, it's somewhere else, or someone took it." She straightened and twisted side to side as if her back was sore. "I guess the neighbor has a key to the studio, if not the house, because Bill and I made sure the door was locked last time we were here."

Lucille had reached the studio door, less exuberant as if she knew it would be empty this time. We entered, and I stood quietly as Penny walked slowly into the soft stillness. Golden beams of sunlight slanted through the back windows, illuminating dust motes that danced in the air. She looked around, then moved slowly to the covered canvas.

"This must be the one she was working on," she said, hesitating momentarily before reaching for the cloth. She carefully lifted the cover, and my heart caught when I saw the nearly finished portrait of Christine and Lucille. In all the works I'd seen, none had included Christine, but here she was, arms wrapped around Lucille's chest, both of them radiating pure joy. Christine smiled, the edges of her eyes crinkling. Her cheeks were pink with health, and a soft sunbeam highlighted tendrils of hair that escaped her headband. Lucille's head tilted back toward Christine, her mouth slightly open, relaxed, and at ease, a glimpse of teeth and tongue partially covered by her big, black bloodhound lips. It was a dog so loved and secure that nothing else existed for her but that moment in time. Christine must have painted this from a photo. I recognized the leather couch as the one right before me, and I imagined David taking the picture that was the basis for this last work.

I'd nearly forgotten Penny, who stood immobilized, eyes locked on her sister's. Her hand went to her mouth, white knuckles pressing hard against her teeth. Her body shook with short, ragged gasps as if the air was too solid to breathe. Before I could react, Lucille slid off the couch and belly-crawled over, pressing herself against Penny's legs. Penny sank down and wrapped her arms around Lucille, crying into her neck while Lucille rolled sideways on the hard floor, a heap of shared misery.

The intimacy of the raw emotion rendered me immobile. I closed my eyes, desperately wanting to be anywhere else. I took a tentative step forward, feeling that I should offer comfort or withdraw, but even while I was deciding, Penny was stoically gathering herself together.

"I'm so sorry," she said, her voice raspy.

"I should go."

"No, please. It was the shock of seeing that." She glanced toward the painting without actually looking at it again. "She looks so happy." Blotchy hives flooded her neck and face, and she wiped at her tears with the back of her hand. "If this wasn't an accident, I need to know what happened. If she interrupted a burglary, then they need to find the hoodlums responsible." She ran her hand along Lucille's flank. "Whoever did this—Lucille and I deserve to know."

CHAPTER SEVENTEEN

By the time I got home, I was wrung out. Penny and I had searched through the studio, and by the time we were done, she was convinced the jewelry was nowhere on the property. She'd pulled herself together, seemingly better than before her mini break-down. In the end, I remembered to give her the CBD oil for Lucille, and she promised to let me know how she was doing and whether it helped. I felt like I needed some CBD oil myself after all that.

I thought about what Penny had said. If the police didn't believe Christine's death was accidental, then it meant someone pushed her. The missing jewelry would indicate she'd interrupted a burglary, but what about Lucille? Wouldn't Lucille have stopped a burglar? Most dogs aren't the protectors people like to think they are; nevertheless, Lucille was a big dog. Who in their right mind would break into a house with a ninety-pound hunk of dog looking out at you? Unless it was someone that Lucille knew.

But now I only wanted to curl up with Addie and forget about everything—Lucille and Penny, Evan and Gabriella. I didn't even want to think about Bertram and my search for love.

I poured myself some chilled hibiscus tea and sat on the couch. Addie was already there waiting for me, leaving just enough space for me to wedge in between her and the arm. I squished in and took a long drink, letting the calming tea swirl around my mouth. This was more like it.

Addie rolled over and rested her head on my lap. I closed my eyes and let my mind drift. I didn't feel like doing much, but I wanted to let my mom know what a loser she'd set me up with. I dialed my parent's home phone, and my mom picked up on the second ring.

"Jessie, honey. I was hoping I'd hear from you. How did it go?" Her question was delivered in the singsong tone of gleeful confidence. She was probably already picking out wedding venues and florists.

"Hi, Mom. Yeah, I wanted to fill you in on my date with Chaz."

"Hold on. Let me get comfortable." She sounded like we were girlfriends about to rehash a hot night out.

"You probably don't need to get too comfortable," I said.

"Oh?" The florists were going out the window, and wedding venues were suddenly on hold.

"He left. He left right in the middle of our date. Wait, no. We never even made it to the middle. He saw a hot girl at the bar and left with her without even saying goodbye."

There was silence on the other end while she processed this. Knowing my mom, this was going to go one of two ways. She would either be outraged on my behalf or—

"You did dress up, didn't you? I mean, I know since you stopped working at a real job, you tend to look like, well, like you work with dogs."

I ran a hand down Addie's belly. "Yes, Mother. I was shockingly clean. I wore nice clothes. I did my hair, make-up, the whole nine yards."

"Well then, I am surprised. Marilynn said her son is a wonderful young man. Chaz is apparently in a prestigious investment banking program that grooms the next generation of executives."

"Yes, he did mention that before he ran out with the bimbo."

"Jessie, there's no need for such vulgarities. You must have done something—" My doorbell rang, and Addie leaped to her feet and exploded in a salvo of barks next to my head.

"Mom, I have to go. Someone's at the door. Anyway, I wanted to let you know what your friend's son is actually like."

She started to say something else, but I disconnected. Addie stood at the door, barking and wagging, which was a weird combination for her. She got excited when Evan came over, hated Larry and all strangers, but I didn't know what to make of this mix. I peered out the peephole.

Oh. It was Evan and Gabriella. I opened the door, and Addie raced out, pushing between them. She herded Evan in before turning and woofing at Gabriella, who stood uncertainly outside.

"Addie," I said, grabbing her collar and pulling her back. "Sorry about that."

Gabriella inched in, reaching out her hand for Evan. He was busy rough-housing with Addie, ruffling her fur and spinning her in wild circles. She twirled and wagged, panting playfully. He finally straightened, and Addie's mouth closed with a snap; her tail stilled, and she turned and sat, facing Gabriella with an unwavering stare.

"Evan?" Gabriella stood unmoving, looking at Addie, then glancing nervously away.

"Oh, she's fine," he said, walking over and sinking onto the couch. "This is Addie." Addie raced over and jumped up next to him. Gabriella started toward him, then stopped as Addie exposed the merest hint of teeth.

"Addie!" I admonished her. I was used to her hackling at Larry, but other than that, she usually had better manners. "I'm so sorry. She's usually not like this." I went over and shooed her off the couch. Gabriella slid timidly onto the cushion Addie had vacated, setting a white box down on the coffee table.

"Dogs really hate you, don't they?" Evan asked with a smile. Gabriella punched him in the arm.

"They do *not!*"

"Well, Henry does. And now Addie does. Is there something I should know?" His tone was playful, and he leaned over and pulled her back against him. "Dogs know things, you know."

Addie had taken up a position six feet away, sitting ramrod straight and staring unblinkingly at Gabriella.

"Henry doesn't like you?" I asked. Addie tended to have opinions, but Henry liked everyone.

"He's just not very friendly, I guess," Gabriella said. I glanced at Evan, and he shrugged.

"So, what are you all up to tonight?" I asked. I noticed Gabriella giving me a once-over, and I self-consciously brushed at my hair. "Can I get you something to drink?"

They looked at each other, apparently communicating telepathically.

"That'd be great," Evan said. "Do you have any beer?"

I picked up my tea from the coffee table and headed for the kitchen. "Sure. Gabriella? What can I get you?"

"What are you having?"

"I was drinking hibiscus tea, but I can get you something else. Wine? Beer?"

"I'll try the tea. If you like it, I'm sure I will too," she said, standing and picking up the white box. She sidled toward me, giving Addie a wide berth. "I brought you a little something from work," she said, holding the box out toward me. "I wasn't sure what you like, so I got you a couple of different things."

"Well, that was sweet. You didn't need to do that." I took the box, the scent every bit as appealing as when Kip and I were downtown. I peeked inside the lid, spotting a chocolate cupcake and a white-topped red velvet.

She looked into the box with me. "I hope you like them. I helped come up with the recipe for the chocolate one." She pointed to one side. "The secret was to add a little coffee to the batter. It gives it depth to the flavor. Oh, and cut back the sugar. They were adding too much sugar. It was making them too sweet."

"Really? You must be a great baker. This looks and smells amazing." I said. "Do you guys want to have some? I don't think I can eat all this."

Evan patted his stomach. "No. I've been eating plenty of those," he said. I did detect a slight mound rising under his shirt. Maybe it was just the way he was sitting.

"They're for you," Gabriella said. "I hope you like them." She had the air of a child proffering an artwork that she'd toiled diligently on, both proud and uncertain.

"I'm sure I will," I said.

She smiled at me, and I felt a wave of her allure envelop me in its warmth. Maybe my first impressions had been wrong. Maybe she was just a nice, sweet girl who had a crush on Evan. Perhaps I'm just way too judgmental. Then I thought about how Penny felt—this was her own flesh and blood.

"I've been thinking about it, and I'm, like, so impressed that you started your own business from scratch," she said. I reached into the refrigerator and pulled out a beer for Evan. "I know I told you that I want to start a business of my own—you know, be a designer. Evan thought maybe you could give me some pointers." She twirled a lock of hair around her fingers. "Or maybe I'll be a design influencer. That's what I'm super passionate about."

I took the top off the beer bottle and watched her turn in a slow circle, appraising my design choices.

"Like, if you want, I could make some easy changes here and post them. It would help my portfolio."

I walked the beer over to Evan. Addie was back on the couch, claiming her place beside him. I walked back to the kitchen. "You know, I think I'm okay with how things are right now," I said.

"Oh, sure!" she said. She raised her eyebrows, her face puckering. "It's not bad." She should never play poker. "It's not like Evie, who needs so much done." She turned and smiled at Evan. He looked down at his beer bottle.

I pulled the pitcher from the refrigerator, added ice to a tall glass, and poured the vibrant red liquid. I topped my glass off and handed Gabriella her drink. "It's pretty," she said. She took a tiny sip and hesitated briefly before giving me a full smile. "It's delicious!" She sounded as if she was trying to convince both of us.

"If you don't like it, I can get you something else," I said.

She reached out and touched my arm. "Oh no, I do! It's good." She looked over at Addie, then scooted closer to me. "I like your top," she said, running her fingers down my front. She glanced up at me, her thick lashes framing eyes that were a near-perfect color match to her hair, reminiscent of a sleek chocolate lab. The overhead light caught the gentle curve of her cheek, and her skin looked as soft as a peach. Her pink lips curled up in a half smile. The moment felt vaguely intimate, and I understood what had Evan hooked.

"Thanks," I said, taking a step back. I was flustered. There was something intense and mesmerizing when she locked her attention on you. I felt charmed and uncomfortable at the same time. And if I was being honest, there was something so appealing about that level of directed interest that I found myself wanting her to like me.

I took my drink and moved Addie off the couch, opening a place for Gabriella. I hauled Addie over and held her in front of me while I plopped in an armchair across. Addie rumbled deep in her chest and locked her eyes on Gabriella. I shushed her, but there was no stopping a border collie stare. There was a small silence.

"So, about your business," I said. "I'm not sure how you start an interior design business. Are there design schools you're looking at? Or do you even need a degree? I don't know how that all works."

Gabriella smiled indulgently at my ignorance. "You sound like my mom. I mean, yeah, I'm sure there are, but that's so yesterday. I think if I had some clients, I could post my results and then, like, go from there." She raised her glass, letting the tea touch her lips before shuddering slightly. "My dad says I can do whatever I want. He thinks when we get some of this settlement from my aunt, I can use that to buy a good computer and some software or something. He thought Aunt Christine should have helped me. She was an artist and had all that money. This is kind of the same thing." She looked around my living room again, redecorating in her mind even though I'd said no. "I think there're software programs that let you show the before and afters of a room. Or move stuff around to see how it would look. You've seen it on those shows on TV, right?"

"I have. It's pretty cool."

Evan sat quietly, drinking his beer. He'd heard all this before.

Gabriella started twirling her hair. "I think I could do one of those shows. My dad thinks if I went to Hollywood, they'd for sure give me my own series. He said I'm prettier than all the women in the ones we've seen. We watch 'em together all the time." She turned and smiled at Evan. "You should watch them with me too."

He smiled a goofy smile I'd never seen before. "Anything you want."

Gabriella turned her attention to me. "You know, you're pretty too. You should do some videos to grow your business. I'm sure you could get a lot of followers."

I felt a blush creeping across my cheeks. "That's a thought," I said. I cast around for something to deflect the attention off of me. "It's nice that your parents are so supportive. I'm sure that means a lot."

She shrugged. "My dad is, for sure. He'll do anything for me. My mom's a pain. She's still acting all mad that he's excited about getting some money. Like, she wasn't exactly close to my aunt; what does it matter? And when she does say the money could help, she's got lame things she wants to do with it."

"Like what?" Evan asked.

"I dunno. Like, the air conditioner keeps going out. I mean, my dad fixes air conditioners as his job, but it still keeps going out. He said we need a new one. And her car needs something. But look at my car. It's worse than hers. I need a new car more than she does. And she's working two jobs; it's not like she can't afford to buy herself one." She paused to examine one of her nails.

"Where does your mom work?" I asked, finding Gabriella's logic interesting. Maybe her mom worked two jobs because she loved them both and enjoyed the challenge, but I doubted it.

"She works at The Dollar Box store. You know, the one on Polk Street? And she works nights cleaning offices. I don't really know where. Maybe downtown?" She set her drink down and gave Evan a pointed look, blatantly tired of the conversation.

"You ready to go?" he asked. She nodded. "Hey, we're gonna go grab some food," he said to me. "Do you want to come?"

I hadn't eaten and was too tired to cook, but I couldn't tell from Gabriella's expression if she wanted me to join them or not. I declined. She was trying hard to make friends with me, but I was too tired to deal with that tonight. Not to mention, I still hadn't decided if she was a cold-blooded killer or not.

CHAPTER EIGHTEEN

Saturday morning, I poured my first cup of coffee, hoping to infuse life into my cells. I'd slept poorly, first interrupted by Addie kicking me with flailing paws and barking a string of muffled woofs, followed by my own series of weird dreams. I don't think I barked or flailed, but I can't swear to it, nor did I remember the dreams that were probably trying to tell me something important.

I took Addie walking, my thoughts turning to yesterday. Gabriella had turned on her charm last night, and I saw how fully magnetic she could be. It wasn't only about physical attraction; she had a way of captivating and pulling you in, somehow coercing a flutter of desperation for her to like you. I'll bet all the girls in her school had wanted to be her best friend. The boys, well, I'm sure the boys had wanted something else. Either way, she knew how to make her audience react. Evan didn't stand a chance.

Penny's reaction to her own niece was interesting. It sounded as if Christine hadn't liked her either. Of course, they'd had years to see her for who she was deep down, and what appeared to be charm was likely just one of her tools to be used as she saw fit. What lurked beneath might not be as pretty.

As for Wayne, it sounded like he would do anything for his little girl. She'd said so herself. Pressing Penny the day after Christine's funeral for money, or for the jewelry Gabriella wanted, was distasteful at best. Would he go so far as to kill his sister if it made his princess happy? Penny didn't think so. And Gabriella killing Christine for her jewelry seemed even more of a stretch. Neither of these scenarios seemed correct.

However, if the police thought this wasn't an accident, then someone had helped facilitate Christine's death. With no sign of a break-in, it stood to reason that someone had access to the house. And that someone definitely had something to gain.

After breakfast, I found myself on my computer looking for Wayne Goodman. I didn't unearth much. He didn't have any social media accounts that I could find. He didn't have a LinkedIn account. Gabriella said he fixed air conditioners, but I didn't know if she meant he did that professionally or if he was just handy. I didn't see any Goodman Air Conditioning companies. I did find their address, and for lack of anything else on my agenda today, I decided to drive by.

I poured the rest of my coffee into a travel mug, plugged the Goodman address into my maps app, and headed out. They lived east of downtown, beyond the ballpark and the fast-developing neighborhoods springing up around it. I didn't have a plan, exactly. Mostly, I wanted to see where Gabriella came from and maybe catch a glimpse of her father. Despite what Penny thought, he seemed to have the most motive, lazy or not.

I made my way downtown, ignoring my maps app as it yelled directions at me. I thought I'd swing by the building where I used to work and where Evan still worked to get a sense of Gabriella's commute. It had never crossed my mind that she probably lived near downtown in order to make a minimum wage job worthwhile, but as I cruised the relatively empty weekend streets, I realized that was the case. It also meant that while she was on the opposite side of downtown from Evan, she was still pretty close to him. For some reason, that made me uncomfortable. I was still processing the fact he had this whole other life I wasn't entirely privy to.

At the Convention Center, I picked up Polk and headed southeast. The road was narrow but well-paved. I cruised past quirky night spots, dozens of warehouses, a local brewery, and the old Houston Power and Light Company building, now mainly looking abandoned except for the man lying on a heap of blankets near the door. In all my years living in Houston, I'd never been here before. I drove slowly since no one was behind me, feeling like a tourist—not that this was exactly a hot spot.

I'd nearly passed a large parking lot before realizing it was shared by a Kroger grocery store and The Dollar Box. This must be where Gabriella's mother worked. I made a quick right turn and skidded into the lot. I had no idea if she was working or what I might do if she was, but I was here, and I might as well go in and look around.

I'd never been in one of these stores and was surprised at how vast it was. It had to be at least the size of the grocery store next door. A quick look around wouldn't hurt. Maybe I'd run into Gabriella's mom stocking on one of the aisles. I grabbed a plastic basket, discarding it when I saw the crusty used tissues crumpled in the bottom. The second one I picked up had a sticky handle that made me want to run and find the cleansing wipes. The third one was marginally less gross. Right off, I was drawn to the book section about fifteen feet in. They had paperbacks for less than three dollars. I picked through the jumble, snagging two mysteries and two chic lit books, excited by my finds.

Next, I picked my way through a random selection of spices,

jellies, cereals, and canned vegetables, selecting a jar of apricot preserves. I wondered where they got their inventory. Everything was cheap, but it was definitely an odd assortment. In the pet section, I found a towel guaranteed to remove twice as much water from your dog as a standard towel. I took five. These would be great on rainy days during my dog walking.

I added measuring spoons, two silicone spatulas, and a muffin tin I couldn't pass up. My basket was getting full, and I'd nearly forgotten what had brought me in. I hadn't seen any workers, so I cut to the front before being enticed to buy more things I didn't need.

Near the front of the store, crowd control belts stretched between movable bases, funneling shoppers to the next available checker so you never got stuck in the slow line, which I invariably did when left to my own devices. This morning, there were only three people in front of me, and I had a chance to study the two cashiers. It didn't even take a minute to identify Gabriella's mom—she looked exactly like her, maybe a little friendlier. She had dark circles under her eyes that Gabriella didn't have yet, hinting at fatigue and perhaps worry.

I waited, hoping I would get her, but right before it was my turn, another worker came over. Gabriella's mom signed off her register, and the new woman logged on and waved me over. Just my luck. Then again, what was I thinking? That I'd be able to strike up a conversation and ask if her daughter was capable of pushing her aunt down the stairs? If her husband would do the same to speed up an inheritance or steal his sister's jewelry?

At first impression, I wasn't feeling killer vibes from Gabriella's mom. Of course, I could be wrong. But if she had killed Christine and stolen her jewels or thought she'd be getting a big inheritance, I doubted she'd be working her Saturday morning shift at The Dollar Box. The woman who rang me up was nice but distracted, and I was out the door with my bag in minutes.

I saw Gabriella's mom sitting on a concrete bench as I exited the store. She was on her phone and staring off across the parking lot. I stopped in my tracks and tried to move closer without drawing attention to myself. I pulled my receipt from my bag and held it up as if checking every item.

"When's she going to be back? She said she would make the alfajores for Catalina's party." Pause. "Wayne, you said you would make sure she did." Pause. Her voice was low and aggravated. Feeling my presence, she glanced sideways at me, and I began rummaging in my bag as if I wasn't a full-blown eavesdropper. She turned away. "When's she going to be home? Well, that's not enough time! You know those take a while to make." She looked down and rubbed at her forehead. "Because I told her we would bring those. I can't just buy something after I told Catalina—okay, okay. I'll take care of it." She stabbed at her phone to disconnect, then looked up and caught my eye. She smiled as if she was the one who should be embarrassed, unlike me, the eavesdropper.

I smiled back, wondering how to capitalize on this opening, but she hopped up and headed back inside. So, worthless things I'd found out: Gabriella didn't make the cookies she told her mom she would, and no one knew when she'd be home. I wondered if she was with Evan.

I put the bag in the back of my car, still intent on driving by their house. Her mom seemed nice, and I was curious about her father. From what Penny had said, Wayne wasn't nice at all. I wondered how Gabriella's mother had ended up with him. Maybe he was incredibly handsome and put on a good act.

Busy pondering these dynamics, I drove forward, intending to pull through to the next aisle. A loud crunch and popping sound stopped me cold. I reversed and eased backward, hearing the sound of something dragging.

No, no, no, no, no.

I put the car in park and got out, moving slowly toward the passenger-side front wheel. I hadn't noticed anything in front of my car, although, truth be told, I hadn't looked. Now, something was jammed between the tire and the wheel well. I'd never studied my wheel wells before, and now I realized the space was tighter than I would have thought. Something was caught at the back of the tire, and there was a whole mess underneath that I couldn't get to. I grabbed the edge of a black plastic garbage bag and gave a tentative pull. Broken glass tinkled inside, and I could make out the jagged neck of a wine or champagne bottle that had ripped through the plastic and was stuck. Some metal thing, maybe a pot of some kind, had been crushed under the weight of my car but was now acting as a wedge, holding the bottle in place.

No, no, no, no, no.

I studied the situation, not wanting to make it worse. My wheel rested on the metal object, crushing part of it while the rest rose toward the inside of the tire. There was a giant black spring near the top of my wheel, and I touched it, realizing it was part of my car. A fat lot I know about cars. Pushing the bag, I could make out the metal thing was a galvanized ice bucket. I pulled out some sodden napkins and greasy food containers that were caught, then gently pulled at the bottle, but there was no way of dislodging it until I freed the bucket. This did not look good. What were the odds I could get this untangled without ruining my tire?

Normally, I would call Evan and make him come help me, but I wasn't going to be able to explain why I was hanging out at a discount store that was nowhere near my house—the exact same discount store that Gabriella had told us about last night.

I curled my fingers around the unbroken portion of the bottle and tried to ease it loose. It wiggled a little, but until I got my car off the ice bucket, I didn't see any way to remove the bottle. If I backed up, it looked like the jagged edge of the bottle might get pressed into my tire, but if I went forward, I wasn't sure if the pail would come loose.

Sighing heavily, I started my car, crossed my fingers, and pulled forward, rolling inch by inch, praying whatever was causing the grinding sound wouldn't make my tire suddenly pop. I only made it about a foot forward before stopping, unable to stand the noise. When I went around the front end this time, I could see I was off the ice bucket, but the bottle was still in place. The glass was wet and sticky, and after a couple of tentative wiggles, I went and got one of the new dog towels I'd just bought. I rolled the towel tightly, slipped it over what was left of the bottle, and began a gentle see-saw motion back and forth. I started soft, got irritated, and then pushed down on the towel, shoving the bottle down and out from its resting position. It hit the pavement with a clank.

I held my breath, expecting my tire to suddenly deflate, but it looked okay as far as I could tell. Not seeing any trashcans, I kicked the mass of garbage into a pile and shoved it into a cart corral where no one else would run over it. My hands were sticky, and my knees were brown with dirt and pebbles. I used the dog towel to clean myself up as much as I could before dropping it down with the rest of the trash.

I considered going home, feeling deflated after that experience, but I was literally less than a mile from the Goodmans', so I might as well continue. I was only going to drive by anyway. What could it hurt?

CHAPTER NINETEEN

My mood had soured, and I drove with my mind still on the garbage debacle. It was my own fault for not checking around my car before pulling forward, but in my defense, what kind of idiot leaves glass bottles and bags of garbage sitting in a parking lot? My maps app told me to turn at the next intersection, and I dragged my attention back to my surroundings.

The neighborhood was quiet and leafy, made up of mostly older homes with a few small apartment buildings randomly sprinkled around. In spite of being Saturday, work trucks lined the curb, and various tradesmen went about their business. I made two more turns as directed and was approaching the right address when I noticed my tire light flash on.

No, no, no, no, no.

I pulled to the curb, feeling an odd tilt to my car. I did not want to deal with this. I sipped my coffee and looked out the window, spotting the address I'd been looking for: one house up and on my right. It was small-scale and brick with a roof that looked older than Gabriella. The yard was hard-packed dirt with a green swath of crabgrass stretching along a low-lying area near the driveway. A battered pickup truck sat in the shade of an expansive crepe myrtle, and a row of potted tomatoes lined a sunny spot near a side door. Two men sat in mesh folding chairs on a concrete pad that doubled as a front porch.

Great. One was probably Wayne. So now I'd seen Wayne, although I wasn't sure which one was him, and I'd seen where Gabriella lived. And what had it got me? A collection of cheap things from The Dollar Box and a flat tire that I was going to need help with. I took another long drink of coffee and climbed out of the car.

Crap. The tire was decidedly flat. How had it gone from looking fine five minutes ago to fully deflated now? I'd never changed a tire before, and since I'd only had my car a couple of months, I'd never even poked around to find my spare. Did I have a spare? I reached in and pulled the manual from the glove compartment. Then I fished around in my purse for my AAA card. Of course, I didn't have it. I had renewed my membership, hadn't I?

Another thought popped into my head, equally trouble-some. There was something about cars with all-wheel-drive. Something to do with towing—they needed a flatbed or some-thing like that? I glanced over as a metal chair frame scraped concrete. The men were standing up and walking my way. I opened the manual and flipped to the index as if I could fix this with a little light reading.

"Looks like you got yerself a problem."

I looked over, squinting against the sun. "Yeah, you could say that." I closed the manual. "This doesn't look good."

They walked closer. One looked to be in his late forties and bore a striking resemblance to a beluga whale—only not as cute. His forehead was oversized and oddly shaped, a bony protrusion providing shade to his tiny eyes. Random patches of grizzled hair sprouted from fleshy jowls, and the right side of his mouth curved up in what appeared to be a perpetual sneer. The other was thinner, darker, younger, and had a skittish look, his eyes darting to and fro as if afraid to land directly on me. He tossed a cigarette, not bothering to stamp it out.

"It's flat, alright," said the skinny one kneeling down. "Didn't your tire indicator light come on? Usually, if you have a slow leak, you'd a' known about it for a while."

I sighed. "I ran over a garbage bag in a parking lot a few minutes ago. It looked okay when I got the stuff out, but now..." We all turned and studied the rubber pancake.

I tried to guess if one of these men was Wayne, and if so, which one. Judging by age, probably the beluga whale, but he certainly didn't seem to be a match for Gabriella's mom, and if he was Gabriella's father, he hadn't contributed much to her looks—thank heavens. He leaned forward, resting his hands on meaty knees. "Lucho, get down in there and see if you can feel anything." He heaved upright and turned his attention to me. "What'd you run over?"

"It was a bunch of stuff in a garbage bag," I said, feeling like an idiot. "I didn't notice it in front of my car, and there was a wine bottle and an ice bucket and, I don't know, a bunch of junk."

He looked at me and shook his head. "Women."

Lucho stood up and dusted his hands off. "It's flat alright. I don't feel anything exactly, but looking like that, I doubt it can be fixed."

We stood in silent vigil.

"I tell my daughter all 'a time to look out where you're driving," said the one I presumed was Wayne.

"I'm usually careful," I said, the slightest bit of defensiveness coming through.

"Mm-hmm. That's what she says."

Lucho leaned over and poked at my tire again. "I could

change it out for ya," he said. "That'd at least get ya to a station to get a new one."

"Oh, I couldn't ask you to do that," I said. "I have AAA. I just need to find my membership. I'm sure I renewed." I scrambled to get to my email, popping AAA into the search bar.

"It's no trouble. He don't mind. Do ya, Luch?"

Lucho straightened up and gave me a wink. "There's not much I wouldn't do for a pretty lady."

"I can pay you," I said. "Or seriously, I don't mind calling my service."

The bigger guy cracked his knuckles, first one hand, then the other. "Don't be silly. They'll take forever to get out here. And I always hope if somethin' happens to my little girl, some nice person will take care of her. Kind of like, you know, what'd they call it now? Payin' it forward. Yeah. So let us take care of you, and maybe you can be payin' it forward to someone else sometime."

I felt like a jerk. I'd been coming over here to spy on this very man that I thought might be a killer, and here he was, being kind to me. Looks notwithstanding, he appeared to be a much nicer person than I'd thought.

"I'm Wayne," he said, tapping his chest. "And that there's Lucho."

"I'm Je—" I stopped, stuttering to a halt. I certainly didn't want him telling this story to Gabriella only to have her figure out it was me. "I'm Jerri."

He squinted at me. "Kind of boyish. You're a pretty girl. I'd think you'd call yourself something more feminine. I call my daughter Gabe, so same kind of thing, but her given name is Gabriella which is one of the most beautiful girlie names I've ever heard." He glanced over at Lucho, who was back on his knees studying the placement of my car next to the curb. "And I'm the only one who calls her Gabe, so it's okay."

"That's a beautiful name," I said. "Actually, my real name is

Jerrilee, but sometimes it's easier to shorten it." He grunted, apparently not impressed by the more feminized version of my made-up name either. "How old's your daughter?" I asked. I might as well see if I could get a conversation going while I was stuck here.

"She just turned twenty-one. She's a hellion, that one." He was unashamedly proud of her hellion status. I thought about the tired circles under her mom's eyes and knew which parent was the worrier.

I smiled. "Twenty-one is a good hellion age. Does she have a boyfriend?"

His face shut down, and he moved over and gave Lucho a little kick. "How's it looking?"

"We're gonna need to pull it out a little farther from the curb," he said. He looked at me. "You got a jack?"

At my blank look, he popped to his feet. "I prolly got one in my truck," he said, loping away. "Wayne? Do you have one in case I don't?"

Wayne ambled up the driveway, and I was left standing alone. Okay, so don't bring up boyfriends. I wondered what generated that response. Did he know about Evan and didn't like him? Or was he adverse to thinking of his little girl with anyone? From what Kip and I had seen at Chonk, she was pretty free and loose with her affections. Maybe Wayne preferred to think of his little girl as sweet and pure, although I sensed it had been many years since she'd been sweet and pure. Maybe that was his issue.

Lucho was back in seconds with a scraped-up orange jack. "I got one!" he yelled toward Wayne, who was listlessly rooting through the back of his pickup truck. "Can you pull forward a little and maybe a little bit farther away from the curb?" he asked.

I did as he asked, following his lead as he waved and shouted to direct me where he wanted. Once he was happy with the placement, we went to the rear of my car. He waited while I moved my bag of new purchases and took out the cargo mat. Then he went to work unearthing my spare tire and the associated tools that Subaru had so kindly provided. Turns out I had a jack after all. Lucho appeared to be having a great time. Wayne, on the other hand, had turned sullen and was poking at the screen on his phone. He saw me looking at him and turned around, holding the phone to his ear.

"When you going to be home?" he asked. Despite turning away, his voice was loud and clear. "Your mother said you're supposed to be making something for Catalina's party this afternoon."

A sudden dread washed over me. What if Gabriella came home now? What could I possibly say if she came home and found me camped out in front of her house? I couldn't think of any excuse for being where I was. I would have to run away down the street and leave my car behind.

"Can I help you with this?" I asked Lucho as he carefully arranged the tire and the tools in a neat line.

"Nah, I got it," he said, looking up and giving me a shy smile.

"Well, you better be," Wayne was saying. "I'm not gonna listen to your mother bitching about this all night." He paused and glanced over at me. I looked away so fast I nearly pulled an eye muscle. "Nothing. Me and Lucho just hanging out. Yeah, I'll tell him."

He hung up and waddled over. "Gabe says hi," he told Lucho. "She said she'll save you some of those alfa whatevers she's making."

Lucho smiled. "She's sweet." He had positioned the jack with expert precision under the frame of my car and was pumping it up, inch by inch. Seeing how careful he was being made me relax a bit. I would relax more if I knew for sure Gabriella wouldn't be home until I was long gone, though.

There were so many questions I wanted to ask Wayne, but I couldn't pose any of them. It wasn't like I could bring up Christine or inquire where he'd been last Saturday evening. Nor could I ask if he'd stolen her jewelry or shoved his sister down the stairs. Then, a thought struck me. If Wayne thought Christine's estate was being split between him and Penny, there would be no reason for him to steal the jewelry—he'd assume it would be a part of the final distribution. In fact, it would be easier for him if everything was liquidated and split up. It would save the pesky trouble of finding a fence because, at some point, these jewels would be listed on a stolen goods report. Then again, if he knew the jewelry was destined for a dog rescue, I could see a motive to take them. I'd gotten the sense from Penny, though, that he had no idea what the terms of the will were.

Wayne moved closer and hunched down next to Lucho. "How's it looking?"

Sweat had begun running down Lucho's face, and his t-shirt stuck to his chest. "It's good," he said. He reached for a wrench and began trying to loosen the first lug nut. His thin arms strained like taught rubber bands, his teeth clenched, and he grunted loudly.

"Here, lemme do that," said Wayne. He grabbed the tool and put his bulk behind it, shoving downward with a powerful thrust. The wrench tilted, and he repeated the move until it nearly hit the ground. "You should be able to get it now." He straightened, rubbing at the small of his back.

The last thing I wanted was for someone to get hurt helping me. "You okay?" I asked.

"Fine. Just an old injury. Acts up sometimes."

We stood in silence, watching Lucho laboring over my tire. Wayne sucked in breath through his mouth, a wheeze sounding from the back of his throat. In and out. In and out. I stared at him out of the corner of my eye, hoping he wasn't having a heart attack, but neither he nor Lucho seemed phased by this rasping. I felt twitchy and nervous. I grabbed the end of my ponytail and ran my fingers over the smooth strands, trying to soothe myself.

"I'm sorry," I said. "But do you have a bathroom I could use? My coffee..." I trailed off and bit my lip. "I could probably wait."

Wayne wheezed again, then jerked a thumb toward his house. "Yeah, in the side door. It's past the kitchen on the right."

I took off at a trot as if this was indeed an emergency, but truth be told, I couldn't stand there listening to his breathing anymore. He needed to get that checked out, probably sooner rather than later. I opened the door to the kitchen and took a quick glance around. Now that I was in the house, I wanted to poke around, but my nerves were feeling as tight as Lucho's arm muscles.

"Hello?" I called softly. As far as I knew, the entire Goodman clan was out of the house, but better safe than sorry. "Hello? Anyone here?"

I moved through the kitchen, doing a quick survey. It was neat and clean, except for some soft drink cans on the counter and a couple of cereal bowls with dried cornflakes stuck to the sides resting in the sink. Toward the front of the house was a den area, dominated by an overstuffed maroon recliner, which undoubtedly housed Wayne's bulk much of the time. It pointed toward a flat-screen television that rested on a laminate console table. A smaller sectional sofa hugged the wall, two pink blankets wadded up and covered with half a dozen throw pillows. The walls were bare, and there were no knick-knacks. There didn't appear to be much in the way of feminine influence here. There also didn't appear to be an overabundance of money. I could see why they hoped to get an influx of cash from Christine's estate.

I headed down a short hall, peering into the open doors as I passed. The main bedroom was at the far end, the bed unmade and a string of manly-looking underclothes strewn along the floor toward a bathroom. Two smaller bedrooms were at the back of the house, one serving as a storage area; the other was Gabriella's bedroom. A small bath was across the hall. I hesitated, the desire to snoop around Gabriella's bedroom nearly overwhelming my good sense. When I spotted a pink jewelry box on top of her dresser, reason fled, and I walked into the room.

If Gabriella had stolen Christine's jewelry, there was no chance she'd have tucked it into a little girl's jewelry box. Right? Well, what if she had? What if no one ever came in here, and she thought it would be safe? What if she put all her prized possessions in there? I would be remiss to pass up this opportunity. Before I could stop myself, I had it in my hand, flipping the tiny clasp and raising the lid. My heart nearly stopped when the music box began tinkling forth the notes to Swan Lake. I slammed the lid shut and thumped it back down on her dresser. I needed to get out of here. What if someone caught me?

I was rounding the corner to the hallway when I heard the door open and Wayne's heavy footsteps hitting the kitchen floor.

CHAPTER TWENTY

I froze, half in and half out of Gabriella's doorway. Wayne stopped mid-step, too, his eyes narrowing menacingly as they locked onto mine.

"What are you doing in there?" His voice was hard, his thick body planted, blocking my way to the side door. Maybe I could outrun him to the front door, but even if I could, then what? My car was up on a jack, and the tire was probably off the rim by now.

I could hardly breathe. "I needed a tampon," I said, my voice cracking with stress. "I thought maybe..." I fluttered a shaking hand toward Gabriella's room.

"Oh, Jesus." Wayne's pale beluga head turned crimson, and he looked away. "I don't wanna hear about this. Did you look in the bathroom?" He turned and waved a disgusted hand as if dismissing me entirely. "Hurry up." Then he thumped out the door, leaving me alone to catch my breath.

Well, since I had his permission to snoop around the bathroom, I might as well take a peek while I was here. I went into the dated hall bath and shut the door behind me, turning the tiny loose lock. I took a second to prop myself against the counter and stare at my wide-eyed self in the mirror. I would never make it as an undercover cop.

The bathroom was disgusting. I could only suppose that Gabriella's mom had given up on playing maid and was letting her fend for herself. So far, the strategy didn't seem to be taking. Every inch of counter space was covered with makeup, hair care products, and assorted lotions and creams. I pulled at a drawer that opened only two inches before a curling iron wedged against the wood. I shoved it closed and tried the bottom drawer. That one also appeared to be the final resting place for a myriad of hair styling tools: flat irons, hair dryers, and another curling iron, their wires tangled and twisted into knots and covered by a leaking jar of something pink. Gross.

I availed myself of the facilities while there, my bladder having been tweaked by nerves. Those nerves hadn't fully calmed down, and I still felt jumpy with tension. A quick glance past a filthy shower curtain revealed bands of gray dirt overlaid with splotches of pink bacteria creeping up the sides of the tub. Blobs of multicolored shampoo coated the far corner as thick as dried candle wax. I shuddered. I would rather shower at a roadside motel than set foot into that thriving petri dish.

I bypassed washing my hands, convinced that touching the handles on the sink would add far more bacteria to my hands than I currently had. I'd only been in here about three minutes, but I felt the pressure to get out before Wayne came back in looking for me. I fumbled with the lock, then raced down the hall and out the side door.

Lucho had the spare on and was working to tighten a lug nut as I hurried over. Wayne stood a few feet away, arms crossed and studiously avoiding looking at me.

"How's it looking?" I asked Lucho, leaning down for a peek.

"I'm about done," he said, glancing up and rubbing a forearm across his brow to stop a trickle of sweat before it hit his eye. "Hey, Wayne? You wanna give me a hand tightening this up?"

Wayne grunted but moved in our direction. I guess while he didn't like me and suspected me of rooting through his daughter's room, he still didn't want to see me killed when my spare tire rolled off the rim in traffic. I stepped away and checked my wallet while they were busy. I slipped a twenty out and folded it in my hand for Lucho. He certainly deserved something for his trouble.

It only took a few more minutes before he was done. He replaced my tools under the cargo liner and hefted the discarded tire into the back. Wayne had wandered back to his chair on the concrete pad, for which I was thankful.

Lucho turned to me. "So now, ya can't be driving far on that, okay? It's an all-wheel drive car, and you shouldn't even be driving with the spare on the front. Can you go straight to a tire place?" He looked so concerned that I began worrying whether I should be driving it at all.

"Is it safe?"

"Yeah, you should be alright, but like I said, you ought to get this taken care of. Today, if you can." He wiped his hand across his forehead and flicked a stream of sweat off, leaving a black dirt mark in its place.

I thanked him profusely and slipped him the twenty. He tried to refuse it, but I insisted, hurrying to get in my car before he could argue. He smiled, waved, and tucked the bill in his pocket before bending to retrieve his jack.

I needed to check my phone for the nearest tire place, but I just wanted to get out of there. The fear of Gabriella pulling up before I could get away was still foremost in my mind. I waved to

Lucho and pulled slowly away from the curb. The smell of rubber filled the hot car, and I turned the air on high. There was a Discount Tire on the Southwest Freeway. I'd been there before, and their service was good.

I gripped the wheel tightly in my sweaty hands as I rolled slowly past the Goodman's house. From the corner of my eye, I could see Wayne leaning back in his chair, his arms still folded across his chest as if angry and offended. This would be a story I should be able to laugh about someday, but I wasn't sure there was anyone I'd ever be able to tell it to.

The drive to the tire place did nothing to calm my strung-out nerves. The steering wheel vibrated oddly in my hands, and I drove so slowly that people kept honking at me. I couldn't believe how many people were okay with making rude gestures at me—couldn't they see this dinky donut tire? Houston had an abundance of potholes, but I'd never felt them as severely as I did now. Every rut caused my car to judder and pitch as if my spare tire was a solid hunk of hard rubber. I sure hoped I wasn't damaging anything.

By the time I reached the tire place, nervous sweat rings lined my armpits, and relief washed over me like a marathoner crossing the finish line—until I saw the line. Discount Tire on a Saturday is like The Honey Baked Ham store on Christmas Eve. I dutifully marched to the back of the line and hoped for the best. The young advisor I finally reached went outside with me to look over the damage. He pulled the tire from the back of my car, bounced it down onto the pavement, and shook his head sadly as he examined it.

"Yeah, it can't be fixed," he said decidedly. "And that's a shame because you've got an all-wheel drive car here." This was the second person to bring this up like it was a bad thing. He explained the situation using words like uniform diameter, differential, and drive-train. I stared at him, trying to keep up, but mostly, I was getting a sinking feeling that this would be expensive.

"So, bottom line?" I asked.

"You're probably going to need four new tires."

"But only one is bad!"

He sighed and launched into his talk again. I rubbed my temples and tried to pay attention this time. "Okay, I think I get it," I said. "But my car is new, and these are essentially new tires, so replacing one now should be okay, right?"

He bent to look at the tread. "How many miles do you have?"

"Less than a thousand."

He smiled. "Okay, I think we can work with that!" He took a moment to slide behind the wheel to check my mileage as if he didn't quite believe me.

We went back in and made our way past the new line to his terminal. He clacked away on the keyboard, bending, frowning, scrolling, and muttering to himself. Finally, he looked up. "You're in luck! And I mean, you are in luck. We have one of the same in stock." He looked down again, tracing his place on the screen with a finger. "You have no idea what a small miracle that is."

"I believe you," I said, feeling a wave of gratitude for this buzz-cut teenager. I refrained from hugging him.

"It is gonna be a while," he said. "We're pretty full today, and most of these people have appointments. Is there any way you can leave it and come back? It'll probably be late afternoon."

I thought through my options, but none were very good.

"I'll wait," I said.

He shook his head like he thought this was a poor decision on my part but continued to enter all the information he needed before taking my keys and telling me they'd let me know when it was ready. I paced for a while, hoping a chair would open up, and then I went outside and paced the sidewalk out there. This was going to be a long day.

At twelve-thirty, I walked across the parking lot to the restaurant next door. I lingered over the menu, drank three iced tea refills, and picked my way through a Cobb salad. When I finally noticed my waitress giving me the eye as if I was holding her up from leaving, I paid the bill and wandered over to one of the benches near the door. I might as well sit in here for a while since I was already sick of the tire store. It was hot here, and my thighs stuck to the vinyl seat, but at least I could entertain myself watching people come in and out. I started playing games, making up stories of those who passed by.

I had already assigned people roles of spies, embezzlers, serial stalkers, and secret prostitutes when a woman walked by. I immediately appointed her as a home wrecker. You could tell by the tight dress, swiveling hips, and cat-like look of satisfaction that she was out to steal a man. And, oh my God, the man she sashayed up to literally removed his wedding band as she approached. My mouth dropped open, and he caught my eye, realizing I'd seen everything. He was my age, or maybe a few years older, and he immediately got flustered, grabbed the woman by the arm, and hustled her inside. Well, well, well. I wondered where his wife thought he was this fine Saturday afternoon. Judging from his clothes, I'd say he told her he had to go into the office for a little while. What a creep. Then again, maybe I had it wrong. It was only a restaurant; it wasn't like I was sitting in the lobby of an hourly motel. But the ring removal was definitely a bad sign.

I sat back, my thoughts suddenly drawn to Christine's neighbor, David. He'd absolutely had feelings for Christine, but Christine didn't seem like a home-wrecker. What I'd seen pass by was about sex. I got the sense what David felt for Christine was about love. Sometimes love happens when people spend time together, and judging from his grief, he'd had more than just high-level neighborly feelings for her. I didn't know if she'd reciprocated his feelings. I didn't know if they had a full-blown relationship. It sounded like Penny didn't know either.

I wondered if his wife suspected anything. Maybe they were one of those older couples who went to dinner and sat in silence, each leading their own lives with nothing left in common. Perhaps she'd welcomed his attention being directed elsewhere, but I doubted it. Not many people were okay with sharing a spouse, particularly if that spouse might be falling in love. Her stable, wealthy little world would be at risk. And what might she be willing to do to protect that? Would she be prepared to shove her rival down the stairs? David had a key to the studio; I wondered if they had a key to the house. Many neighbors share their keys in case of emergency. And then there was the key that Penny thought should be under the flower pot that wasn't. Might Irene have taken that?

I thought back, trying to picture Irene. Mostly, I recalled how her hands clutched at her silk bathrobe and the oversized slippers she'd shuffled back and forth in. Besides that, she was essentially a series of background impressions against the stress of seeing Christine's lifeless body. She'd seemed scared and vulnerable. Or had that been the security guard? At the time, my attention had been focused on Christine and Lucille. I wished I'd paid more attention.

But Irene killing Christine over jealousy didn't explain the missing jewelry. I still wanted to blame Gabriella for that, although deep down, I wasn't convinced that rang true. It was also possible that the jewelry wasn't missing, just somewhere that Penny hadn't found yet. That didn't ring true in my gut either, but nothing tied up exactly right in this situation. I wondered how the police investigation was going. Maybe I'd check in with Penny tomorrow and find out if the CBD oil was helping Lucille and whether the police had any new information.

As for now, I wanted my car to be done.

CHAPTER TWENTY-ONE

I didn't get home until after five. I'm unsure who was more irritated by my long day, Addie or me. I felt like I'd been gone on a road trip to nowhere for days. Addie bounded around using her super-sniffer nose to determine where I'd been and with whom. I don't know what she thought, but my inefficient human nose picked up the sour stench of dried stress sweat. I was pungent.

I was halfway up the stairs to shower when the doorbell rang. I slumped down the stairs and squinted through the peephole as Addie barked beside me. An oversized, distorted eyeball stared back at me, and I jerked away, letting out a small yelp.

"Hey! I know you're in there. I saw you drive in."

Addie continued barking. I slowly opened the door several inches, blocking the opening with my body.

"Hey, Larry."

Addie kept on.

"That's what I wanted to talk to you about," he shouted. "Can I come in?"

I put my arm along the edge of the door and rested my head against it. "It's not a good time. I'm headed for the shower."

Unlike the other morning when Larry looked relatively spiffy on his way to work, today he wore a dingy t-shirt and gym shorts that looked overwashed and in danger of disintegrating off his waist. There are things in this world that I'd rather not see. He made a face and fanned the air in front of his nose as if dispelling an offensive odor.

"Whoa, yeah. Have you heard of deodorant?" He stepped back and studied me. "I always thought you were one of those princess girls. I didn't think princess girls ever smelled bad. What have you been doing?"

"It's been a long day. What did you need?"

Addie continued to bark but at a woof level, her mostly closed lips muffling the sound.

"It's about that," Larry said, pointing at Addie. "Your dog barked incessantly all day long." He repeated himself, this time clapping between each word. "All day long."

"Really?" That was odd for Addie. She was usually good when I left. Granted, I typically wasn't gone this long, or at least since I'd quit my full-time job, but she was left alone plenty of times and seemed fine. Or at least I thought she was. How would I know if she barked every time I was gone? "Does she normally bark when I'm not here?"

"I don't know. I work for a living. But it's Saturday, and I was trying to relax. It's not very relaxing listening to that!" He pointed an accusing finger at her.

"I'm sorry. I didn't expect to be gone so long." I looked at Addie, who stopped woofing and looked at me. "I'll tell her not to do that next time." Larry looked like he had more to say, but I eased the door shut and snapped the lock, too late to miss his loud belch. There was something comforting about Larry reverting to his disgusting-neighbor status. I'd started to worry about myself earlier in the week when I found him semi-appealing.

Clean, dry, and comfortable in an oversized t-shirt and shorts, I took some time to play with Addie. She wasn't keen on fetching things, but she did relish a good game of Find It, whereby I ran around trying to find a good place to hide her toy, and she immediately tracked where I'd been and raced back with it. Sometimes, she returned with the toy before I'd even sat down again. Tonight, she was at the top of her game, running straight to the toy like a heat-seeking missile every single time.

"Why did you bark all day?" I asked her. "Were you trying to annoy Larry?" She had nothing to say; she just raced off and started her zoomie loops. "Too much energy?"

The doorbell rang again. Addie redirected mid-loop and careened down the stairs. I followed more slowly, dreading a Larry repeat, but before I was halfway down, she began wiggling her entire backside so hard I marveled that her spine could move like that. Evan was the only one that elicited that kind of reaction.

I opened the door automatically, remembering after the fact that he might have Gabriella with him. Henry raced through, and Addie shot off after him, nipping at his back feet as he flew in mock terror toward the couch. Leaping onto the cushion, he twisted around and play bowed, yapping in her face now that he was level with her. She vaulted up, knocked him sideways with a paw, and they tumbled in a pile.

I looked back, relieved to see that Evan was alone. "Hey," I said. "This is a nice surprise."

"I wasn't sure you'd be home, but I hoped you would be. I needed a break."

We settled in our regular spots, and he filled me in on the project he'd been working on. It was a complicated model, and as team lead, he was also responsible for the other team member's work. He looked haggard.

"Why can't they do what they're supposed to?" he grumbled.

"Like this new guy, he's smart and all, but he waits till the last minute. No, it's not even that—he goes over the last minute. It doesn't matter how many times I tell him we need his data before we can run the model. He tells me to 'chill, man.' What am I supposed to do about that?" He slumped back and put an arm over his face. "I needed his data yesterday. They want the first pass at our deck Monday morning. Do I have it? No! I've spent most of the day running his stuff because he doesn't 'do weekends.' I don't want to be a jerk. I've worked with jerks. But geez. And Susie, she's sweet, but it turns out she's not that smart. No matter how many times I show her how to do something, she says she gets it, but she doesn't!"

"Team lead's not all it's cracked up to be, huh?" Addie and Henry had arranged themselves on either side of him. "Is there anything I can do to help?" It had been a while since I'd run any modeling spreadsheets, but I could probably do some simple number crunching if he needed it.

"Thanks, but no. I just need a mental break. What'd you do today?"

I gave him a condensed version of my day, carefully avoiding mentioning where my tire disaster had originated. I had to dance around it because he was incensed on my behalf and wanted me to complain to the store owner, if not present them with the bill for my new tire.

I finally redirected the conversation by asking how Gabriella was doing.

"Her little cousin's having a birthday party tonight, and she had to go," he said. He sounded vaguely relieved. "She was getting pissy because I have so much work to do. She doesn't get why it can't wait till Monday. I don't think she understands how work works." He sighed. "She sounds like our new analyst. What's with kids these days?" He laughed like we were decades older rather than a few short years.

I wanted to tell him about Christine's missing jewelry, but I wasn't sure what he would share with Gabriella. I hated having to censor what I talked to Evan about—it was so unnatural.

"Any news on her aunt?" I asked, trying to approach the subject from the side.

"Like what?" Henry had draped himself across Evan's lap and was batting at Addie's ear.

"Oh, I don't know," I said. "I saw Penny and Lucille Thursday evening. She said the police don't think Christine's death was accidental."

"Really? How come you didn't say anything last night?"

"I don't know. I'm not sure what Gabriella knows or doesn't know."

"What difference does that make? It was *her* aunt."

He was getting affronted on Gabriella's behalf. I needed to refine my approach. "I know, but I didn't want to upset her if they hadn't told her that it might not have been accidental."

He considered. "Yeah, that makes sense. She can get pretty worked up about stuff. So, what do they think happened?"

"I'm not sure they know. I guess they're looking at anyone who might have had a motive."

Evan sat up a little straighter, his exhaustion falling away. "Do they have any leads?"

We'd found ourselves trying to figure out suspicious deaths before, and I knew he imagined himself some kind of super sleuth. I debated again, telling him about the jewelry.

"Well, I think they're not sharing something yet." I had no idea what 'they' were or weren't sharing, but I paused, waiting for Evan to volunteer himself to secrecy.

"What?" He was on alert now, like Addie spotting the first flick of a squirrel tail.

"I don't want to put you in an awkward position with Gabriella," I said.

"We're basically not even talking about this," he said. "Well, other than her droning on about getting some money from it." I sat and stared at him until things began clicking in his brain. "Wait, you don't think Gabriella did it, do you?" His voice had an odd tone, as if he was halfway excited he might be dating a murderer and halfway outraged at my audacity.

"No, that's not what I'm saying at all," I said. Maybe she did, maybe she didn't. "But when I was there, Penny said all of Christine's expensive jewelry is missing."

"So...it was a robbery?"

"Maybe. But there was no sign of a break-in."

His eyes narrowed as he gazed across the room in thought. "So, someone with a key?"

"Maybe."

"But this is the jewelry Gabriella was talking about last night, isn't it?" he asked, finally catching up.

"Yeah. The thing is, Christine had recently had it appraised and had added something to her will, leaving it all to the dog rescue that she'd gotten Lucille from."

"So, Gabriella wasn't going to get it anyway?" he asked.

"No, apparently not."

We lapsed into silence while Evan digested all this.

"How much was this jewelry worth?" he asked.

"I'm not sure. There was a full appraisal, and Penny showed me the catalog detailing all of it. I didn't see a total, but these were some really expensive pieces. I'd have to guess in total—at least a hundred thousand? Maybe a couple of hundred thousand."

"*Dollars*? For *jewelry*?"

"I know, right! But this was absurdly nice stuff. It was everything her ex gave her."

Evan lapsed into silence, absently flicking a finger against Henry's tags and listening to the tink, tink, tink they made. "I was with Gabriella for at least part of that Saturday night," he said. "We were hanging out in Midtown. There were a bunch of bands and food trucks, stuff like that." Tink, tink, tink. "Do they know when Christine, um, died?"

"I think they know, but I'm not sure myself. I haven't wanted to ask Penny anything that specific. Christine's ex was ruled out because he was with plenty of witnesses at the fundraiser, so it sounds like it must have been fairly early."

He let out a long breath. "Then, I don't think it could have been Gabriella either. I was with her till at least midnight. And I'm not sure she was steady enough to go do something like that."

I considered a drunk Gabriella climbing the stairs and somehow causing Christine's fall.

"What about the sister?" he asked. "This Penny lady. Maybe she wanted the money. She's got as much motive as anyone else."

Truthfully, she might have more. What had she said about Wayne's expectations? 'He thought he would be getting,' then she'd stopped. From that, I inferred that he wasn't getting an even share he felt entitled to. Maybe she'd said they. Well, Gabriella had been clear about wanting money out of this too. I wasn't sure Penny was inheriting Christine's estate, but I was at least sure her grief was real.

"It seems like she and Christine were close. And I've seen her. She is broken up over this."

"So then, it still seems like a robbery."

"True," I said. If there'd been any sign of a break-in, this would be a slam dunk. "She did say Christine usually kept a spare key under a flower pot, but she didn't find one when we looked."

"Let's go," he said, shoving Henry aside and standing up.

"Go where?" I asked.

"I want to see for myself. Maybe we'll spot something no one else has and figure out who killed her. This is just like those other times we've solved crimes." He said this as if it were the most natural thing in the world. "Or maybe we'll find the jewelry! And then the dog rescue can get their money. C'mon, Jess! You know you want to help the dogs. I'll bet there's something everyone missed. Come on. What's it going to hurt?"

I didn't think we would find anything poking around Christine's yard, but he was right—it reminded me of some crazy things we'd done in the past couple of years, which led me to wonder why I kept running across dead people. I'm an average person; it shouldn't be like that. Nevertheless, Evan's enthusiasm made it feel like old times between us, and I was all for doing anything that felt like the old us.

CHAPTER TWENTY-TWO

We sat on a bench in the park overlooking Christine's house, holding tall plastic bottles of slowly warming water. It wasn't even seven o'clock, and the slow-moving June sun was taking its sweet time going down. Evan had wanted to rush into the backyard and start poking around, but too many people were hanging out at the park. For all we knew, some of them were Christine's neighbors who would wonder what the strange couple was doing trespassing at a house where someone had recently died.

So, we sat catching up on things, the conversation bouncing around. I told him about my date with Chaz and how he'd walked out on me. We touched on how weird it was that Henry didn't like Gabriella, and we speculated the reasons, from her perfume to her lack of experience with dogs. I refrained from pointing out that maybe she was just a bad person. Eventually, Evan grew restless and paced before me, wanting to start his investigation. Frankly, after the morning I'd had 'investigating' Gabriella's house, I was more than content to stay on the bench.

He stood staring at the house, looking first at one side, then the next. He'd started his investigation.

"Okay, we have the tennis courts on one side and a house on the other." He tilted his head. "It sits alone, doesn't it? For being in the middle of River Oaks, at least. Someone could have hopped the wall from the tennis courts. Right?"

The courts were empty, and he headed that way. I hauled myself from the bench and trailed along. Pushing through a squeaky gate, we approached the wall that bordered Christine's. A nearly ten-foot high cinderblock wall wouldn't be impossible to scale, but it wouldn't be easy. Evan walked along, running his hand as close to the top as he could as if checking for grips.

"Okay, maybe they didn't come this way," he conceded.

"And then they'd still have to get in with no sign of a break-in," I added.

The tennis courts were clean—no litter, debris, or even any leaves scattered in the corners. From the far side of the court, the house's second floor was visible but still heavily screened by the thick branches of the backyard oak. There were no direct lines of sight to the windows, so anyone watching the house would be limited to glimpsing an occasional light flick on or off.

Evan was at the far side of the courts near Christine's, trying to propel himself up by wedging his sneakers against the corner of the two walls. He evidently had no ninja genes whatsoever and couldn't get more than two feet up before falling back each time.

"Okay, I don't think the killer came in this way," he said, confident that his test was conclusive. "What about the other side?"

"Evan, I don't think we need to worry about whether someone hopped the fence. We need to figure out who could have gotten into the house with no forced entry. There's not even a locked gate to the backyard—someone could have walked up the driveway. And actually, the front door was unlocked the morning that Christine was found. Presumably, someone could have gone in that way. Or maybe she let someone in."

He dusted off his knee, which had lost a few layers of skin on his last attempt. "Right. Okay. Let's think about that." We exited the courts, closing the squeaky gate behind us. "If she let someone in, they must have gone upstairs in front of her in order to turn around and push her down, right?"

"I guess so," I said. "Or they could have reached forward and flung her back." I told him about finding David, her neighbor, and how distraught he was at her death.

"Oh, that's good!" Evan said. "Maybe she let him in, and he killed her accidentally, and now he's guilt-ridden."

"Maybe," I said, considering. "But I don't know. I'm trying to picture how that would happen."

"They were fooling around on the stairs, and down she went."

It was a possibility. "I wonder if he has an alibi?"

"Is the neighbor married?" Evan asked. "Maybe the wife snuck in and waited at the top of the stairs."

"That seems more likely," I said. I didn't want to think of gentle David having killed Christine, no matter how inadvertently. But Irene—I could get behind that. "She was the one who found Christine," I said.

"Oh! Oh! She went in and destroyed evidence." Unlike traditional investigators, Evan didn't believe in finding and following evidence; he believed in deciding who the killer was and looking for clues accordingly. "Okay, this is good. She either had a key, like neighbors sometimes do, or she found the key."

We stood at the park's edge, waiting as people slowly cleared out. Dusk had begun edging in, darkening the corners and ushering in a fully rested mob of mosquitoes. I swatted at my exposed legs.

"What do you want to do?" I asked, hoping to get in the car

and go home. We could speculate all evening from the comfort of my couch.

"Let's go see if we can find anything," he said in a near whisper. "It's why we're here!"

He was so excited and so much like ordinary Evan that I decided it was worth a few bug-bites to reconnect with him. We glanced around before making our way up the driveway.

The backyard was darker than the park, thanks to the heavy canopy of leaves blotting out the remaining daylight. A tiny porch light glowed yellow outside the studio, most likely hooked to a light sensor. We crept toward the back of the house, and I pointed out the flower pots that Penny had expected to be hiding a key. Evan lifted each one, peering close and feeling underneath as if he didn't trust that Penny had been thorough enough. Not finding anything, he crept toward the bushes and studied the dirt behind them using the flashlight on his phone.

"What are you looking for?" I whispered.

"I'm not sure," he whispered back. "But maybe there's a fake rock or something where she hid a key." A twiggy shrub poked into his abdomen as he leaned down to examine the space behind it. "Or maybe there's footprints. They could have gone in this window."

It seemed unlikely since the bush he was mangling looked as if no one had disturbed it, except him, in the last few years, but I let him search anyway. He was having fun. I wandered back toward the studio, drawn again to the adorable structure. I wished I had room in my backyard for something like this. Like Evan, I lifted all the flower pots in front of the studio and squinted underneath in the dim light. I wasn't about to feel beneath them like he was doing in case ants, roaches, or other multi-legged creatures were hiding out. The last thing we needed was to draw attention to ourselves with an ear-splitting shriek if I touched a wiggly.

Convinced no keys were hiding under pots or within hidden rocks, we converged in the middle of the yard. Evan was staring at the fence blocking our view of the house next door.

"I wonder if we could go look around over there," he whispered.

"No! We can't go over there; they're probably home. Anyway, what exactly do you think you'll find?" I whispered back.

"I'll know it when I see it."

He approached the wooden fence slowly. It wasn't ten feet tall like the concrete block wall on the other side, probably only seven. Judging by the scent, the boards were cedar and relatively new, and they overlapped enough to ensure no gaps. A row of azaleas ran along the base, split near the middle for a nicely placed concrete bench. Evan hopped up, stretching slightly to see over the top. Not to be left out, I climbed beside him, feeling the top of the bench wobble slightly. I grabbed the top of the fence, steadying myself and hoping we wouldn't go down in a heap.

The yard was dark, the only light a warm yellow glow radiating from the windows. They didn't have any window treatments that I could see, and my love of peeping into other people's houses went into high gear. I didn't have to stretch to see the upstairs windows, so I started there. Unfortunately, besides what looked like the side of a well-polished cherry wood dresser, there wasn't much to see in the closest window. The following window appeared to be a continuation of a bedroom, but the angle prevented me from seeing anything besides a bit of wall. I've never cared for that shade of mauve.

I was pulling myself up higher to view the downstairs windows when three things happened simultaneously. The smell of cigarette smoke hit my olfactory nerves at the same time I spotted the glowing orange tip of a cigarette hovering in the darkened niche of a covered porch. Just as I was processing that, a phone began ringing. My heart flew into my throat as I reached for my back pocket where I'd shoved my cell. Almost immediately, I knew it wasn't mine, but my brain seemed to be working on a delay. The ringtone wasn't familiar, and the sound had come from the covered porch. I felt Evan reach out and wrap his fingers around my wrist as if willing me to remain silent.

"Hello?" It was a woman's voice, probably Irene's, but I couldn't be sure. "Oh, nothing. Having a quiet evening in." I heard the ting of a glass being set down on a metal table and a long inhale as she took a drag of the cigarette. Evan and I ducked down—his eyes were still level with the top of the fence, but I couldn't see anything without stretching. I held a hand against the fence for balance and leaned my head closer so I could still hear. Evan released my wrist as he shuffled his feet to a more comfortable position, readying for a long surveillance.

"No, he's out with clients tonight. Yes, I know it's Saturday night. He's been out with clients every Saturday night this month." Her voice was bitter and more than a little bit slurred. "Mm-hmm. Mm-hmm. Well, 'those clients are what pay the bills, Irene.'" Her voice had dropped into a presumed imitation of her husband. "No, I'm fine. He's just been...he's just been going through some things. I'm glad he's out of the house." I heard a clank as if her glass had hit something on its way to her mouth.

A mosquito flitted against my thigh, and I quashed the instinct to smack it, waving noiselessly instead, trying to shoo it away. It moved to my other leg, and I felt a sudden prick on the back of my hamstring. I shooed harder, and the top of the bench wobbled. Evan flapped his hand at me to stop.

"Oh, did'z you? Yeah. Yes," Irene said. "She was our neighbor. Mm-hmm. No, I don't watch the news. Mm-hmm. Oh, yeah, years, actually. I didn't know her as well as *David* did." She nearly spat the word. I heard the sound of glass clinking on glass and then the soft glug glug glug of a hefty pour. An extended silence followed. Enough time for her to drain her glass and pour some more.

"I don't want to speak ill of the dead..." Whatever she was drinking was starting to catch up. "But between you and me, she was a huzzy." Pause. "Hones'ly, whatz he supposed to do? She's actin' all helpless over there. You know he's weak." Another pause. "He's been unbearable this week. Just moping around. Gawd, stiffen up and be a man. I don't need anyone to know this. I didn' need to have his little huzzy up in my face every day, either. Mm-hmm."

The sudden notes of a ringtone on high blared from Evan's pocket. He jumped off the bench and fumbled for his phone, stabbing at it in the dark.

"What is that? Is someone over there?" A sudden whoosh of light illuminated the yard as Irene hit their flood lights. She suddenly sounded more sober, but her voice quivered with fear. "Who's there?" I leaped off the bench and followed Evan, who was already at a dead run across the yard and rounding the corner to the driveway. We pounded down the drive, and he veered into the park, slowing to a quick walk as we made our way down the path. He'd lowered the volume, but it began to trill again.

"Turn it off," I hissed. He suppressed it again, this time ensuring he switched to silent mode. We walked hastily to the other side of the park, where we sank onto a bench at the far side of the play area.

"Why aren't we getting out of here?" I whispered, breathing heavily and flapping my shirt to cool the sweat running down my chest.

"She might see your car and take down the license plate or something," Evan said. "Let's hang out for a few minutes and see if she's called the police." Another mosquito danced near my upper arm, and I slapped at it hard, hitting myself but missing his agile little blood-sucking body. "We're just a couple of people hanging out in the park. What do they know?"

Evan's phone lit up yet again, and this time he answered it. "Yeah, hey, sorry I didn't pick up in time. Are you having fun?" He turned away from me. "Of course, I miss you too. No, I'm, ah, working."

A River Oaks patrol car cruised past and rolled to a stop at Irene's. Bushes and trees blocked my view of what was happening, so I sat and listened to Evan drone on in a remarkably irritating voice about how he 'did too miss you more.' It was all I could do not to make junior high gagging sounds, which would have been entirely appropriate.

My own phone rang, and I checked the screen but didn't recognize the number. I declined the call and switched to vibrate. Evan wrapped it up with Gabriella and looked over.

"Who was that?" he asked.

"I don't know. Not anyone in my contacts."

"Was that the police I saw go by?"

"River Oaks patrol," I said. Evan popped up and walked closer to the street to see what was happening.

"There's a guy walking along the driveway," he hissed. "He's checking the windows." I glanced around to see if anyone was close enough to hear him, but the park was empty. Evan gave me a whispered play-by-play until the patrol car finally pulled away and left.

I have to say, I was wiped out. My desire to snoop was gone, and I doubted it would return anytime soon.

CHAPTER TWENTY-THREE

Sunday was mercifully quiet. Frances called me early, and we headed out for brunch. Houston is a big brunch city, but Frances had managed to secure a corner table at one of our favorite restaurants, and we were there before the crowds got large.

I'd never told her about Christine and saw no need to bring it up now, but this required me to edit myself. I'd been so involved with trying to figure out what happened this week that most of what bubbled up in my immediate conversation had to be considered and, for the most part, discarded. Instead, Frances seemed intent on gently probing to see how my search for a partner was going. As bad as my experience with Chaz had been, I could see its value as a funny story in the future. If you skipped past the humiliation of being left almost immediately for another woman, it could be amusing. Frances didn't see the humor. She smiled sympathetically but had a few choice words to say about Chaz and his family.

She brightened considerably when I told her about being rescued by Martin and his father and proceeded to ask me numerous questions about each of them. Even with this, though, I had to cut out any references to Martin's tangential tie to Christine and the fact that we'd met briefly before this encounter. She never inquired about Evan and Gabriella, and I never brought them up.

The break with Frances was exactly what I needed to feel grounded again. By the time I was home, I was relaxed and feeling more myself. Having neglected Barker Street Bones lately, I devoted myself to a few hours of catch-up. I did a complete inventory review of my ingredients, updated my spreadsheets with distributor data, played around with website ideas, and downloaded some articles on how to set it up. I was halfway through a rather technical article I didn't understand when my phone rang.

I didn't recognize the number, but I thought it was the same one I'd ignored yesterday.

"Hello?" I sounded curt, ready to disconnect whatever telemarketer had the effrontery to bother me on the weekend. There was a pause and a breath. "*Hello*?" I repeated.

"Ah, hi? Um, is this Jessie?" It was a man's voice, and he sounded convinced he must have the wrong number.

"Yes. Who's this?"

"It's Martin. Martin Amos? We met the other night? Well, we've met twice. Remember?" He paused as if running through a mental sequence of events.

"Oh, hi, Martin. Sorry, I thought you were a telemarketer."

"I tried to call you yesterday?" This was painful. Someone needed to help him with his conversational skills. I would have thought an attorney would be more polished.

"I must have missed it." There was another lengthy delay as if we were speaking on a trans-Atlantic line from a century ago.

"Right. Anyway. How've you been?" We suffered through a few more minutes of trivial back and forth until he finally reached the point. "I was wondering if you'd like to have dinner with me Tuesday night?"

I bit back my initial refusal. Martin seemed nice enough. He wasn't exactly my type, and he wasn't exactly what I imagined as my future husband, but not everyone finds love at first sight. In fact, it's probably better to build a relationship slowly. The whole love at first sight thing seems nothing more than a myth. And this definitely wasn't love at first sight, so maybe it had potential.

"Sure, that sounds nice," I said. He offered to pick me up, and I gave him my address, ignoring all the articles directing one to arrange your own transportation. In theory, this was our second date. And I *had* met his father, which was equivalent to a background check. He rambled on, his giddiness acting as a repellent, and I cut him off before I changed my mind completely.

I pushed Martin out of my mind for the rest of the day and for all of Monday as well. I threw myself into biscuit baking and dog-walking. I would go on this date, decide if it was worth pursuing, and go from there. No need to twist myself in knots about it.

Tuesday came quickly. I was taking my final dog client home when my phone began buzzing in my pocket. I shifted the leash to my other hand, keeping a tight grip as the oversized Labrador retriever I was walking spotted a squirrel. The squirrel raced up a tree, flicking his tail as he ran. My client dragged me along as he lumbered toward the tree, sniffing furiously at the squirrel's track. I regained my balance and answered the phone. It was Kip.

"Hey—"

"Omigod, you have to come here right now!" I held the phone away from my head as his piercing scream threatened to damage my eardrum.

"What's—"

"It's out—the dog! She was here! Omigod, you have to get here! Here doggie..."

"Kip! What are you talking about?" This didn't even sound like Kip. Okay, maybe like Kip huffing helium, but his panic set my pulse racing. "What's going on? What dog?"

"Jessie! You need to get here! What's its name?" His voice grew fainter as he moved farther from his speaker. "Here, doggie. Here, dog...C'mere. It's okay. I won't hurt you." Judging from the shrillness of his tone, no sane dog would come anywhere close to him.

I started race-walking the Lab toward his house. Luckily, we were only two houses away, and I had him up and through the front door before Kip turned his attention back to me.

"He won't come to me! What do I do?"

I shoved my charge into the living room, tossed a couple of biscuits from my bag toward the couch, and raced back out the door, ensuring it was locked behind me. I wasn't sure what kind of drama was happening with Kip, but I had a panicky feeling it involved Henry.

"Kip! Slow down. What's going on? Is it Evan's dog? Is it Henry?" My heart was in my throat. Why would Henry be loose? They were only yards from a busy street, and that traffic could be deadly to a loose dog at this time of the afternoon.

"Henry! Here, boy! Henry...come to Uncle Kip. Atta boy. Come here. It's okay..."

"Kip! Is it Henry? How'd he get out? You've got to get him before he runs onto Montrose. Where's Evan?"

"Okay, okay. It's okay. Gotcha!"

"Kip! What is happening?" I put the phone on speaker, tossed it on the passenger seat, and peeled away from the curb, heading toward Evan's house.

"Well, aren't you a licky little thing? Ergh."

"Kip!"

Through the line, I heard a squeal, like rusty hinges being forced open. "Jessie? Are you there?"

I braked hard for a light, and my phone flew onto the floor. "Kip?" I leaned over and fished around, trying to reach it without rolling into the intersection. "Kip?" I finally snagged it, pulling at least two muscles with the effort. I shook the phone to see if we were still connected.

"I'm here," he said, sounding more like his usually suave self. "You would not believe what I've gone through to save this, this canine creature. I hope your friend appreciates it."

"What happened?" I asked. "How did he get out? What did you mean she was here?" The light turned, and I jerked forward, still in crisis mode.

"Omigod, that girl! She was here with the silver suit, and she let the dog out!"

"What do you mean, she let the dog out? Where's Evan? Is he there?"

"Well, wouldn't that have made it so much more interesting? A threesome. My, my, I didn't know your mind worked like that."

"Kip, stop! I am trying to understand what's happening. Look, I'm like ten minutes away. Do you have Henry safe?"

He assured me Henry was safely tucked away, which, knowing Kip, didn't give me as much comfort as you might think. I made good time and only sort of ran two lights. Turning onto Evan's street was anticlimactic. I'm not sure what I expected, but the road was quiet, devoid of traffic, people, and escaped dogs. I pulled to the curb and cut my engine.

Evan's driveway was empty, and no cars were parked at the curb. Kip waved at me from his front steps—no sign of Henry. I trotted over, anxiety making me prickly.

"Where's Henry? Is he okay?" As I said his name, I heard a sharp little bark coming from the back, and I headed immediately toward the sound. "Henry? Henry!" My voice carried the panicked note of a parent whose toddler had wandered off in a store.

Kip raced along at my heels. "He's fine. He's fine. Although had I not been home, it would have undoubtedly been a different story." He stepped in front of me and slowly pushed a side door into the garage open, hunching over and holding his hands against the opening so Henry couldn't shoot out. "Hey, little mongrel! How are you doing in there?"

I knocked him out of the way, needing to see for myself that Henry was okay. Henry pushed past Kip and launched himself against me, crying and whining with excitement. I wrapped one arm around him and curled the fingers of my other hand around his collar, afraid he might run off even though he was trying to attach himself directly to my body. Lifting the wriggling mass of fur to my chest, I stood and held him tight, breathing in the soft doggie scent, and—was that cologne?

"What happened to you?" I cooed. Kip reached over, surprising me by murmuring high-pitched baby talk and gently rubbing Henry's ears. When Henry finally began to still in my arms, we moved to Kip's steps and sank down. "Tell me what happened," I said.

He leaned back and stretched his legs out, crossing them neatly at the ankle. Now that Henry was safely ensconced in my embrace, Kip was suddenly Mr. Cool. The shrill shrieks I'd heard through the phone—a forgotten memory. "It's as I said. I was home working in my design studio in the front there," he flicked a finger at the front windows. "And I heard the muffler of the little floozy's beater car. Believe me, there's no mistaking it. At first, I didn't think much of it, but a few minutes later, another car pulled up, and I saw that hot Boomer we saw last week in the food basement get out. She must have been in the house already because I saw him go in then."

Had Evan given her a key? And what was she doing?

Kip plucked a leaf from the bush beside him and began shredding it. "I was possibly staring out the window by now, not that I'm nosy," he explained. "But it was like having a telenovela playing out right in front of me!"

"I'd have been watching too." I nudged Henry slightly to the right to ease his leg bone out of my ribs.

Kip relaxed. "Anyway, it was quiet for a while. At least I couldn't hear anything going on. I'm pretty sure we both know what was going on. I went back to work figuring an old guy like that might take a while." He jostled me with his elbow. "He left, I don't know, maybe half an hour later. Maybe not that long."

"What about Henry?" I asked. "When did you see he was out?"

"I might have seen flashes of him near the fence or at the house next door. I wasn't looking for a dog. But after the suit left, the nymphette came out. She ran around from the corner over there, looking panicked. You could tell she'd lost the dog. I don't know if she thought that yard was fully fenced or what."

I leaned over Henry's warm little body and stroked his silky ear. "She must have let him out when her trick arrived," I said, fury burning in my chest. "How could she be so stupid?" I closed my eyes and took a deep breath. "So, then what? She couldn't find him, so *she left*?" The breath hadn't helped; anger licked through me like dry kindling catching fire.

Kip resumed plucking at his leaf. "Yep. She looked near the porch and a little bit next door, but then she boogied out of there."

We sat in disbelieving silence, listening to the thrum of traffic only yards away. I wanted to kill Gabriella, and the longer I thought about it, the more my anger began to spill over onto Evan, even though he presumably didn't know about this.

Maybe because he'd brought her in and allowed her to be so careless with something so cherished.

"Now what?" Kip asked. "What are you going to tell your friend?"

"I'm going to tell him what happened. He needs to know what she did."

Kip bounced beside me. "Can I be there when you tell him?" he asked, clapping his hands lightly.

I stood up, still clutching Henry to my chest. "Sorry. I'm taking him home with me, and I'll call Evan from there." I suddenly remembered my date with Martin. Glancing at my watch, I realized I needed to get moving. Knowing if I mentioned my date, I would lose another half hour while Kip grilled me—I refrained, promising him I would call him when I had the chance.

Henry was ecstatic when he arrived at my house, even though the greeting from Addie could be considered lukewarm at best. He found her toy basket and climbed inside, flinging toys from side to side like a kid going crazy in a toy store. Addie and I stood watching, although my brain had snapped into battle preparation for my call to Evan.

I finally gave up preplanning what to say and jabbed Evan's work contact on my phone.

"Evan Petty," he said, sounding aggravated.

"Evan, it's me," my own voice sounded harsh and clipped. "I have Henry."

There was a moment of silence. "What do you mean you have Henry?" I could tell he thought I was playing at something that he didn't have the patience for today.

"I have Henry at my house. Your *girlfriend* let him out this afternoon and then left. He was *out*, Evan. If Kip hadn't noticed and gone out to get him, he probably would have been hit by a car."

There was silence on the line.

"Jessie, what are you talking about? How could Gabriella have let him out? She can't get in. Gah, what did that guy do? Did he break into my house or something?" His voice was rising. "I want to know how he got Henry. If he does anything more to any of my stuff, I'm calling the police."

I thought I was going to burst a blood vessel. "Kip didn't do anything but save Henry from getting killed! You should be thanking him that he did. Gabriella was over there with some guy doing God knows what, and she let Henry out while they did it!"

He hung up.

He hung up? My heart raced with rage, and a nerve in my forehead began to twitch. I redialed. I thought he wouldn't pick up, but he finally did.

"Jessie, I don't have time for this. I don't know what kind of drama you're cooking up because you don't like Gabriella or you're jealous or something, but I don't have time for this."

"Evan, listen to me. I am not making up anything. You don't want to believe me, then don't believe me. But you need to take a good hard look at what's going on. I don't really care about her. But I *do* care about Henry and the fact that she is willing to be so reckless as to let him out to get lost or get killed—I do care about that! He is at my house. I'm not even sure I want to give him back to you if you're going to be like this."

"He's not your dog. I will be by after work to get him, and I expect you to hand him over."

This level of wrath couldn't be healthy for me. I breathed in through my nose. "I'm going out tonight. If you can't come by before six-thirty, you'll have to wait till tomorrow."

He said something I couldn't quite make out and hung up again.

I sat on the floor and leaned back against the couch, trying to quell the vicious wave of emotion flowing through my body. Addie crept slowly past me, trying to figure out this unfamiliar vibe. Henry, oblivious to the mood in the room, lasered in on an old stuffed hedgehog of Addie's and began tearing at a seam. I closed my eyes and took several deep breaths, counting slowly as I inhaled, held it, then exhaled. This could have been so bad. By some miracle, Kip had been home, had seen what was happening, and had saved Henry from being lost or worse.

I absolutely didn't know how Evan and I could get past this. It was one thing to speculate about Gabriella stealing Christine's jewelry or shoving her down the stairs, which I didn't fully believe. And the fact that I felt weird about Evan suddenly being in a relationship was just a matter of adjusting to changing circumstances. But when Henry's life was at stake? No. This was not okay.

I sat fuming, my date with Martin nearly forgotten until he texted me a happy face emoji and said he was looking forward to our evening. I groaned. The last thing I was in the mood for was a date, but it was too late to cancel. Maybe it would be good to get out and distract myself.

CHAPTER TWENTY-FOUR

The only redeeming part of the afternoon was that I hadn't had time to get nervous about my date with Martin. By six, I was ready. I fed Addie while distracting Henry upstairs. By six-fifteen, I was stomping back and forth in front of the window, looking for Evan's car. At six-thirty, the older model car I'd seen Saturday night crawled slowly down the street before ultimately pulling into my driveway. Martin emerged, looked around, then cupped his hands in front of his face, huffing out and breathing in. Oh God, he wasn't checking his breath with the idea of kissing me, was he? I wasn't feeling a ton of chemistry with this guy. Dinner, okay. But I hadn't thought beyond that.

Where was Evan? The doorbell rang, and both dogs charged, trying to outdo each other. I hunched over, trying to block them with my knees and one hand while opening the door with the other. Martin took a step back, the smile fading from his face.

"Hi," he said, shouting over the din. "I didn't know you had so many dogs."

Henry bounced up and down, emitting a staccato series of yelps while Addie transitioned to a deep-throated growl.

"Sorry," I said, slipping a finger under Henry's collar and

turning to hiss at Addie. "Stop it!" She backed up a couple of feet, then planted herself, a small ruffle of fur rising on her neck. "Addie, stop it." I waved a hand at her, trying to get her to move back and act like a friendly dog. "Would you like to come in?"

Martin frowned and glanced pointedly at his watch. "No, we should get going if that's okay."

I heard my phone ping from its resting place on the coffee table. Maybe it was Evan. "Yeah, okay. I need a minute. This one," I scooped Henry up. "He's not mine. A friend of mine is supposed to be coming to get him any minute now." I walked backward toward my phone while Addie and Martin squared off. I couldn't hear her growling anymore, but she was pinning him with her most intimidating stare. Truthfully, I might be a little scared if I didn't know her. Martin refused to engage with her, instead picking nervously at his fingernails. He looked up at her once and then resorted to biting his cuticles.

Evan's text was short and to the point. *I'll be there in a minute.*

"My friend will be here in a minute or two. Are you sure you don't want to come in?" I asked Martin.

"No, um, do you think it'll be long? I made a reservation." The slightest hint of a whine had crept into his voice.

"Okay, tell you what, let me leash this guy up, and we can wait outside. Then, as soon as my friend gets here, we can go. It should just be a minute or two." I grabbed one of Addie's spare leashes and fastened it to Henry's collar. I set him down, picked up my purse, phone, and keys, and hustled toward the door.

Seeing us all departing, Addie wasted no time jumping on the couch and settling into her favorite corner. I pulled the door closed behind me and locked the deadbolt. Martin stepped farther away as Henry and I made our way outside.

We stood without talking while we waited. Henry took advantage of the lull to explore the small row of ratty bushes in front of Larry's house. I heard Evan before I saw him, the rev of his engine out of proportion to a sedate drive down a residential street. He squealed to a stop at the curb and hopped out, slamming the driver's door behind him. Henry strained and pulled toward Evan, yipping in delight. When I didn't move fast enough, he raced behind me, twisting the leash around my legs and knocking me off balance. I dropped everything I held but managed to hold on to the lead. I untangled myself and quickly gathered my things—on my feet before Evan reached us.

He held out his hand for the leash without saying a word.

"Evan."

He looked furious. Well, so was I.

"Evan!" I was still holding the leash, but he was close enough for Henry to jump up on his legs, dancing his happy dance, seemingly unaware of the tension swirling around him. "Look, I don't know what you're so mad about, but you really need to be aware of what happened so it doesn't happen again." He bent down, his face hidden behind Henry's bouncing head. "Gabriella let him out. She did. And then she left. I don't know what she told you about that, but that is what happened."

He lifted Henry and stood up, unclipping the leash from his collar. His eyes, when they met mine, were cold. "I know what happened. I talked to *her*. I don't need anyone else throwing their opinions in here."

I stood waiting, wondering if he was going to give me an explanation. From the sidewalk, Martin cleared his throat. We both turned and stared as if only now becoming aware of his presence.

"Uh, Jessie? We need to get going."

Irritation washed over me. "Yeah, I know. In a minute." I turned back to Evan. "So, she let Henry out and just left? And that's okay with you?"

He let out an exasperated breath. "It was an accident, okay? Everyone screws up sometimes, *even you*." He turned and headed for his car. I wondered how she explained what she had been doing there in the first place. I wondered if the silver-haired guy had even come up in the conversation.

"Are you ready now?" Martin was very much starting to get on my nerves. I dropped the extra leash near my front door and watched Evan rocket away with Henry.

Once Martin and I were on our way, I stared out the window, trying to alter my mood but seething in a way I never had before. We appeared to be heading toward the Galleria. "So, where are we going?" I asked, trying to keep my tone light and attempting to thrust down the newest 'disturbance in my energy.' My energy was so disturbed I felt like a hazardous black cloud. And wouldn't you know, I'd forgotten to bring my rose quartz or wear the tourmaline. I wondered if either of those could help me dispel this anger. Maybe I should call Bertram later.

"There's a place on Post Oak that some guys from work talk about a lot," he said, glancing over his shoulder before drifting into the right lane. "It's supposed to be really good."

"Nice. What kind of food?"

"I'm not sure," he said, his hands tight around the steering wheel. "I think they go mostly for happy hour."

Great. I wondered if this was another two-for-one something like Chaz had selected.

"So. Your friend is a guy?" Martin stared straight ahead as he asked this, trying to sound nonchalant but sounding constipated instead.

"Yeah, Evan. We've been friends for a long time. We used to work together."

"Did you ever date?"

"No, we're just friends."

Martin grew quiet, and I sank back in my seat, trying to think of conversational topics, but I was still hung up on Evan,

Gabriella, and Henry. I knew she wasn't a dog lover, and the fact that Henry didn't like her made me wonder if she'd deliberately tried to get rid of him. If things got serious with Evan and it became a problem that his dog didn't like her, what better way to bypass that situation than to get rid of the dog? How could Evan get involved with someone like that? And furthering that thought, if she could do something like this with a dog, imagine what she might do to get jewelry worth hundreds of thousands of dollars.

"So, Martin, do you like dogs?"

He turned his head without, in fact, looking at me. "Um, I guess so."

He hadn't seemed like it when he saw Addie and Henry, but it probably wasn't fair to judge off that. They hadn't exactly been welcoming. Anyone would have reacted as Martin had. Well, I wouldn't have, but I'm a crazy dog person. I didn't think he would actively try to get rid of my dog, but I certainly wasn't going to get into a situation to test that out.

Martin pulled carefully into a shopping center a few blocks from the Galleria. The lot was full, and he drove slowly down the rows, searching for an open space. I scanned the signs, wondering where we were going. All I could see was a sporting goods store, a toy store, and a shoe store up the way. He drove until he found a less crowded section farther down the lot and closer to the street. We walked through the parking lot with Martin leading the way.

As we reached the sidewalk, I saw a flurry of activity up ahead. Cars waited in a long valet line, and groups of well-dressed professionals mingled with couples as they headed for a neon-lit restaurant around the corner. We now had enough room to walk side by side, but Martin continued to lead by a pace or two. He was losing points, although I told myself not to be so judgmental. Maybe he was nervous.

Closer to the vibrant purple door, we were suddenly swept along in a sea of bodies. Separated momentarily from Martin, I found myself wedged between two good-looking guys in suits.

"Hell-o!" said the one, placing a steadying hand on my elbow as a woman rushing by knocked her giant purse into my shoulder.

"Hi," I said, glancing around for Martin.

"Are you here by yourself?" asked his friend, dazzling me with a complete set of bleached-white teeth.

"No, I'm with someone." I looked around and spotted Martin ahead, nearing the door. "Oh, there." I waved a hand, but he wasn't even looking for me. A couple more guys joined my two new friends.

"Who have we here?" asked one. He looked vaguely familiar and stared back as if trying to place me.

Eventually, Martin turned and noticed I was missing. He scanned the crowd, a look of dismay crossing his face as he spotted me.

I pushed forward until I reached his side. "Hey, wow, this place must be pretty good," I said, determined to set aside my own issues and get through this date.

"Oh, my God! Look who it is!" said one of my new escorts. "Anus! Look, boys, Anus is here."

Martin's face flushed scarlet, and his left hand began to flick back and forth before he raised it to his face and began gnawing at a nail. The guys around me moved forward, jostling into a raggedy circle around him.

"Marty Anus, how'd you get out of the office so early tonight?" one asked. "Did you finish that update to the trust I told you I needed?"

"Hey, guys," Martin mumbled. He seemed to shrink perceptibly. The circle tightened. I was pushed back as they moved forward.

"No, seriously. Did you finish it?" It was white teeth, and he moved his face closer to Martin's. "I need it, and if it's not literally sitting on my desk at this precise moment, then I need you to get your ass back to the office and finish it."

Martin chewed harder at his nail. "You'll have it," he said, not looking at his tormenter.

I slid between two of the guys and touched Martin on the arm. "Don't we need to go in? I think our table is ready."

There was a stunned silence, but only for a second.

"Whoa! Wait just a minute! Marty has a date?"

"Yo, Anus, is this a date, or is this your sister?"

"Who says she's not both?"

"She's too pretty to be your sister."

"Hey babe, what're you doing going out with someone like this? You're too hot for this whiner."

"Yo, Marty—did you drive her over in your beater? You should have told me you had a date; maybe I'd have let you borrow my Porsche."

My face had started to burn with sympathetic humiliation for Martin, but now the irritation and anger at my whole day began to roil up. I stared harder at the guy who looked familiar. Where did I know him from?

"Marty had a party, and nobody came..." he sang in a singsong voice. Wait—I did know him. But, wow, it had been a long time ago. Like, second or third grade. But his mocking tone was the same now as it had been in elementary school. Hard to forget.

"Edwin? Is that you?"

All heads swiveled toward me. Edwin's face flushed red, and he drew back.

"Wait, what?" laughed one of his friends. "Edwin?"

"Edwin Tottenham, right? Gosh, I haven't seen you since, what? Third grade? Remember how you made us call you Edwin

Rhodes Tottenham the Third? Like, the whole thing every time someone addressed you?"

The group doubled over, laughing and clutching at each other. "Edwin?"

"Edwin Rhodes Tottenham, your highness!" They were removing imaginary hats now and bowing with sweeping arm gestures. One of them fell onto the sidewalk. "Edwin Rhodes Tottenham," he burbled.

"It's Ed. I go by Ed."

Ed was suddenly not amused by the banter. Funny how that works.

"Yeah, okay, that's easier. It's been a while, right? Gosh, last time I saw you, there was something…" I closed my eyes as if trying to remember. "Something happened at recess?" I opened my eyes and laughed. "Oh yeah. Remember that time—"

He cut me off and began herding the group away, grabbing the fallen one by his arm and dragging him along until he managed to find his feet.

"Wait, you don't want to stick around and share memories?" I called after them, but Ed suddenly seemed in a hurry. From the direction he was headed, it looked like they'd changed their minds about eating here.

Martin stood motionless, still worrying at his cuticle. "That was something," he finally said, looking at me with a mixture of admiration and fear. "Thanks."

I didn't actually feel great about the whole thing. I was no better than a bully myself with that outburst. Seeing Martin stand up for himself would have been a lot more gratifying. I turned and headed for the door. "We gonna eat?" I asked.

CHAPTER TWENTY-FIVE

We entered the restaurant and were seated at a tiny table near the far wall. A busboy hustled past, dropping off two small glasses of water from his tray. Within the first minute and a half, Martin kicked my legs twice and stomped my foot once before I turned sideways in my chair and crossed my legs to the side. Then he knocked over one of the water glasses, causing a stream to rush across the small space and cascade down onto my lap. I unfolded myself and hopped up, but the damage was done. Cold, wet fabric clung to my thighs, and I thought I was going to have to brandish a fork to keep Martin from patting at my crotch with his napkin.

"It's fine," I said, blotting at the fabric, although that did nothing more than transfer white fuzz from the napkin to my skirt. Our waitress swooped in with a couple of clean bar towels, and we managed to sop up most of the flood. Thank heavens the glass had been small. Martin fluttered around on his side of the table, waving his napkin in the air as if this would somehow help.

The waitress caught my eye and gave me a sympathetic smile.

"Can I get you a drink?"

I ordered a white wine, Martin ordered a light beer, and we sat back down.

"Tell me more about—"

"You work with those—"

We stopped.

"You first," Martin said.

"You work with those guys?" I finished. "They don't seem very...nice."

He grabbed his silverware and began fiddling with it, turning the fork this way and that before doing the same with his knife.

"Yeah. We're all junior associates, but those guys get better breaks. The partners always give them more opportunities and more client face time. Basically, more everything. I get all the grunt work." The waitress returned with our drinks, and Martin didn't even wait for me to pick my glass up before he lifted his and took a long swallow.

"Why is that?" I asked. I was starting to understand why, but I wondered what he thought.

"I don't know. Most of them went to—" he set his glass down and raised his fingers for air quotes, "—*prestigious* schools. And they're all...well, look at 'em. The glitterati. They kiss up to the partners and weasel their way into golf games on the weekends, and they have their fancy cars and their pick of the admins. Most of them come from money, and their dads helped get them in." A foamy blob of spittle landed on his lip. "And they're all younger than me, so they take great pride in that. As if anyone controls their age."

"What about the guy who acted like you worked for him? Is he one of the junior associates too?"

"Yeah, but he works with one of the senior partners, and they let him—" more air quotes—"use resources as he sees fit."

"Why don't you quit? Find another job?"

He stared at me like I'd lost my mind. "And how'm I going to do that?"

He continued to stare as if expecting an answer. "I don't know; send out some resumes?"

"Everyone knows everyone! If word gets back that I'm looking, not only will they ruin any chance I have of getting on with another firm, but then they'll really make my life miserable."

"Wow. Sounds terrible," I said, picking up my menu and perusing for something the kitchen could get out quickly. "It seems your dad is proud of you, though."

Martin sat back in his chair and smiled, his face softening. "Yeah. That's what keeps me going. I can't let him down. He's sacrificed so much for me. My mom left when I was young, and it's just been the two of us." He was better looking when he let go of his grievances.

"He seems like a great guy," I said. "I really enjoyed our dinner the other night."

Martin reached across the table, grabbing my hand as it rested near my wine glass. He managed to snag my pinkie and ring finger and wrapped his fingers around mine. "I'm so glad you said that. I did too."

I stiffened, feeling my lips move into something that should have been a smile, but I knew it didn't even look close. Our waitress materialized as if on cue. "Do you want to hear about tonight's specials, or are you guys ready to order?"

I slipped my hand away from Martin as if I needed both hands to prop up my single-sheet menu. "I'm ready to—"

"What are the—" He smiled at me. "We keep doing that," he said, nearly giggling, as if it was the cutest thing in the world to start talking simultaneously. "If you're ready, then let's order." He looked at the waitress. "Bring me whatever she's having." He smiled at me again. I ordered, and the waitress confirmed he was okay with it.

"Two Pollo Romanos coming up."

Once she was gone, I sat back, folding my hands in my lap so as not to encourage further hand-holding. Martin leaned forward, resting his arms on the table, and I cast nervous glances at my wine glass. He stared at me with a small smile.

"You're just so pretty," he said. One hand lifted from the table and reached toward me as if he was about to brush at my hair. I grabbed my wine and leaned back, nearly toppling backward in my chair.

"Thanks," I said, taking a long swallow of the chilled wine. "So, tell me more about your work. Or your childhood. Or, whatever." I smiled, willing myself to give this guy a chance. Okay, maybe he wasn't the best lawyer in town, and maybe he was a little awkward, and maybe his coworker was on to something when he said he was a whiner. Or—perhaps he was a nice guy struggling with his job. I'd struggled at work and spent plenty of time grousing over work events with anyone who would listen. If nothing else, this made me realize how very much I needed to stop complaining about things.

Once he started talking, he kept going. He told me how his mom left when he was ten. She'd packed her car while he was at school, and his father was at work, and that was that. They'd had a couple of phone calls and a Christmas card here and there, but mostly, she'd cut and run. I couldn't imagine. He talked about his and his dad's financial and emotional struggles after she left, and I started to better understand how Martin had become the man he was. He had a loving, doting father but had been abandoned by his mother. That could explain some of his gracelessness.

We'd finished our drinks before the entrees arrived, and the waitress brought another round. I was beginning to relax, and

Martin seemed to be unwinding too. By the time we finished our meals, I'd told him a bit about my background, being careful to avoid mentioning my relatively affluent upbringing, the time spent at boarding school, or the college degree I'd never had to worry about paying for. Instead, I talked about my job at Astor Oil, how awful my boss had been, and how I'd found her murdered. That brought us around to Christine.

"Have you heard any more about what happened?" he asked me.

"I was going to ask you the same," I said. "Since your firm was handling her affairs, I would imagine you're going to know more than me."

He looked away across the restaurant, seeming to study the other diners. "Not really," he finally said. "Obviously, we will be handling things from an estate perspective. Sometimes it takes a while to get the death certificate. That can take almost a month. And since she wasn't at a hospital or anything, it can take longer while they do whatever investigation they're going to do. Accidental deaths like that can take a while to wrap up." He reached out for our waitress as she raced past and asked for the check. "You didn't want dessert, did you?" I assured him I didn't.

There was a lull, and I debated mentioning that the police didn't think Christine's death was accidental but decided this was more for Penny to discuss than me. Martin was already on again about his work.

"You wouldn't believe the assets some of our clients have. So much money, it's insane. And the things they do with it. There are people out here struggling to pay the bills who can't afford the basics, and some of these people are setting up trusts for their cats! Their cats!"

I laughed until I realized he was categorically working himself up. "Well, I guess when you have money, you get to decide what to do with it."

His eyebrows drew together. "Well, some of it's ridiculous. Fine, leave your money to your heirs or a worthwhile charity, but some of this other stuff." He glared across the restaurant as if convinced the other patrons were opulent idiots intent on leaving their fortunes to Fido or Fluffy.

"I'm sure you've seen a lot of weird stuff," I said, trying to sound neutral. He seemed hypersensitive about the wealthy. Perhaps he'd be better off changing his job or his specialty. Maybe he would have more passion for his work if it involved suing well-to-do clients and redistributing their wealth as he saw fit. Like a modern-day Robin Hood. "What's the weirdest thing you've seen in a will?"

"Oh, I don't know. There's always a lot of drama when one child is left out, which happens much more than you'd think. We had one estate where everything was to be split equally among four, but the fifth child—well, he was, at the time, an adult—he was left a tiny painting of a daisy. None of them knew why. I still think about that. Imagine growing up with so much wealth, thinking you'll never have to worry about anything, and suddenly you're cut out and left with nothing but a painting of a daisy."

"Was it valuable?" I asked. "Maybe it was a masterpiece, and it was worth more than everything else combined."

He laughed. "I don't think so."

I wondered briefly about my own parents. They'd never disclosed what they would be doing with their wealth. I'd always thought it would be split evenly between me and my brother, but maybe I shouldn't assume that. Overall, this talk about estates was beginning to depress me.

We wrangled briefly over the check. He'd paid last week for both Jerry and me, and I offered to pick this one up, but he insisted. On the way back to the car, he took my hand and swung it in gentle arcs like a little kid would do.

"Look at that car," he said, pointing with his free hand at a black muscle car backed into the front spot by the valet. "I'm going to get one like that soon. Maybe in red. What do you think the guys at work will think of that?"

I pictured them, most of them like the guys I'd grown up with—born into money, trained from a young age into understated displays of wealth: dark German cars, bespoke suits in muted tones, memberships to country clubs that cost more than most people's homes. Sure, there were flashy displays as well—private jets, exotic vacations, grand mansions on massive lots, and second and third homes all over the world. But generally, muscle cars weren't at the top of the list—unless you counted the midlife crisis guys.

"I'm sure they would be impressed," I said.

He turned to me with a grin. "What about you?" Before I could answer, he leaned forward and gave me a wet peck. His lips felt like October worms, cold and wiggly. "Would you be impressed?"

I refrained from wiping at my mouth but could barely contain a slight shudder. "What? Oh, yeah, sure."

We continued walking, his arm swinging growing more energetic. I feared that we would begin skipping soon. I *knew* I should have driven my own car. Fortunately, his car was reasonably wide, and by pressing up against the door, I was too far away for any convenient touching. Several blocks from my house, I started going on about how early I had to get up, how tired I was after a long day, how much I'd enjoyed dinner, but— here I gave a big yawn—how exhausted I felt. As he pulled into my driveway, I began fishing in my purse for my keys. Flutterings of misgiving assailed me as I frantically pawed through the contents. I hadn't left them at the restaurant, had I?

"What's the matter?" asked Martin.

"I can't find my keys. I know I had them. I locked the door.

Do you remember? You saw me lock the door, right?" It had been chaotic. Between my anger at Evan, and Henry pulling me in various directions, I was still almost positive I'd locked the door, meaning I had to have my keys. Unless somehow they'd fallen out of my purse at the restaurant, but that was unlikely; I hadn't even opened it.

Then I remembered dropping everything when Henry's leash had twisted around me. I'd probably dropped them in the yard. I jumped out of the car and made my way over to where we'd been standing. It was dark, and I couldn't see much. Pulling my phone from my purse, I turned on the flashlight and began walking in a small grid pattern, hunched over and looking for anything shiny.

Martin joined me, throwing himself down and crawling on his hands and knees, patting the ground in exaggerated sweeping motions.

"You see them?" he asked.

"No."

We spent a few more minutes searching to no avail. I finally straightened up.

"You know, I can get into the garage with my keypad, and I have a spare key in there—somewhere." I punched the code into the keypad, and the door groaned up. Now, if I could only remember where I'd left the spare key. It used to be under a can of paint, but I'd used the paint a while ago, and I'd move the key. I went to the shelves on the back wall and began picking up each item and peering beneath in the faint light of the garage opener light. Martin went to his car, and I saw him rummaging around in his trunk. I continued wracking my brain to remember where I'd left my key. I'd looked under a can of WD-40, two dried paint cans, a car duster, and a container of azalea food. I was running my fingers along the baseboard, praying nothing hairy would crawl up my arm, when I heard a click.

Addie began barking furiously. Martin stood beside the door, smiling broadly at me and holding it open just enough to show he'd gotten in while keeping Addie's snarling face safely at bay.

"How'd you do that?" I asked. "Was it open? I usually keep that locked."

"My secret," he said, slipping something into his pocket.

I wasn't sure if I should be relieved or scared. "No, seriously. How'd you do that?" I moved over to take over the door handle, leaning toward Addie and telling her she was a good girl. She snuffled at the gap, assessing that it was indeed me, but continued to growl at Martin behind me.

"Unlike the glitterati, I had to do a lot of jobs while I worked my way through school," Martin said, stepping back from the door as Addie began pawing at the opening. "One of them just happened to be with a locksmith."

"Interesting." Well, at least I could get in the house now. I'd grab my big flashlight and hunt for my keys after Martin left.

"I also worked for a tire place and a gutter cleaning company. So if you need your tires rotated or your gutters cleaned, I can help you with that too."

I might have called him to change my tire last weekend if I had known that. "Good to know. So, anyway, thank you for dinner. That was nice." I still held the door handle while Addie pushed her nose more aggressively toward the crack. Martin stepped closer as if hoping for another kiss, but as soon as he moved, Addie reverted to barking loudly. "She's not particularly friendly," I said, smiling and giving a little shrug. He stared at me until the garage light flicked off. "So..."

I could see him trying to work out how this had come to an end when clearly he wasn't ready to go. "If you want, I could help you look for your keys," he said thoughtfully. "And don't you have one of those cages you could put your dog in?"

That did it. "No. Thank you. I don't need to crate my dog.

Thanks for dinner." I lifted my hand to the garage door button, waiting for him to take the hint and leave. He sagged a little, realizing his defeat, before turning with a little wave and walking toward his car. I hit the button and went inside to Addie.

I waited to make sure he left, peering through my upstairs window like a creeper until I saw his car move out of sight. Then, I sat there for an additional five minutes to make sure he didn't come back around for any reason. Convinced he was gone, I grabbed my big flashlight and headed outside. Luckily, it didn't take me long to find my keys. They were half hidden under an overgrown clump of muhly grass about three feet from where Martin had been crawling. Speaking of crawling, I couldn't deny my skin crawled every time he touched me. I hoped he wouldn't call me again, but judging from his overeager manner, I guessed I'd have to find a way to let him down easy. Or hard. His choice.

CHAPTER TWENTY-SIX

If anyone had watched me interact with my phone on Wednesday, they'd probably have wondered about my mental stability. At intervals, I would snatch it up and stare at the screen, willing it to buzz, then almost immediately toss it aside as if I'd been shocked unpleasantly. On the one hand, I wanted to hear from Evan. I foolishly thought he would contact me to apologize. How could he not?

On the other hand, I did not want to hear anything from Martin. Not a text, not a phone call, not a happy-faced emoji. Literally, not one thing. I feared that even thinking about him would trigger some sort of communication. So, I spent the day grabbing it up and throwing it down. When it finally did buzz late in the afternoon, it was neither of them.

"Jessie, this is Penny." Thank heavens. "I needed to share this with someone who'd understand. Lucille wagged her tail at me today!"

"Penny, that's great!" I said, feeling as relieved as she sounded. A wagging tail was routine in everyday dog life, but for one as messed up mentally as Lucille, it bordered on extraordinary.

"And she came out of the corner and laid down next to Bill while he was working yesterday! Well, only for a few minutes, but it was more than she's done before."

We chatted about how Lucille was adjusting. There were more positive but subtle signs that you had to look for: she watched them more, made eye contact on occasion, and brushed up against Penny while she was in the kitchen. It seemed she was making small forays into her new life. As tempted as I was to ask if Penny knew anything more about the police investigation, I didn't want to sound like I was prying. Fortunately, she brought it up first. She'd told the police about the missing jewelry, and they'd taken a copy of the appraisal to send to pawn shops and jewelry stores. So far, no suspects in Christine's death, though.

"I know this wasn't an accident," she said. "I just know it. Do you ever feel something deep in your bones? This jewelry, Christine's death, it has to all be tied."

"You would think so, but what if it isn't?" I asked. It *seemed* like it should be, but I had doubts about Irene now, and there seemed to be no reason for Irene to steal the jewelry. Unless it was to confuse things. I didn't want to cast aspersions on Irene if she was just an innocent neighbor, but from what Evan and I had heard, she seemed to view Christine as a threat to her marriage.

"What'd you mean?"

I didn't know how to tell her what I'd overheard without telling her about me and Evan poking around, so I jumped in. "Well, this is embarrassing, and I hope you don't get mad. But my friend that I told you about, the one who's going out with Gabriella, he wanted to go look around. We've been caught up in crazy things before similar to this, and he thought maybe he could spot a clue. So Saturday evening, we went by Christine's and looked around the backyard." I paused, waiting to see if she was mad.

"Did you find anything?" she asked. She didn't sound mad.

"No, but Irene, the next-door neighbor, was sitting on their back patio. We didn't realize she was there until we heard her start talking. She was on the phone, and it sounded like she thought something was going on with her husband and Christine. What if she found the key and, I don't know, was overcome by a jealous rage or something?" I refrained from mentioning the hussy comments.

There was a silence while Penny seemed to digest this. "That's interesting," she said. "I've been wracking my brain trying to figure it all out. I've been halfway suspecting Wayne might have something to do with it, the way he's been pressuring me about the money. But it doesn't make sense that he'd steal the jewelry if he thought he was getting it anyway."

"The thing is, I don't want to accuse her of anything. It's literally just a thought. I don't know anything," I said.

She sighed. "Yeah, I don't want to start accusing anyone either. That's why I haven't said anything to the police about Wayne. It's the same thing. It's just a thought." We lapsed into silence, and I could hear her gentle breathing into the phone. "Actually, we know the neighbors have a key," she said. "At least they have a key to the studio; I'm not sure about the house. I should make a trip over and get whatever keys they have. We haven't had time to pack up Christine's canvases yet. Those are the only things I'm worried about. I can't see the neighbors doing anything to those, but if she's a jealous wife...well, I've seen those movies. I'd hate for anything to happen to Christine's works."

That thought had never entered my mind, but I'd seen those movies too. Knowing how far out Penny lived, I asked if she wanted me to run by and get them back. We wrangled for a minute over it, but I could tell she was relieved at not having to make the trip.

I was sitting in front of Christine's house twenty minutes later, reflecting on how strange it was that everything seemed perfectly normal. You'd never know the tragedy that had taken place here. I made my way up the sidewalk to the Pierces' front door, trying to think of what I would say.

The door was opened by a maid in full uniform. I didn't even realize this was a thing anymore. Her dark gray dress appeared to be made of some thick fabric that looked as if it repelled stains and couldn't be wrinkled, no matter how hard you tried. The collar was white and matched the half-apron that wrapped around her waist. Thick white hose encased her legs and disappeared into white crepe-soled shoes built for long hours on your feet. I must have been gaping because she cocked one eyebrow at me and gave me a half smile.

"How may I help you?" she asked.

"Is Mr. or Mrs. Pierce available?"

"Who shall I say is inquiring?"

"I'm Jessie Gallagher. Um, Penny..." I paused, not knowing Penny's last name. "The sister of the lady next door, Christine?" I had not rehearsed this nearly well enough. I cleared my throat. "I understand Mr. Pierce has a set of keys to the art studio next door, and the family asked that I come by and retrieve them."

She gave a demure nod and asked me to please wait where I was. The foyer was grand, with a curving staircase leading to a second story, and the marble on the floor looked like a match to next door. Heavy curtains hung from the windows, blocking the natural light. Two small lamps had been switched on, casting pools of yellow onto a heavy console table. A maroon and gold striped wallpaper dated the space by at least thirty-five years and further contributed to the gloomy atmosphere. It was hard not to compare to the airy openness Christine favored. If I were David, I would have preferred being next door too.

"Right this way." The maid was back and ushered me down the hall, through a large kitchen, and out a side door. We were on the porch where Evan and I had seen Irene the other night. Irene sat in the same cushioned chair, her legs tucked under her and a highball glass in her hand. A bottle of bourbon rested on a side table beside an ice bucket and a pair of silver tongs. The top of the ice bucket lay slightly askew, and I heard a soft sploosh as the ice melted in the heat. She'd been sitting out here for some time.

"Can I get you anything more, Mrs. Pierce?" the maid asked.

"No, thank you, Cora. Have a nice evening." Cora retreated, closing the door behind her. Irene took a slow drink, studying me over the top of her glass. Her stare was disconcerting, and I looked away, taking a moment to check out the backyard. The space was lovely, professionally planted, and manicured. A stone path wound throughout, stopping at intervals where one could admire a fountain, rest on a decorative bench, or smell a bed of roses that occupied the lone sunny spot along the fence. When I looked back, Irene's eyes were still trained on me, but I could detect a slight glaze and a lag in the normal blinking process.

"Do I know you?" she asked. She wasn't slurring her words like she'd been the other night, but I got the sense it was taking a lot of effort to control her tongue.

"I'm Jessie Gallagher. We met that morning when you found Christine."

"Oh, that's right. You insisted on going in to remove that wretched beast." Her nose wrinkled in disdain as if reliving the memory of Lucille's nerve-strained intestinal purge. She waved a hand before her face and took another swig of her drink. "Oh well, it's been much quieter without that thing around." I pressed my lips together in an attempt to curb my temper. "It's been quieter without both of them, as a matter of fact." She tilted her head and directed a sly little smile at her glass.

"Okay, anyway, Christine's sister wanted me to get the keys back that your husband has to the studio or any other keys you have," I said.

Her focus shifted, and she patted her hand along the cushion beside herself, searching for the box of cigarettes that were just out of her line of sight behind the ice bucket. Not finding them, she settled for another drink, closing her eyes as the liquid filled her mouth. Her cheeks puffed slightly as she lifted her chin and swallowed with odd little gulps like a baby bird reflexively enjoying regurgitated worms from its mother.

She gave a little sigh and opened her eyes, seemingly surprised to see anyone there.

"Oh, hello," she said. "What was it you wanted again?"

"I need to pick up any keys you have to your neighbor's house."

"What makes you think I have any keys to the neighbor's house?" She dropped her tone and mocked my voice, inserting verbal air quotes in a most obnoxious way.

I sighed. "Perhaps I should come back when your husband is home."

"If I knew when that would be, perhaps you could," she said. Her s's were getting more fluid as her blood alcohol level began its ascent. "I do not know where he is spending his free time now."

I could have felt sorry for Irene. I imagine it wasn't easy watching your husband develop feelings for someone else. Then again, maybe if she wasn't such a miserable person, David wouldn't have found Christine so appealing. One could argue that Christine had had every right to be bitter, having been left for a younger woman, but instead, she chose to blossom. Irene seemed committed to drowning herself in a bottle.

"My husband can be flighty," she continued, her gaze slipping sideways from my face and landing on the bush beside me. "I dare say most men are." Her eyes cut back to me. "Are you married, young lady?"

"No, I'm not."

She shrugged one shoulder. "You're just a child." She twirled her glass and watched the remaining bits of ice bounce off each other. "You probably think you'll never be old like me. You'd never be with a man who could look at another woman. You'll always be your husband's dream." She looked up again. "Isn't that right?"

I shrugged. "I don't know."

"It's what you think. It's what everyone thinks when they're young and naïve."

She was depressing me. "So, about those keys?"

She sighed. "Do you know what I thought when I saw Christine's body lying there?" She paused as if waiting for a reply.

"No."

"I thought, well, thank heavens I don't have to watch David lighting up anymore. I hadn't seen that glint in his eyes in years. Isn't that sad? I didn't like my husband looking happy." I transferred my weight from one foot to the other. "And now you think I'm a horrible person." She gave a minor hiccup. "Perhaps I am. There wasn't much I could do about getting younger. D'ya know..." She patted the chair cushion next to her as if hoping I'd curl up with her for a nice gossip session. I pretended not to notice. She shook her head as if momentarily confused. "Where was I? Oh, yes. D'ya know what I did last month? Last month, while my husband was mooning around over the hoozie next door? I went to Chinatown."

She rearranged her legs, crossing one over the other and swinging her ankle. I thought I'd lost her. "What's in Chinatown?" I asked.

"What'z in Chinatown? Young you."

"Excuse me? I'm not sure I'm following."

"Yung Yu." She spelled it for me, then laughed, a cackling sound. "See how clever the name is? Yung Yu for guaranteed taut skin. Only you have to let them wrap you." She shuddered. "A man put this foul-smelling muck on me." Her hands were moving now, up and down her body. The little bit of bourbon in her glass splashed up and out, leaving round, wet splotches on her shirt. "He touched me in places that David hasn't touched me in decades."

I wondered if Cora was still in the house. Perhaps she could go find those keys for me.

"I bet you have taut skin, don't you? Of course, you do. Look at your legs." She leaned forward for a better look and was reaching out a finger to touch my leg when the backdoor opened, and David walked out. I jumped back as if I'd been caught in a compromising position with his wife.

"Hi," I said, my voice too loud.

"Hello." He walked over to Irene and leaned down to kiss her cheek, deftly taking her glass away at the same time. He straightened to face me, his hand resting on Irene's shoulder. She reached one hand up and covered his. "It's Jessie, isn't it?"

"Yes, hi. Christine's sister had asked if I could come by and pick up the keys you all have. She and her husband are trying to work through the estate, and they haven't had time to secure everything." I stopped, realizing I sounded accusatory. "They can't get down here easily, and I'm in the area."

"Of course." He turned to his wife. "Irene? Would you like to come in? It's rather warm out here." He helped her stand and steadied her as she stumbled across the patio to the door. "I'll be right back."

I didn't know where he deposited Irene, but he was back in moments with a blue leather keyring.

"I apologize. I only have the key to the studio. I should have given this to you the other day. I don't know why I didn't."

I assured him it was no problem. In fact, I felt terrible taking it from him because I got the sense he might still be escaping over there for comfort. If Penny and I hadn't imagined Irene shredding the canvases with a set of sheers or throwing buckets of red paint all around, I would happily have left it with him. He walked me out, both of us avoiding the topic of his pickled wife.

CHAPTER TWENTY-SEVEN

I was trying not to be overly dramatic, but the very real possibility that my friendship with Evan may have suffered irreparable damage loomed over me like a cloud of doom. I was missing him, and while I was still so furious about how he was putting his infatuation for Gabriella ahead of his concern for Henry, I still lamented what had happened.

I thought about our friendship over the years. We'd gotten to know each other so well while working together that I always felt comfortable being myself. I never had to pretend to be someone I wasn't. I'd grown up in an environment where status was everything. My friends' parents had made up most of the Who's Who list of Houston, as had their families before them. There were unwritten rules on How-to-Be. You had to dress in precise accordance with the ever-changing, nebulous imperatives that were never stated, but somehow everyone knew. You had to belong to the River Oaks Country Club. You had to have the appropriate trendy hairstyle and the most fashionable shoes. Expensive jewelry was given on birthdays, and my friends and I wore posh pieces to the most mundane events because we could. Girls would disappear over holiday weeks and reappear looking slightly different—better, prettier. Manners were nonnegotiable, even if it was just for show. We were all unfailingly polite, but manners couldn't override the spiteful comments that permeated most conversations. It was exhausting to always feel like you had to be *on*.

With Evan, it was different. He'd seen me at my best. He'd seen me at my worst. He'd literally seen me looking disgusting, being hysterical, and doing all kinds of things that were questionable, to say the least, and he'd never batted an eye. He was always just Evan—goofy, immature, sometimes selfish, yes. But he was also kind, unpretentious, and non-judgmental. He was probably my first friend who didn't care where I came from, how much money my family had, or what my father did. I don't think he'd genuinely understood my background until I quit working at Astor Oil without having anything else lined up. In his world, that spelled financial ruin.

But lately, he'd been changing. I'd sort of known we'd drift apart when we no longer worked together. Nothing melds people together tighter than day-to-day life. When we were working together, there was no way he would have started dating someone without me knowing about it. Heck, I'd have been with him at the cupcake place, and Gabriella would never have had time to coerce Evan into suddenly being her boyfriend. But here we were. It was time I started considering if this friendship had a future. Right this very minute, I wasn't so sure. But the overwhelming sadness I felt when I tried to picture my life without Evan made me think it was worth trying to sort out.

It was late Friday afternoon, and another long weekend was upon me. I'd been home less than an hour after my dog walking and couldn't settle down. I decided to take a quick trip to Kip's to drop off the CBD oil for his cat. I had no idea if he'd be home or even wanted to try it on his crazy cat. And driving over there had nothing to do with the fact that he lived directly across the street from Evan. I was not stalking Evan. He probably had plans with Gabriella tonight, anyway. And by the way, I was still mad.

I turned onto Evan's street and pulled along the curb in front of his house as I usually would before realizing if he was home, he'd think I was there to see him. So instead, I executed a rough three-point turn and parked in front of Kip's, as if that wasn't weird.

As luck would have it, Kip was sitting on the steps outside his kitchen door holding a tumbler filled with an unnatural golden-orange-colored liquid. A tiny blue cocktail umbrella poked from between fat ice cubes, and he raised the glass as I exited the car.

"Jessie! Just in time to begin the weekend with us!"

Bertram waltzed out the door, answering the question of who the 'us' was.

"Oh, your friend!" Bertram gushed, sloshing some of the same liquid onto Kip's shoulder as he passed. He bounded over and gave me a quick hug. "I'm so glad you're here! Tell us about the search for your lover! Is good?"

"Hi, guys," I said, glad one of us felt optimistic about my search for love.

"Let me get you one of these fabulous cocktails," Kip said, rising to his feet. "Bertram invented them this afternoon, and they are to die for! What did we decide to call these?"

Bertram giggled. "I don' think I want to say in front of your friend."

Kip disappeared into the kitchen, and Bertram took his seat on the step, patting the concrete beside him. "Come. Come sit. Tell me everything. Are you being careful? Do you carry your stones like I said?"

I sank down on the hard step and pulled the cord, extracting the black stone from where it rested inside my shirt, glad I'd remembered to wear it this morning. "I am." The pink stone, however, was still sitting on my dresser.

"And the love stone?"

I was hoping he wouldn't ask. I made a face, afraid to lie, in case he really was psychic. "I forgot that one on my dresser."

Bertram made a tsking noise, but he didn't look at all upset, instead taking a long, slow drink. "Is okay. Rose quartz is for love, but sometimes self-love most. I think there is work to do on self-love, yes?"

Kip reemerged, holding out a glass toward me. "Here you go, dear." I took the drink, and Kip sank down, squeezing his narrow hips onto the step, shoving me closer toward Bertram. "Cheers." He clinked my glass, and Bertram did the same, hitting his against mine so hard I feared they would crack.

I took a tentative taste, letting the cool liquid run over my tongue. "That's good," I said, lying only a little. I had no idea what I was trying.

"So, Jessie, fill us in," said Kip. "What has transpired with you? How's your little friend? I can tell you right now he's still with the harlot. In fact, I would expect she should be here soon."

It had only been two days since I'd seen Kip, and yet so much had happened.

"I'm not sure where to start," I said, taking another sip. "Oh," I turned toward Kip. "I don't think I told you, but the police don't think Christine's death was an accident. Or at least they're not sure."

He looked unimpressed. "Well, of course, it wasn't an accident. I told you that."

"Okay, well, you didn't know she had a bunch of valuable jewelry that she'd had appraised and recently added an amendment to her will, leaving it to the rescue group where she got her dog."

He shrugged. "You did mention the jewelry, and people leave money to all kinds of places," he said.

Bertram leaned against me, not to be left out. "Yes, mi tia abuela left her house to the restaurant next door. They always gave her meals, and so when she passed, she gave them her house so they could, how I say, get bigger?"

I patted his arm. "That was nice. But anyway," I turned back towards Kip. "The jewelry is missing, we think. At least her sister hasn't been able to find it."

Now I had his interest. He sat up straighter and peered at me. "I'll bet I know where it is!"

"Where?"

He jabbed a pointy finger toward Evan's house. "I'll bet either they're in on it together, or else...Oh, I know! That's why she's with him. He's a slobby rube who won't notice the jewels stashed somewhere in his piles of laundry. She *is* a sly one, isn't she?"

I started to protest, but now that he'd aired the thought, I turned it over in my mind. Okay, if I was being honest, I didn't really see Gabriella as a killer. She might do something in a fit of pique, so I couldn't totally rule out her killing Christine in a semi-accidental way. But there was no way Evan was in on it. I knew him well enough to know that for sure. Then again, Evan was a slob. He might not notice something hidden in his house; it would be a great place to stash things.

He was getting ready to expound on his theory when an earsplitting rumble came around the corner, drowning out any hope for conversation.

"Speak of the devil," Kip shouted over the roar. Gabriella pulled along the curb in front of Evan's house, her car reverberating with a clamor of competing noises. It seemed she turned her stereo all the way up to try and drown out the racket from her defunct muffler. At this rate, she'd be hard of hearing by the time she was Evan's age. In addition to the clamor, her tailpipe spewed out a noxious cloud of black smoke that wafted along the car's undercarriage. Her lungs might give out before her ears. She was pandemonium on wheels.

"I don' like this noise," Bertram shouted. "It is, how I say, destructing energy."

She didn't turn off the engine; instead, she sat vibrating and belching, staring down, presumably at her phone. She should consider investing in a booster seat because I could hardly see her head above the window. The smell from the black cloud drifted up the driveway, and I pulled my shirt over my nose, unwilling to let myself be gassed. Then she turned off the engine, and it was as if I'd suddenly gone deaf.

Evan's Jeep rolled smoothly around the corner and into his driveway. Oh boy. I shrank down on Kip's step as if hiding behind Bertram would render me and my car invisible. Gabriella emerged from the depths of her car, the door creaking as if on the verge of falling off, before she slammed it shut with a forceful heave.

"Hey, bae!" she said to Evan as he exited his car. She wiggled toward him, shoulders and hips swinging as loosely as an inflatable air figure at a carwash. I saw him glance at the street and take in my car. He flinched and scowled, looking first at his porch before turning and spotting us on Kip's step.

Kip raised his glass in acknowledgment. "Hey, neighbor!" he said. "Happy Fri-yay!"

Evan puffed up like a rooster, his shoulders drawing back and his slender chest jutting forward. Gabriella turned and looked in our direction. When she saw me, her expression mutated from sultry to assassin in less than a second.

"Oh my God!" she squawked. "What is *she* doing here?" She turned on Evan. "You said you'd make her leave us alone and stop spreading lies."

I had a flurry of emotions churning through me. The thought of Evan talking to this... this... girl about me...about *me* was not okay. I started to rise, but Bertram gently touched my shoulder.

"'S okay, 's okay," he said.

"Is her energy getting disturbed again?" asked Kip, turning to look at us. He gestured toward my glass. "Honey, have a drink. That skank is not worth disturbing your energy over."

Evan corralled Gabriella and hustled her across the porch to the door. They went in with a bang. Bertram shuddered beside me and took a long swallow of his own cocktail.

"Uff," he shuddered again. "That lady is bad energy. I tell you, it's like, how I say, pollution aura."

I couldn't come up with a better description of Gabriella if I tried, and I laughed.

"That's better," said Kip. "Sit tight. I'm going to mix up a new pitcher of cocktails. I think we could all use one. Bertram, you stay here and make sure Jessie doesn't go over there and cause a scene."

He slipped into the kitchen, and I looked at Evan's house again. My energy surge had faded, and I felt a creeping sadness, thinking I might never go in there again. I'd had a lot of fun with Evan in that house. Okay, there were some not-so-great things too, but overall, we'd had fun. I missed hanging out with him and the dogs.

"Can I say something?" Bertram asked.

"Of course," I said.

He took a deep breath and looked into his glass, swirling the ice around. "I feel you chasing things—like not good chase," he said slowly. "Like, you still not filling you."

I didn't say anything.

"You know?" he asked.

"I'm not sure," I said. My own ice cubes were beginning to

melt, creating little pools of pale liquid surrounded by darker orange depths.

"Finding a lover starts here," he said, thumping a fist against his own chest. "Here." He thumped again. "You are looking out there." He waved his hand in the air.

"I'm not looking there," I said, a little more snappishly than intended. "Evan and I are just friends."

Kip reemerged from the house carrying a swirling pitcher of orange liquid. This time, there appeared to be random chunks of fruit floating in it. "Okay, who's ready for a topper?" he sang out. Bertram and I didn't respond. "Oh no. What did I miss?" He sank back down, filled his glass, and set the pitcher on the concrete between his shoes. "C'mon, kids. What happened?"

"Nothing happened," I said.

Bertram hung his head. "I say something wrong."

"Oh no. What did you say? Did you tell her she was going to meet a different kind of animal? What is it this time? Bertram, I think you need to work on your skills a little. Most of your customers won't be as forgiving as Jessie here." He sipped his drink, and I wondered how much he'd already consumed.

My own drink warmed its way to my belly. I hadn't eaten in a while, and these were pretty strong, but the flavor was growing on me.

"It's fine," I said. "And you're right. I'm just in a mood."

"Oh honey," said Kip. "Of course, you're in a mood. I mean, look. One of your best friends has thrown you over for a murdering whore. And you deserve so much better, doesn't she, Bertram? So stop telling her useless things and help her find her man."

Bertram sighed. "It's how I was telling her. Finding love starts here." He thumped his chest again, but not as forcefully this time as if even he had doubts about his wisdom.

"Oh, pshaw," said Kip. "Finding love starts out there. You

can't hang out with dogs wearing God knows what all day and expect to find a hot man. It doesn't work that way."

"I don' say she only looks here," Bertram massaged his heart with his fingertips. "But she starts here."

They might have gotten into a full-blown brawl over my love life if they hadn't been interrupted by Evan and Gabriella sailing out of the house. Evan had his arm wrapped around her neck, but instead of looking romantic, Gabriella dragged along in his wake like a drowning victim fighting her rescuer. She made it five yards before shoving him away to adjust her dress and smooth her hair. They studiously avoided looking in our direction, although I could tell Evan was trying to see us out of the corner of his eye. I'd made that move before myself, and I could tell he was feeling the eyestrain.

CHAPTER TWENTY-EIGHT

We watched them leave. Evan reversed out of his driveway so fast that he nearly rammed the side of my car. I leaped to my feet, jaws clenched, awaiting the crunch of metal on metal, but he braked in time, threw his car in drive, and peeled out. I sank back down.

"Time to top off!" said Kip, picking up his pitcher. He refreshed all the glasses, and we relapsed into silence.

"I want to help," said Bertram, finally breaking the silence. "But I think I am not, how I say, conversing the message right."

"It's fine," I said, my negative emotions beginning to be dulled by the orange cocktail. "I know you're right. This whole thing with Evan has thrown me off my game. I wasn't that worried about being in a relationship before. But seeing that..."

"Seeing that would make me not *want* a relationship," said Kip. "I mean, puh-lees." He shuddered.

"Well, she's adorable," I said. Both guys huffed. "Well, she is," I insisted.

"You're much cuter," said Kip. "But you could maybe take some pointers about fixing yourself up."

"She is no' cute," said Bertram. "She is cold, dead energy."

I was starting to like Bertram more and more. "Tell me what else you pick up from her," I said, feeling my muscles beginning to relax into loose, tingly bands.

He looked at me from the corner of his eye. "No, I don' want to open myself to that." He set his drink down and cut at the air in front of him like he was slicing through a forest of cobwebs. Then he made a series of small spitting sounds, "Pfft, pfft, pfft." He finished by grasping one of the cords around his neck and extracting a black stone similar to the one I wore. He held it in his palm, pressing it against his heart before shoving it back inside his shirt. Then he picked up his drink and relaxed once again. "I am done with that girl."

I pulled my own necklace up and held my stone in a similar manner. It was warm from my skin, and I clutched it in my palm.

"So, back to the first thing," said Kip. "The stolen jewels."

"We don't know they're stolen exactly," I said, slipping my black tourmaline back inside my shirt.

"Of course, they're stolen," said Kip. "The only question is whether the person who stole them is the same one that killed the lady."

Maybe Irene killed Christine, and Gabriella showed up later, saw an opportunity, and snagged the jewelry. The more I thought about it, the more plausible it seemed.

"What if Gabriella did take the jewelry?" I said slowly. "How would she get rid of it? I don't see her keeping it for sentimental reasons."

Kip snorted. "Honey, that girl doesn't know sentimental. But I'm sure she knows people who could help her liquidate."

"Maybe. But if she's sitting on a fortune, why is she doing the sugar-daddy thing if that's what it is? And why is she still with Evan?"

"Tell me sugar-daddy thing," said Bertram excitedly.

"Oh, it was a scene!" said Kip. He launched into a spirited

description of Gabriella's tryst with the well-dressed older man and his own heroism in saving Henry from certain death. Bertram was enthralled, an excellent audience with a wide range of exclamations, each emoted at the perfect beat. When he reached the end of his involvement, Kip sat back and cocked his head. "And maybe the question isn't why is she still with your friend, but why is *he* still with *her*?" he asked. "How is he okay having tricks turned in his house? And by someone who nearly got his dog killed?"

My newly relaxed muscles stiffened with tension. "I have no idea what she told him. Whatever it was, it seems like he believed her."

"Well, I think we should go look for the jewelry," said Kip.

A vague, uneasy feeling sent tendrils of anxiety licking at the edges of my stomach. "Where?" I knew I shouldn't have asked.

"Where do you think?" asked Kip, adding another ounce to my glass. "Don't you have a key for emergencies? I'm almost certain you would," he said calmly. "Because of the dog, of course."

Of course.

"Kip, we can't go in there," I said. "No way. I won't violate Evan's trust like that."

We sat and listened to traffic noises.

"But if the dog was in danger, you would go in, right?" he finally countered.

"That's different," I said. "Going in to snoop is not the same as making sure Henry is safe."

"Let's look at this," he said, with the patient air of a professor explaining complex answers to a dull student. "Your friend is dating a girl who is a parasite." I was with him so far. "She doesn't care for you and is trying to isolate your friend from his normal support system." He paused, waiting to see if there was any pushback. There wasn't. "She wants what she wants when she wants it and won't let anyone get in her way. We can clearly see she doesn't care about your friend. I think we can safely say she doesn't cherish dogs. She had no compunction about letting the dog out once, yet she's still the girlfriend. She brought a man over to do what her kind does while your friend was at work. And yet, she's still the girlfriend!"

Bertram shook his head and laid a hand on my forearm. "Is bad."

"If you don't get involved, you will lose your friend."

"Evan is a grown man."

"He's a man-child," said Kip. Bertram murmured assent even though he'd never met Evan. "I think it's going to take some effort to open his eyes," he said. "And even if you're willing to let him learn some hard lessons, which, hey," he held up a hand. "I'm not arguing against. But I can't constantly sit at my front window and watch out for his sweet little dog. I guarantee you, that girl will get rid of the dog one way or another, and then aren't you going to feel bad that you didn't do anything to stop it?"

Okay, I'd like to blame the orange drinks. And while they probably contributed, it was as much my dislike of Gabriella, my anger at Evan, and, of course, the overriding concern for Henry that made me pull the keyring from my purse and hold up Evan's house key.

We'd made it across the street and onto Evan's porch, with Henry barking at us from the other side of the door before I began coming to my senses.

"Wait, hold on. We're going snooping to save Henry and my relationship with Evan—only if he knows I've been snooping, we will no longer be friends, and I will have no idea what happens to Henry."

Bark, bark, bark.

"Well, you're not exactly friends right now," Kip said. "Okay, how about this? You give me the key, and Bertram and I will go in and find the jewelry."

"Then what?"

"Then we've caught her red-handed."

"And Evan will know we've been snooping."

Bark, bark, bark.

Kip tapped at his lip, trying to get around my reluctance. It was still light, but the sun had dropped low enough to cast broad swaths of shade around the house. Birds fluttered in the big oak tree, swooping down and hopping along the gravel drive while traffic noises hummed nearby. It felt like almost every other Friday afternoon I'd been over here, getting ready to hang out with Evan, but we weren't hanging out this time. In fact, I was considering illegally entering his house. My heart was beating too fast, and I felt as skittish as a feral cat. I patted my chest, trying to calm myself.

Speaking of calming, a thought popped up. "Oh, by the way, I came over to give you some CBD treats I got for your cat. They're supposed to calm him down." I started rummaging in my purse, thinking I should try a handful.

"That's very sweet." He reached over and plucked my hand from my bag. "But let's focus, okay? How about this? Bertram and I will go in and get the jewelry, and you can return it so that the money goes to the dog rescue. I know that is important to you."

"I'm not sure that helps with the Gabriella situation. If she stole them, then she needs to be held accountable."

"Karma will fix," muttered Bertram. I'd noticed he'd become very fidgety as we stood there. "Kip, I dunno about this. I feel, how I say, not good here."

"That's it. I'm with Bertram," I said, turning around.

"You don't feel good because this house is haunted," said Kip. "Jessie, do you remember that lady who came to remove the ghost?" He started to laugh. "Oh my, what was her name? She nearly burned the place down."

"A ghost is here?" asked Bertram. I have to say, for a psychic, he didn't seem too keen on dealing with the other side.

"No, I'm sure there's not," I said. "And even if there had been, Mrs. Gray got rid of it."

Bertram began reaching for his necklaces again. "Kip, I don' want to be here. Let's go back to your house. We have more of that nice drink."

"Yeah, this is a bad idea," I said. Bertram and I turned and made our way off of the porch. We'd just reached the bottom step when I heard a car approaching. I glanced up and saw Evan's Jeep turning off Montrose.

CHAPTER TWENTY-NINE

"They're back! They're back!" I yelled. Bertram and I raced for the far side of the house, and Kip vaulted over the rail, all of us ducking around the corner just as the car turned into the drive.

"Why are they back so soon?" hissed Kip. My heart was hammering so loud I could hardly hear him. Thank heavens we hadn't gone in.

I waved a hand to shush him, and we huddled beside a straggly bush. I could feel Bertram's warm breath on the back of my neck—his breathing as ragged as mine felt. Evan's tires crunched on the drive, and I could hear their raised voices before they even opened the doors.

"Yeah, I know," Evan was yelling. "But I didn't *give* you a key —you *took* it! And I never said you could bring in a decorator. I said I would *think* about it!"

"I was trying to do something *nice!*"

"You never told me his name. Why is that? If he was a decorator, I'd like to see his website."

The car doors slammed almost simultaneously.

"You said you didn't want to do it." Gabriella had moderated her tone as if transitioning into appeasement mode. "Evie, please don't be mad at me. C'mon. We can take Henry for a walk and still go out after."

Footsteps clumped up the sagging porch steps. "So what was the decorator's name then?" asked Evan, his voice lower but still angry.

I felt Kip's hand grasp my shoulder. He leaned against my head and whispered softly in my ear, "His name was John." I clamped a hand over my mouth to still the laugh that nearly escaped.

"C'mon, forget about it. Let's have a nice night, okay? It's Friday. I've hardly seen you all week. Let's not fight."

Henry was still barking, high-pitched, and excited as he recognized Evan's approach.

"Hey, bud," Evan's voice lost all animosity as he addressed Henry. That, at least, gave me some comfort. "C'mere." His voice drifted away as the front door snapped shut behind them.

"Oh, that was so scary," whispered Bertram. "Why my guides no tell me sooner?" He looked up at the sky as if searching for his wayward guides.

Kip giggled, a soft little hiccup indicating he was at least somewhat tipsy. "A little trouble in paradise," he whispered. "Perhaps he's starting to figure out there was more to that story than he wanted to believe."

I was trying to figure out how to cross the street without being seen when the front door opened again. We froze.

"You're still going to take me to dinner, right, Evie?"

"Hey, look out! You nearly stepped on him." I heard Henry's nails scratch against the porch, and he whined, an excited little tracker on the hunt.

Oh no, he must smell me.

"Henry, stop it. What are you doing? C'mon, we're going this way."

I pushed backward, nearly knocking Bertram over. I grabbed his arm to steady him and waved frantically at Kip, gesturing to follow me. Henry was going to give us away. We moved as quietly as we could down the narrow side yard, although I could tell we weren't being quiet at all. Dead leaves crunched and skittered underfoot, and I could hear Kip giggling and hiccupping as we went.

"Shut up!" I hissed. I couldn't think what we would tell Evan if he caught us back here.

Fortunately, Gabriella was nattering on, her voice projecting an annoying whine that surely must drive Evan crazy.

"What about the other thing?" she asked. "My dad is driving me crazy. You don't even know. He literally won't shut up about Aunt Penny and Aunt Christine. Like, oh my God. I get it! She's being a bitch and won't give us anything. But what am I supposed to do about it? She's *his* sister. Are you even listening to me?" I heard a grunt, which must have been Evan. "I don't know why I can't stay here." The whine began to intensify as we reached the backyard. I wanted to hear the rest, but it wasn't worth getting caught for.

I led Kip and Bertram into the backyard, intending to circle around. A small strip center abutted Evan's property on the other side, and we could slip around the fence over there. Then we could stroll down Montrose as if we'd been out for coffee or something. No big deal.

Kip had been back here before, so I wasn't sure why he acted like this was some new horror he'd never experienced. In all fairness, though, the weeds *had* reached an impressive height. Evan hadn't mentioned the rat infestation he'd been battling for months lately, so hopefully, they were gone. Then again, he'd been busy, and maybe he hadn't had time to deal with it. Perhaps Kip's dramatically high steps were appropriate.

"Why you walk like that?" whispered Bertram.

"My friend, there are monstrous rodents in here," said Kip softly. "I've seen them."

Bertram let out a squeak and began running across the yard toward the far side of the house.

"Wait," I whispered as loudly as I could. "Wait, you can't run out there!"

I caught him as he reached the corner and pulled him back by his shirt. His hands waved near the sides of his face like inverted jazz hands that had malfunctioned at high speed. I hoped that was how he calmed himself to keep from screaming, but I wasn't sure.

"Bertram, it's fine," I whispered. "It's fine. We'll go along the side here and see where they are. I think they were taking the dog the other way so we can go around the fence there." I pointed. Little whimpering sounds vibrated in his throat, and I feared I'd have to slap him.

"I don' like rats," he said. His hands fluttered, and I grabbed one wrist.

"It's fine. There're no rats."

"You promise?" he hissed.

"I promise." I hate lying. I kept a firm grip on his wrist as we crept along the side of the house. Kip slunk behind us, and as we approached the front, I could hear Gabriella's voice still going on. It sounded like they hadn't gone as far as I'd hoped. In fact, it appeared they were still in the front yard. I held up a hand like a platoon leader on nighttime maneuvers.

"I'm not saying, like, forever," Gabriella said. "Just, like, a few days. I don't know why you're being so mean." I heard a scuffing noise as if she were kicking rocks in the driveway. I slowly poked my head around, careful to stay hidden by a bush. I parted the branches and felt Kip crawl up close next to me.

Evan held Henry's leash loosely as he watched the dog poke

around. He wasn't responding to Gabriella at all, which only encouraged her further.

"So, why not? It's not like you're even here that much. You work all the time anyway. I could get home early and make you dinner. Come on, bae." She moved up behind him and ran a finger along the hair at his collar. "It would be so fun."

Evan leaned forward toward Henry, pulling the leash and dragging him backward. "What is that? Henry, drop it." He reached down, trying to wrest something from Henry's mouth. Henry turned suddenly and pulled back, ready for a good game of tug-of-war. We watched as whatever he had stretched between the two of them.

Beside me, I felt Kip stiffen.

"What is that?" asked Gabriella.

Suddenly, Evan let go, the object snapping back toward Henry. "Oh, my God! Henry, drop it." Evan wiped the hand he'd been pulling with reflexively on his pants and shook the back of Henry's neck with the other. "Drop it! Drop it!"

Gabriella leaned forward, then turned quickly away. A saggy length of pale rubber dangled from Henry's mouth as he shook his head from side to side, trying to entice Evan to continue the game.

"Henry, drop it!" screamed Evan. Something in the high-pitched tone got through, and Henry dropped the thing, his ears and tail drooping as if he'd done something bad. Evan bent at the waist, staring down before glancing towards Gabriella. "It's a condom, Gabriella! What is a condom doing by my porch?"

Next to me, I felt Kip's body begin to heave, and he held a hand to his mouth as if suppressing a gag. I felt much the same. It would be a long time before I'd want Henry's little tongue licking my face.

Gabriella stepped back. "How would I know?" She was

trying to sound outraged, but there was a hesitation, and Evan pounced.

"Are you *kidding* me? You're going to look me in the eye and say you don't know anything about this?"

She grabbed her hair, pulling the mass forward over one shoulder and running her fingers along its length as if soothing herself. "How would I know, Evan? I didn't put it there. That's disgusting. Someone probably threw it out of a car. It's gross." She was starting to sound more sure of herself.

Evan knelt beside Henry, prying his jaws open and examining the inside of his mouth. "Well, I've never had this issue at my house before. And it's too far from the street for something like this to end up here." He stood up. "Gabriella, look at me. Tell me the truth. What happened that day that Henry got out?"

Her back was to me, but I could see her shifting her weight from foot to foot. "Nothing! I told you. I had a decorator friend over to help me with ideas. You know, like, I have my own ideas, but I don't know how to do them yet. That's all. And then you said you didn't want to do anything, so I dropped it."

"So why won't you tell me your friend's name. If he's a decorator, I should be able to look him up."

"He's not an actual decorator. He just does stuff on the side. You couldn't look him up."

Evan moved closer to Gabriella and leaned down, his face inches from hers. "Did you sleep with a man in my house that day?"

"No! I did not *sleep* with a man in your house that day."

I could feel everyone holding their breath, myself included. Evan clenched his fists, his arms shaking with anger. Henry dropped down on his belly, his body tense and his jaws yawning with stress. "Don't mock me, Gabriella. You know what I mean. Did you have sex in my house with someone that was not me?" He was yelling now; each word shot precisely into her face.

She flinched and ducked her head. "Fine. Whatever. It's no big deal. I had someone over. *So what?* I'm sure you hook up with girls all the time—like that friend of yours. You can't tell me you're not doing the same thing."

Even in the shadows, I could see the side of Evan's neck mottling into an alarming network of red patches.

"You were hooking up with someone in *my* house, and you let *my dog* out while you were *doing it*?" I wasn't entirely sure Evan wouldn't have a heart attack. Gabriella must have thought the same because she moved toward him and touched his arm.

"Bae, it's not a big deal. Everyone does it."

Kip leaned toward me, his lips brushing my ear. "Gurl, the everyone does it defense never works."

"It is too a big deal! On top of the part where you were sleep —" Evan cut himself off. "Having sex with some other guy in my bed..." He shook her hand from his arm. "You let my dog out! You were willing to let my dog get killed so you could shag some...some guy?"

Kip and Bertram crowded beside me, all of us too enthralled by the drama to look away.

"I don't know what you're so pressed about," she said, her own anger rising. "Gah, you're so pathetic. If you're gonna be like this, I don't even want to stay here. My mom's less a prude than you. Shit, my grandma's less a prude than you." She muttered something else I couldn't make out. "And nothing happened to your stupid dog, anyway. Look at him, he's *fine!*"

Henry didn't look entirely fine. He looked like he would need therapy to convince him his new tug-o-war game wasn't the cause of this uproar.

Gabriella waved a hand at the deflated sticky mess near Evan's foot. "And by the way, I had nothing to do with that." They both stared down at the offending item.

"I don't believe you," said Evan, his voice as low and as angry as I'd ever heard it.

"Well, I didn't." She paused as if evaluating whether any life was left in this relationship. Deciding there wasn't, she changed her tone. "My friend probably left it there," she said, her voice as biting as she could make it. "He was considerate enough not to leave it in your trash can where you might find it, but like, who wants to carry a used condom around?" She swiveled her hips and started toward her car before turning back. "I need my purse." She stomped up the porch steps, shaking the rickety wood so hard I feared she'd break one. Evan stood as rigid as a post, holding Henry's leash and staring at his shoes.

Within seconds, Gabriella was out again, stomping back down the steps and across to her car. The three of us ducked down, listening as Evan went into the house, slamming the door with a bang. Seconds later, Gabriella fired up her car and roared down the street with a squeal, a belch, and a cloud of black smoke.

Kip, Bertram, and I rose slowly, looking at each other in disbelief over what we'd witnessed.

"Well, that was something," Kip whispered. "It's always so much fun when you're here," he told me.

"C'mon, I don't want Evan to see us and know we saw all that," I said softly. I wasn't sure if I was still angry at him or not —I probably was, but nevertheless, I didn't want him to know we'd witnessed something so humiliating for him. After all, in the end, he'd stood up for Henry.

I ushered them into the alley behind the strip center. I didn't think Evan was sitting looking out his front windows, but who knows? Maybe he was staring forlornly after Gabriella's car.

"This is not nice," whispered Bertram. He frowned at the dumpster before us, its rancid smell permeating the humid air.

Kip grabbed Bertram's arm and led him along the side of the

building as I followed along behind. So, it seemed that Evan was done with Gabriella, right? That should make me feel better, but I felt flat, unsure that we could return to normal even if she was gone.

"How are we going to find the jewelry now?" Kip asked. "Maybe you can make up with your friend and go poke around."

"Forget it, Kip. I don't think Evan has the jewelry."

We reached the street and stopped. Bertram peered north, then south. "I am hungry," he said. "Is there somewhere we could get food?"

"There used to be a Mexican place right here," I waved an arm at the restaurant directly in front of us, but the space was vacant, brown paper blocking the windows. "I thought it turned into a French place."

"Oh, it wasn't good," said Kip. "That didn't last long."

"Look, a sign," said Bertram. I wasn't sure if he meant a physical sign or a sign from his guides, but he began to walk north. Up the block was a small Thai restaurant looking no bigger than a storage container. Bertram bounced on his toes. "Yes! Let's go there. I am, how I say, starfing." Kip shrugged his indifference. I was starving too, so we headed over.

CHAPTER THIRTY

Atiny bell tinkled as we entered a space so dim that my eyes struggled to adjust. Before I could express concern over eating in an establishment where you couldn't even see your food, a tiny, wizened woman with a curtain of dark hair approached, took Bertram by the hand, and deposited him at a table next to the wall. Kip and I followed. The first chair I sat in wobbled so wildly I feared it would collapse under my weight, so I moved to the fourth one, which, while unsteady, would hopefully not collapse. The woman handed us each a plastic menu and disappeared through a swinging door. We were the only diners, and while it was a little early for dinner, I didn't take it as a good sign that we were alone.

"This is much fun," said Bertram, sitting back and beaming at us. "Dinner with my friends after such an excitement!"

Kip seemed to be coming down off his jaunty buzz, and he rubbed a hand over his face. "We should have brought the drinks. Had I known we were going out after that, I would have carried the pitcher with us."

"I think I've had enough of those," I said, hunching close to my menu and trying to make out the smudged print. "Do you think this place is okay?" I looked up at Bertram. "Can you ask your guides what I should order that won't give me food poisoning?"

Bertram giggled, sounding like a junior high girl. "Oh, silly." He swatted at my arm. "It smells good. I'm sure is good."

It did smell good. I perused the menu in earnest now, my stomach beginning to growl. I hadn't even had lunch today, and the orange drinks had hit me hard. The little lady returned with water for each of us, then stood at attention with her notepad.

"Are there any specials today?" asked Kip. The woman began speaking rapidly, gesturing with her pencil-holding hand. Kip sat listening as if he understood every word. When she was done, he said, "I'll have the first one."

"I have that, too," said Bertram, handing his menu over.

"I'll have the chicken Pad Thai," I said when she looked at me. She collected our menus and disappeared again. "How did you understand what she said?" I asked.

"Oh honey, I didn't. But you have to assume in a place like this, the special will have the freshest ingredients."

"Really? I would assume the specials might be the chef trying to use up the old leftover stuff from earlier in the week so he doesn't have to throw it away."

"Well, that's another perspective," he said, sounding uncertain.

"You think?" Bertram asked, looking alarmed. "But it smells good."

"I'm sure it's fine," I said.

Kip leaned forward. "So, oh my, gawd! Let's talk about what we just saw!"

Suddenly, I wasn't sure I wanted to dissect Evan's humiliation. Luckily, my phone began buzzing. I pulled it from my back pocket, wondering if it was Evan. But it wasn't. It was Martin.

"Oh," I said.

"Who is calling?" asked Bertram.

"It's this guy I went out with Wednesday night."

"Answer it!" squealed Kip. "Wait, was he hot?"

My finger hovered over the screen. I wasn't in the mood for Martin.

"You say you look for love, but now Universe sends you love, and you don' want it?" asked Bertram. He shook his head slowly at my foolishness.

I swiped to answer, pushing away from the table and standing as I did. "Hey, Martin."

"Hey to you!" he said loud enough that my dining companions could hear every word. I stepped across the small space and out the door. The bell tinkled as I exited, drawing the little lady from the back. I waved my phone at her to indicate my call.

"What's up?"

"Hey, I know it's a little late notice," he said. "But I was wondering if you'd like to have dinner tomorrow night?"

Ugh. I tried to come up with something fast, but my brain was still on a delay from the drinks. I couldn't even claim dinner with Frances since she'd called to tell me she had a charity function Saturday night. Two weeks in a row, we'd missed our dinners. "Um, yeah, I'm not sure..."

"My dad wanted to see if you could join us. He likes to cook, and he's planning a whole Italian-themed evening. You know, pasta, vino, lots of carbs. He'd love for you to come. Oh, and I would too, of course."

I sighed. I really liked his dad. He was so nice. On the other hand, Martin was, I don't know—not what I was looking for.

"It's no big deal, just the three of us at my dad's house. I could pick you up, or you could just come there if you like?"

Not having to deal with Martin at my house was a plus. And his dad *was* sweet. Maybe I'd give this one more chance to let the Universe know I was genuinely trying.

"Um, okay, that sounds nice," I said. "What can I bring?"

"Nothing, just your pretty self!" he said. I cringed. He gave me his dad's address and said to come anytime tomorrow afternoon, although we'd probably eat around six thirty. I told him I'd be there after six. In my mind, I was planning for six twenty-nine.

I went back inside, where our food had been delivered to our table. How in the world could they cook chicken that fast? In spite of my misgivings, the food looked fresh, colorful, and blossomed with savory aromas. I peered at Kip and Bertram's food, trying to figure out what I was looking at. Something with a dark protein, glass noodles, green beans, and an orange-looking sauce that smelled of garlic. My mouth started to water.

"You were holding out on us!" said Kip. "You didn't tell us about your date! What's he like? Where'd you go? Was he hot?"

Bertram leaned forward and ran a hand along in front of me.

"What are you doing?" I asked.

"I feel for energy," he said. "I don' know about this date."

"Well, I don't know about this date either," I said, picking up my fork and digging into my fat noodles. "But he invited me to have dinner at his father's tomorrow night, and his dad is nice, so I said yes."

"Hmm," Bertram said. He closed his eyes.

"Oh, Bertram. Don't be fussy. This is the first man Jessie's gone out with—in how long?" He looked at me. "Weeks? Months?"

"Could we talk about something else?" I asked, then remembered he would probably swivel back to Evan's disaster. "Tell us about how your business is doing. What's the next big thing?"

Kip launched into what he was working on, some offshoot on his Japanese pillows. Truth be told, I tuned out pretty fast, my brain going around the loop of dreading my date with Martin, to the drama unfolding in Evan's world, then to Christine, Penny, and Lucille. I thought of Irene's seething anger at her husband's relationship—whatever it may have been—with Christine, and on to the police investigating this as more than an accident, then back to my date with Martin.

I'd eaten about two-thirds of my dinner before I surfaced to rejoin Kip and Bertram's conversation.

"Honey, I don't think you've heard a word I said," said Kip, dabbing his lip with his napkin.

"I'm sorry," I said. "I just have a lot on my mind."

"You know, it struck me while you weren't listening to me that even if the little whore had the jewels, she probably went in and got them while your friend was mad outside."

"Kip, I don't think she has them."

"So, now, we'll never know," he said.

Bertram pushed a noodle back and forth. "I still think about your date," he said.

"Hey, you're the one who just said about me sending mixed signals to the universe," I said. "I didn't want to take the call, but I don't want to ruin my chances with mixed signals either."

"I know I said. But now I rethink."

"Great." I pushed my plate away.

"Is the energy," he said, sounding apologetic. "It's how we said at my house, you put out, what was it? Needy energy, and you attract needy? Maybe this is needy energy finding you?"

I sighed. "Okay, yeah. Martin isn't what I'm looking for. Maybe he's needy. But it's more than that. At dinner Wednesday night, he just complained about everything. Like everything was someone else's fault."

"Was he a weak ass?" asked Kip. "Maybe you're getting the weak ass out of the way. Bertram, tell her what comes after the weak ass."

Bertram pushed his plate away too. "I am no' ready for a reading, Kip. You know I have to be, how I say, ground and have ritual done." He closed his eyes for a moment. "But I think you watch out for face hat."

"I don't know what that means," I said.

"I don' know either," Bertram said. He waved his fingers as if shooing away an annoyance.

"Okay, then just call back and cancel," said Kip. "If you know he's not it, then there's no point in wasting your time."

"I already said yes," I said. "And his dad will be there—he's really nice."

"You keep saying that. Why don't you date his dad then?"

"Kip. Stop."

"Oh, I know! Maybe this Martin is the weak ass, and his dad is the rich one who likes shiny things and will leave you all his money!"

"I don't think he has much money," I said. "Oh, well. I'll have dinner with them and then be done with it."

We packed up the leftovers and headed back to Kip's house. All traces of my buzz were gone, and I declined the offer to stay and finish off the pitcher of drinks. As tempting as it was, especially after Bertram fished out one fly and two mosquitos, I decided to head home. Evan's car was still in his driveway, and I had a moment of sadness. I felt like I should pop over and make sure he was okay, but if he wanted to see me, he'd have texted me. He didn't know we'd witnessed the whole mortifying incident, and I wasn't sure if he'd ever tell me about it.

Just before I reached my car, I remembered the CBD cat treats. I walked back, pulled the bag from my purse, and handed it to Kip.

"Here. I forgot. This is why I came over."

He took the bag and peered at the label, squinting to focus. "Oh, calming treats. This is perfect. Thank you. These should come in handy."

Just as I got in my car, I heard the crinkle of the bag being ripped open and turned in time to see Bertram pouring a handful for himself.

"No, those are—" I started to say.

"So good," he said, tossing a few treats into his mouth. He began to chew, his expression slowly changing as his taste buds registered the fishy flavor. I slid into my car and pulled away.

CHAPTER THIRTY-ONE

I awoke Saturday morning gripped by a dreadful headache. I wasn't sure if it was from the drinks or some strange preservative in the Thai food, but it felt like someone was hammering at the back of my eyeballs. I walked Addie at half speed and tried to decide if breakfast would help or hinder my recovery.

I was lying on my couch, still debating the question, when the doorbell rang. Oh, lord. I hoped it wasn't Larry. Addie pranced to the door, and I could hear Henry's excited whine before I even hauled myself upright. I opened the door, and Addie charged out, nearly knocking Evan off his feet.

"Addie, no! Look out." Evan held a large white paper bag and Henry's leash in one hand while balancing a cardboard drink holder with two large coffees in the other. He also had a flattish-looking package tucked up underneath an arm.

"Here, let me help you," I said, grabbing the coffee cups. He dropped Henry's leash, and the dogs shot through the door. Evan hoisted the bag and the gripped flat thing under his arm. He glanced at me from the corner of his eye without making eye contact.

"Hi," he said, standing inside the door as if unsure of his welcome.

"Something smells good," I said, glad of all the distractions.

"Oh, yeah. I brought breakfast." He looked down. "I should have called first."

"No, no, it's fine." I set the coffee on the counter and unhooked Henry's leash as he raced past me. Evan stood awkwardly, holding the big white bag and looking around like he'd never seen my kitchen before.

"Are paper plates okay?" I asked.

"I don't know. We might need the real deal." He cast another quick glance at me before looking away. "You look a little white. Are you sick?"

"No, I just have a bad headache."

"I saw you at my neighbor's yesterday," he said, taking one of the coffees and heading for the table. He set the bag in the middle and pulled out container after container.

"Yeah, I found some cat treats that are supposed to be calming. I thought it might help Kip's cat. Wow, what's all that?" I asked. I set down a couple of dinner plates and reached into the drawer for silverware.

"I got some breakfast," he said. "I wasn't sure what to bring, so I got tacos, pancakes, a couple sides of bacon, and some hash-browns. Oh, and some cinnamon rolls."

"Evan, this is enough for eight people."

He looked at the spread. "I guess it is a little much." Then he looked up and finally met my eyes. "Jess, I'm sorry. I've been acting like a jerk."

I gave him a half smile, not disputing it. "Things have been a bit much the past couple of weeks," I said, picking up a crispy slice of bacon. "Seems like we're going to have to figure out how to adjust to new things."

His shoulders relaxed, and he let out a breath. "Yeah, I guess so." He slid into a chair and began piling an assortment of breakfast delights onto a plate. He pushed that plate across the table before starting on his own. "I hope you're hungry."

I hadn't been sure I'd ever sit across from Evan like this again, and the relief I felt made me nearly giddy. I wasn't totally ready to let him off the hook, but as we started to eat and he prattled on about work, I felt the comfort of familiarity and realized that this mattered to me. This friendship was worth working on. Surely, we could navigate something a little more complex than the easy friendship we had. It was just going to take a little effort. Then again, as friends, we should be able to express concerns about anything—including potential partners. I felt a tiny frown crease my forehead.

"What?" asked Evan. "Don't you like the hash-browns?"

"No, they're great," I said, shoving another forkful into my mouth. In fact, the hash-browns seemed to be curing my headache. "It's just," I hesitated, not wanting to rock the newly found peace. "It's just that you're one of my best friends, and we need to be able to talk about things. You know? Like, if you were one of my girlfriends, I would totally be talking to you about anyone I was dating. I would want your opinion, you know?"

He looked down, hesitated, then resumed smearing a butter pat across his pancake. "Yeah, I know. And, same here. I don't know what happened to me. Like I said, I've been a jerk. You were right. I'm not seeing Gabriella anymore. I should have listened to you."

I nearly said something that would have tipped him off to the fact I'd heard the whole blow-up between them, but luckily, I caught myself in time. "Ah, Evan, I'm sorry."

"Yeah, I wasn't sure if you saw the whole pathetic thing," he paused, and I thought about coming clean, but I didn't want him to know we'd been planning to break into his house. Before I could respond, he continued. "But you were right about her. She wasn't a nice girl. Jess, you wouldn't believe it! She actually had someone—" He stopped, and I busied myself buttering my pancake.

"Well, whatever happened, I'm sorry if it didn't work out like you wanted," I said when it became clear he wasn't going to finish his sentence.

He snorted. "Straight up, I don't know what that was about. I'm not even sure how I ended up going out with her at all. She's not my type. She didn't even like Henry! That should have been a deal killer right off."

"Yeah. The bare minimum should be that we can only go out with people who like our dogs. For a life partner, I want someone who would throw himself in front of a train to save Addie, not just tolerate her." I thought about Martin's reaction to Addie and Henry and how he'd wanted me to crate Addie for his convenience. If it weren't for the fact his father was going to all this trouble for dinner tonight, I would totally blow it off. As it was, I probably wouldn't be hungry till tomorrow after this breakfast.

Nevertheless, I wasn't going to pass up a cinnamon roll. I reached into the box and extracted the gooiest one, the icing dripping down the side of my hand. Loving the fact that Evan didn't care, I licked the icing off my hand and dropped the bun onto my plate, even going so far as to scoop up a little extra icing with my finger. Evan took two buns, swirling them in the puddle at the bottom of the box. He laid a strip of bacon on top of one and took a bite. My mouth watered seeing that, so I took another cinnamon roll and added my own slice of bacon.

"Wow, that's awesome," I said.

"Yeah, the salt cuts the sugar," said Evan. He sat back, looked at everything that was left, and started scooping small amounts of seconds.

It seemed like we should talk things out a bit more. That had been a doozy of a fight, and there was no question he'd been awful to me.

As if reading my mind, he said. "Jess. I really am sorry. I wish I could take back everything I said. I know it's not a good excuse, but I'm under so much pressure at work. This team lead thing is harder than I thought it would be, and everyone is questioning every last thing I do. It's like I can't do anything right. And then with Gabriella, I don't know, I felt like, on top of all that, you were judging me too."

"Yeah, basically I was," I admitted. "But it seemed so out of left field. And, well, it was weird you suddenly had a girlfriend. Maybe I was jealous or something." He looked at me, his eyes widening. "No, not like that! We've just never dealt with either of us dating. How lame is that?"

He pushed back in his chair and pulled at the waist of his shorts, which looked like they were cutting into his midsection. "Yeah. I've never had a hot girl come on to me like that before, and maybe it overrode my regular good judgment." *Regular good judgment*—I tried not to laugh. "Anyway, I don't want to mess this up, okay?" He circled his finger in the air, ostensibly indicating our friendship. "How would that work? Do we get veto power over prospective dates?"

"I'm not sure about veto power, but how about we agree to listen to any legitimate concerns?"

"That sounds very adult," he said, wiping icing off his chin. "We'll see how this goes. What about you? Seems like you were going out with someone the other night? Does he make the cut on loving Addie enough?"

"It's a long story, and I don't think he likes dogs that much."

"Dump him."

"I was planning on it. But his dad, who's really, really nice, is making dinner tonight, and they invited me over. I didn't feel like I could say no."

"Jess, this is how you always get in trouble."

"What do you mean?"

"You always try to be nice and then end up like this. Doing things you don't want to do. As your friend, I'm telling you, I think you need to work on your boundaries."

I stared at him, seeing Evan but hearing words I'd expect from a girl.

"When did you become so aware?" I asked.

"Did I tell you about the new admin we have? She's addicted to advice columns."

"Well, you probably have a point, but that doesn't help me tonight. I said I'd go even though I don't want to."

"This is the guy I saw you with the other night?"

"Yeah. That's him."

He scowled. "You can do a lot better than him."

"With any luck. He's not horrible, but I don't really like him that much. I'm not going to see him again after tonight."

"Do you want me to call you at a certain time and get you out of there? I could say there's an emergency, and you need to get home."

"You'd do that?"

"Sure. It's one of the tricks our admin told me about. What time do you want me to call you? We can pick code words. Like if you want an out and need me to save you, say 'eagle force,' and if you're okay, say 'sparrow's nest.'"

This was classic Evan. "How in the world would I work either one of those into a phone call without sounding insane? I don't think I need any code words with you anyway. I'll just tell them I have an emergency or something if I want out."

He frowned and finished his bacon. "I guess that's okay." He licked his fingers. "Do you want to give me his address in case you really do need help?"

"We're meeting at his father's house." I pulled up Martin's text with the address. I forwarded it to Evan's phone, just in case. "I'm sure it's fine. But I sent it to you anyway."

Evan reached for his phone, retrieving my text. "Okay, looks like it's down near the stadium. I could probably be there in about twenty minutes."

"Evan, I'm sure it'll be fine. But I do appreciate this safety call. Having an out takes the pressure off. And if it's going good, I'll give you the signal and stay and enjoy the rest of my evening."

He harrumphed and turned back to the kitchen. "We'll see," he said. We agreed he'd call me at seven forty-five. Surely, I would know by then if I wanted to be saved. That should give me enough time to get through dinner without being rude to Martin's dad, and if it was terrible, I could still be home by eight or so.

We packed up the leftovers, stuck them in the refrigerator, and cleaned the kitchen before collapsing on the couch.

"Oh, here. I got this for you," Evan said. He handed me the flat package he'd brought in earlier.

It was wrapped in brown paper, and Addie poked her nose at it, convinced it was for her. "What is it?"

"Open it."

Addie flipped the edge of the paper with her nose and pawed at the covered section. The object was hard and flat, and as I pulled it out and turned it over, I saw a framed photo of Addie and Henry. They were lying on my couch, smiling doggie smiles at the camera, and I remembered Evan taking this—it felt like forever ago. The frame was weathered wood with dog bones and paw prints branded onto the surface.

"Aww, that's awesome, Evan. Thank you! They look so cute here."

"Yeah. They hardly ever get close like that. I was going to see if I could get Christine to make that into a painting. You know, if I'd won the raffle, but now you'll have to settle for a photo."

He couldn't have picked a better way to apologize if he had tried.

CHAPTER THIRTY-TWO

Despite being told not to bring anything besides my 'pretty self,' I knew I couldn't arrive at dinner empty-handed. After Evan left, I ran to the grocery store and bought some break-n-bake cookies. I'd considered bringing a bottle of wine, but cookies seemed more appropriate somehow.

By six-twenty, I was heading to Jerry's house, my plate of cookies still warm on the passenger seat beside me. I'd refrained from eating any while I made them, but the scent of the buttery sugar was causing my mouth to water. I'd dressed conservatively casual, shooting for a dinner-with-friends vibe rather than a find-me-alluring vibe. I felt pretty good about things. Evan and I were back to normal. Gabriella was gone. And I was looking forward to Jerry's home-cooked Italian meal. The only dim spot was that Martin would be there. I should be kinder. He had his moments. Granted, I knew I didn't want to see him again, but hopefully, we could part on decent terms.

The neighborhood I found myself in was almost walking distance to the stadium where the Texans played, although I was willing to bet the cost of an NFL ticket would be out of reach for most residents here. The homes were modest, with neatly

trimmed lawns, colorful flowers, and well-maintained struc-
tures. Ahead on the right, I spotted Martin's car in the driveway
of a small ranch dwelling. While tidy like its neighbors, there
was an air of something missing. They all looked to be built in
the early fifties. Some had been renovated to a more modern
look, but the Amos house stuck firmly to its brown roots. Everything about the place was brown: brown roof, brown trim,
brown brick. Not all the same shade of brown—that would have
been too much, but all well within the brown spokes of the color
wheel.

I parked and took a moment to check my phone, doing
nothing but delay. My enthusiasm for this date had declined
precipitously as I got closer, and it took a will of effort to get out
of my car. At six-thirty exactly, I forced myself to the door. I'd
barely touched the bell when the door flew open to reveal
Martin and his dad jostling for position.

"Jessie, you're here!"

"Sweetheart, it's so good to see you!"

I was enveloped between the two in an awkward three-way
hug, arms wrapping around my shoulders, back, and neck. I
hunched to cradle the plate of cookies, trying to keep them from
smashing against my belly and dropping to the ground. My face
was shoved uncomfortably close to Martin's, and I squirmed
away, feeling guilt over my antipathy while they were being so
warm and welcoming. Nevertheless, they were triggering my
escape response, and I had to curb the urge to flee down the
walk.

"Hi, guys," I chirped, taking two steps back. I shoved a row of
cookies teetering at the edge of the plate back into place and
readjusted the plastic wrap. Martin reached for a strand of my
ponytail, letting it fall softly back against my shoulder. I
refrained from slapping his hand in front of his father, who was
beaming at me.

"Come in, come in!" he said. Jerry was wearing an apron that looked like it had come original with the house. It hung from his neck, covering the center of his chest before poofing out at his waist, where he'd tied the string around in a bow. Keeping with his love of brown, it was a brown and orange floral print that reminded me of the wallpaper in Evan's living room. At least on an apron, it had the benefit of hiding stains. There wasn't much to recommend it on a wall.

"Something smells good," I said.

"My dad's been cooking all afternoon," said Martin.

"Not all afternoon," said Jerry, batting at Martin's arm. "Don't exaggerate. Please come in." Jerry bounced on his toes and waved an arm, ushering me in. "Make yourself at home. Are those for us?" He nodded at my half-crushed plate of cookies. "They look delicious. Marty, don't they look delicious? Would you like me to put those in the kitchen? Can I get you something to drink? Would you like to sit down? Marty, sit down and entertain our guest."

I wondered how many espressos it took to get this jacked up. Or maybe I was the first guest they'd entertained in, I don't know, decades?

I followed Jerry into the living room, then on to the kitchen with Martin close at my heels like a dog suffering separation anxiety. He clipped my foot at one point, and I would have paused to examine the damage, only I was afraid of being fully rear-ended if I didn't keep moving.

I glanced around as we moved, getting a feel for the place. Much like the outside, it didn't appear that many changes had been made inside in a very long time. But while dated, it was neat. Throw pillows on the couch stood in an upright line along the back cushions like a row of army recruits at attention. A row of overgrown houseplants was meticulously arranged on a plantstand, and on the walls were Thomas Kinkade reproductions, hung entirely too high but with the same level of straight-line precision.

The kitchen felt cozy, if a little cramped—no open concept here. It was semi-divided into two spaces: the cooking area and the eat-in area, bisected by cabinets that hung down, forcing a lot of ducking to talk under or popping to the side to chat around. A demo crew could fix that in less than ten minutes. The wallpaper was charming if you liked twirling strawberries. Somehow, it fit the space. The wallpaper border at the ceiling, though, with its row of white teapots, was a little over the top and made the low ceiling seem even lower.

Jerry glanced at me and then around the kitchen as if trying to see it with fresh eyes.

"We could probably use a little updating," he said. He pulled at his apron strap nervously, and I felt a surge of affection for this sweet little man.

"This is nice," I said, meaning it. "It's warm and homey. I love it." He reached over and squeezed my shoulder, smiling so wide I could see the silver crown shining in the back of his mouth.

He turned to the oven and pulled the door open, leaning in to take a peek. "It's getting there," he said. "I hope you like lasagna."

"I love lasagna." Judging by the smell, this was not a frozen chunk of industrial lasagna from the grocer's freezer.

"Dad even made the noodles from scratch." Martin came to stand beside me, taking the opportunity to give my neck a little squeeze. Ugh, why did he even have to be here? It would be so much nicer to have a relaxing dinner with Jerry. I inched away, pretending a sudden interest in the wooden salad bowl on the counter.

"Can I help you with anything?" I asked Jerry. "You need any greens washed? Salad tossed? Table set? Anything?"

"No, no, I've got it all under control. Why don't you kids get something to drink and go enjoy a little quiet time in the living room. Dinner should be ready shortly."

"What would you like to drink?" asked Martin, moving over to a sideboard beside the table. An array of bottles were grouped at one end, and Martin began touching each in turn. "Whiskey? Gin? Amaretto? Tequila?" He picked up the Tequila bottle and started a little mambo dance with it. He hummed a few notes before raising the bottle high and shouting, "Tequila!" He smiled at me and shuffled closer.

"Um, how about a glass of wine?" I asked, backing up into a kitchen chair and sending it scraping across the floor.

"Whoa, she hasn't even had one drink yet, and she's tearing the place up," said Martin, giving me a wink.

I smiled to be polite and slid the chair back in place. The table was set for three, a plastic tablecloth safeguarding against tomato sauce disasters. Dinner plates, salad plates, and an assortment of forks, knives, and spoons were neatly arranged, and trivets were set in the middle, awaiting hot dishes. Also on the table, as close to the center as they could be without getting in the way, was a large vase of pink roses.

"The flowers are lovely," I said, stroking a soft petal.

"They're for you," said Martin.

"We're so happy you could join us," said Jerry.

"You didn't need to go to all this trouble," I said, feeling the weight of my decision not to see Martin again after tonight. They weren't making it easy. This is probably why they say don't involve the kids until you know if it will work out. The same unquestionably held true for parents.

Martin asked if I preferred red or white, and I said I'd be happy to have whatever they were having. Jerry waved a spatula at a giant bottle of red wine resting on the counter next to the stove. "Marty, I thought we could have that with dinner. It's a little Italian table wine."

Little was not the right word. That was the most immense bottle I'd seen outside a liquor store. Martin studied the top before reaching around to twist off the metal cap, presenting it to me with a flourish.

"M'lady would like to sniff the cork?"

I took the cap and gamely waved it under my nose, wondering how soon it would be before Evan would call. "Perfect," I said.

Martin retrieved two wine glasses from the table, using both hands to hold the bottle steady before pouring. At least he wasn't shy about his pours. I might need this to get through dinner. "Dad?"

"Sure, pour me a splash while you're at it."

Wine in hand, Martin and I moved to the living room. I raced to a cushiony recliner, pretending I didn't see him trying to steer me to the couch. Sinking onto the edge of the seat, I crossed my legs and sampled the wine. It was tastier than expected, light and fruity, with only the slightest hint of vinegar undertones. From the kitchen, I could hear Jerry chopping something with gusto. Chop, chop, chop, chop, chop. If I tried to chop that fast, I'd lose a fingertip.

"Your dad must cook a lot," I said.

"Not especially. He only cooks for special occasions."

I glanced around the room, aware that Martin was staring intently at me. Forcing a smile, I said, "So, how's work going? Any interesting wills come your way lately?"

Chop, chop, chop, chop, chop.

Martin frowned a tiny frown. "No. I don't want to talk about work right now. Let's talk about you. I feel like I'm only beginning to know your many fascinating layers. I'm hoping to learn more tonight."

I felt my fascinating layers begin to curl tightly into a protective ball. "Um, okay. Like what?"

He wriggled deeper into the cushion, stretching one arm along the back of the couch and crossing one ankle across his opposite knee. He glanced at the space beside him as if that look alone would entice me to come over and cuddle in his embrace. I looked away.

"Well...tell me something about yourself that no one else knows."

"Hmm, that's hard. I'm pretty much an open book. I'm not sure there's any one thing that no one knows about me," I said.

"Oh, there has to be. Everyone has something."

"Okay, then, how about you?"

I was surprised when he suddenly uncrossed his legs and sat forward, clutching his wine in both hands before jumping to his feet. "I'll be right back. I thought I heard my dad. He probably needs help."

From the kitchen, the chop, chop, chop, chop continued unabated. Martin trotted out of the room and into the kitchen. That was weird. I took the opportunity to pull my phone from my purse and check the screen. It wasn't even close to the time for Evan to phone with my exit call. I leaned back into the recliner and scrolled through my email. Nothing interesting. Suddenly, my phone buzzed.

It was a text from Kip. *Bertram wants to know if you insisted on carrying out your date with Mr. Needy Energy.*

I heard Martin talking to his father in the kitchen but couldn't make out the words.

Yes.

I'd just hit send when Martin was back.

"Who are you talking to?" he asked.

"No one. I was just checking my phone." I slid it into my pocket instead of back into my purse, wanting to have it close when Evan called.

My phone buzzed. Martin stared at me. "No one?" he asked.

If it weren't for Jerry toiling away in the kitchen, I'd go home right now. This was definitely needy energy with shades of controlling coming out.

He hovered uncertainly, then walked back to the couch and plopped down. Sulky was now making an appearance. I wondered how many red flags I could spot between now and when I locked myself into my car later.

"Everything okay in the kitchen?" I asked. For whatever reason, I was feeling more confident in the face of Martin's unraveling.

"Fine."

Outside, I heard the sound of a basketball hitting pavement, rhythm filling the silence until it too moved off. Plates clattered in the kitchen, and Jerry began whistling an off-tune rendition of *Strangers in the Night*. I was going to miss him.

"So, what do you like to do when you're not working?" I finally asked, thinking I might as well try to brush up on my dating conversation. Not that I planned on any more dates soon.

"I don't know," he said. "I like cars. I showed you the one I want to get, right? The other night?"

"Oh, yeah." I recalled him pointing to something after we'd left the restaurant, but I didn't remember what it was, and being that I wasn't that into cars, this could be a long slog. "Some kind of muscle car?"

A mix of emotions wrangled across his face before he decided to bypass sulky and move into a pundit-of-cars persona. "Well, muscle car is a broad term. I'll bet you didn't know that Pontiac first used it to describe their 1964 GTO."

He looked at me as if awaiting an answer. "No. I did not know that."

"Not that there weren't muscle cars before that. During Prohibition, moonshiners needed to move fast and evade the police, so they started modifying their cars. I'd love to see some of those. I wonder if there's a museum somewhere showcasing the original muscle cars. We should look into that. I'm sure that would be a great trip." He glanced at me to gauge my reaction, and I rearranged my features into something neutral. "Don't you think?"

"I'm sure it would be noteworthy."

"Have you heard of the Rocket 88?"

My fingers itched to check my phone. "No."

"It had a lightweight body from the Oldsmobile 76 and a high-compression overhead valve V8. That combination was unheard of before that. Can you imagine how awesome it must have been? Compared to today's cars, it probably couldn't compete. But man!" He looked at me again. "Right?"

"Totally." The smell of the lasagna was getting stronger, and the wine was warming my belly. Only another hour or so to go. Too much more of this, though, and I might need a nap before dinner.

"What do you drive?" he asked. "I know I saw it, but I was concentrating on the pretty lady, not what the pretty lady drives."

I shuddered a little, trying to accept the compliment and not be repelled by it. Was there something wrong with me? Would that kind of statement be appealing from a different man? I wasn't sure. "I have a Subaru."

"Oh." Judging from his tone, this might be a deal breaker, and I immediately perked up.

"Oh yeah, I'm a Subaru girl now, although it's not a muscle car. But it gets good gas mileage, and they last forever. Oh, and my dog loves it! You'd be surprised how picky my dog can be about cars. I had to rent one when my last car was...well, totaled. Anyway, it was this little Kia, and she wouldn't even get it in." He stared at me as if I was describing my time on a spaceship. "What? Don't you like Subarus? Do they make a muscle car? I know they make some little low-slung thing. You know what I'm talking about? I've seen them race past me on the freeway. A lot of times, the owner gets those neon lights for underneath. You've seen them, right? The neon purple undercarriage lighting?"

I now stared at him as if expecting an answer.

"Muscle cars are made in America," he finally said, palpably disappointed in my car views.

"Well, surely there are some foreign muscle cars," I said. This was fun. "For instance, look at BMW. Or Ferrari. Or Porsche."

"By definition, muscle cars are made in America," he said, his jaw clenching and unclenching.

"Marty, you're not boring our guest with your car obsession, are you?" Jerry poked his head around the corner, unquestionably dismayed at our seating arrangement and, unlike his son, able to read a room.

"She has a Subaru," Martin said as if this explained everything.

"Well, those are nice, reliable cars," Jerry said, casting a nervous glance at his son. "At any rate, dinner's almost ready if you want to wash up. Bathroom's right around that corner, first door on the right," he said to me, pointing across the room.

"Great, thanks. I'll do that." I popped up and raced in the direction he'd indicated. The bathroom was indeed the first door, and I darted in, flicking on the light and locking the door behind me. I wasn't surprised by the creamy brown tile covering most of the walls, the brown enamel sink, or the brown hand tiles folded neatly and hung just so on the bar. Even the bar of soap sat in a rich brown ceramic soap holder.

What looked out of place was the raggedy nylon Dopp kit, opened wide and overflowing its contents onto the counter: a toothpaste tube squeezed from the middle and crusty with dried paste, a toothbrush with bristles so curled that it looked like it had been used to scrub the toilet, black hair combs, a brush missing half the plastic knobs off the bristles, bottles of lotions, shaving cream, and a wad of crumbled tissues. Peeking out from the edge, I spotted a row of metallic squares. Using a fingertip, I moved one aside to look. Yep, a half dozen hopeful condoms. I nearly convulsed. Was this Jerry's bathroom, or was this Martin's stuff? I thought Martin had his own place. I shuddered again, then pulled my phone from my pocket and checked my messages.

From Kip: *He says the Universe has something better for you.*

My fingers flew across the tiny keys on my screen. *I certainly hope so.*

I checked that the ringer was turned up so I wouldn't miss Evan's call. Scrutinizing my reflection in the mirror, I redid my ponytail and considered lip gloss. I'd pulled it from my purse when I remembered I wasn't trying to impress anyone, so I put it back, washed my hands, and returned to the living room. Martin stood in the middle of the room, holding both wine glasses and staring as if he'd been trying to watch me through the door.

CHAPTER THIRTY-THREE

I'll admit it was unnerving walking out to such intense scrutiny. Even Addie gives me more privacy when I'm in the bathroom. Martin winked and poked his tongue out of the corner of his mouth, making me wonder if he'd hoped I'd spotted the condoms. Or maybe he was having some kind of seizure. At this point, I couldn't be sure of anything. I suppressed a gag and forced a wooden smile.

"Ready for dinner?" I asked.

He looked down at his hands as if trying to remember which glass was mine. He finally held one out before proffering an arm and bowing. "M'lady." If I never heard that term again, it would be too soon.

I ignored his arm, as if I didn't see it, and nearly ran into the kitchen with my purse still on my shoulder, banging against my side. My phone poked me reassuringly in the hip. Jerry was pulling a giant glass pan from the oven, oven mitts stretching to his elbows. He hoisted the pan onto the stovetop with a grunt before peeling back a corner of foil to an eruption of steam.

"That smells spectacular," I said, moving closer. Martin,

disappointed he hadn't been able to walk me to the table, hovered at my shoulder.

Jerry pulled the foil off, and my mouth watered as the cheese rose up in gooey strands.

"Oh heck," said Jerry. "I was hoping to avoid that." He reached for a spatula, scraped the cheese off the foil, and patted it back into place. "You kids all washed up?" Jerry asked. "We're only moments away. Marty? Did you wash your hands?"

"Da-ad." Martin sounded like he was five.

"Well, did you?"

Martin set his wine glass down on the table with a thunk and stomped from the room.

"Kids," said Jerry.

"Can I help you with anything?" I asked. I was still holding my half-full wine glass and fretting about leaving it unattended with Martin. Jerry turned and pulled a bottle of salad dressing from the refrigerator.

"No, no. You're our guest. Please relax. I want to tell you how happy I am that Marty has found such a nice girl." He smiled at me and reached for a set of wooden salad tongs. I inched closer to the sink, leaning casually against it and hoping I'd have a chance to dump my wine before Martin got back.

I wasn't sure what to say to his last remark. How do you tell such a kindhearted father that his son is creepy?

"I know you're proud of him," I finally said. "It's great you're so supportive." He looked up at me as if aware of what I wasn't saying before turning back to the refrigerator. He bent forward to root for something, and I leaned over the sink, dumping my wine directly into the drain. I straightened up and was twirling my glass before he turned around, and just as Martin came back through the door.

"Well, looks like someone needs a refill," Martin said. He

reached for the giant bottle and topped off my glass. "Dad? Wine?"

"Yes, please. My glass is there." He jerked his chin toward a wine glass on the counter with a small puddle of red in the bottom. Martin topped his off too.

"I don't know if you noticed my stuff in the bathroom," Martin said, giving me a sultry look.

"Marty, did you not straighten up as I asked?" Jerry said.

I swirled my wine and took a sip, hoping if Martin had tried to slip me a roofie, it was down the drain or so diluted as to be ineffective. At this point, I was willing to take the risk.

"Da-ad."

"Well, we want it to look nice, don't we?" He pulled the top off a bag of cheese and sprinkled a liberal helping of cheddar onto the salad. "Marty is going to be staying here a few days. He started bringing things in, and already it's like he never left."

"There was a water leak in my apartment, and they need access to fix it," Martin said, addressing me. "I don't like being there with all the workers coming in and out. And I don't trust them with my stuff."

"Did you bring everything in yet?" Jerry asked. "It seems you brought so much for a few short days." He looked at me. "You should see his room. He's got so many belongings in there it looks like he's recently back from an overseas tour."

"It's my work clothes. You know I have to wear suits to the office. And I brought all my other stuff that I don't want stolen."

I looked at a tiny wall clock that hung over the back door. How was it still so early?

"My son, the lawyer," said Jerry, with the desperate tone of a salesman trying to close a sagging deal. "Hon, could you please grab those rolls." He nodded toward a linen-lined basket of crescent rolls resting by the stove. I squeezed past him and picked it up while Martin grabbed the salad bowl and an oversized pepper shaker. Jerry adjusted his oven mitts, hoisted the lasagna to chest level, and made his way proudly to the table with Martin and I following along like lesser floats in the Rose Bowl Parade. His arms shook visibly as he leaned to place it carefully in the center of the table on two uneven trivets. Next to the giant lasagna, the big wine bottle suddenly looked right-sized. This was enough food for a dozen people.

I stood uncertainly, unsure which seat to take, but the decision was made when Jerry and Martin grabbed the backs of two chairs, leaving the third for me. Fortunately, it was a round table, so I wasn't directly next to Martin. I'd had fears of him grabbing my thigh under the tablecloth, but I was far enough away that it seemed unlikely. They waited for me to sit, and I took the opportunity to scoot my chair closer to Jerry. I tried to pull my placemat over as unobtrusively as possible, but I saw Martin give me a confused look.

Jerry picked up his wine glass and raised it. "To our lovely guest! The Amos men are truly fortunate tonight."

"To my pretty date," said Martin.

"To the sensational chef," I said, refusing to meet Martin's yearning gaze.

We reached forward, clinked glasses, and chimed, "Cheers."

Jerry went to work dishing up giant slabs of lasagna. It took some cajoling before I could convince him I couldn't eat three pounds of food in one sitting, so he cut my portion in half, which was still well beyond my abilities. Chunks of beef, onion, and tomato rolled out from between the noodles like a small avalanche while melting cheese oozed behind like hot lava. We passed the salad bowl around, and any hopes of something lighter to fill out my plate were dashed by the gallon of ranch dressing, a bag of cheese, and mounds of croutons. The actual lettuce seemed more like a garnish. And somehow, when I wasn't looking, someone snuck two crescent rolls onto my plate, dripping in butter. If I got through even half of this, I would need to be rolled to my car.

Despite the behemoth breakfast I'd had with Evan earlier, the warm, garlicky aroma was enticing. I took my first bite but froze my expression as I remembered what Kip said about food appreciation and my sexy face. Jerry watched me like a contestant on a cooking show, hoping to make it to the next round.

"Oh my God, that's incredible," I said, meaning every word. "I'm not sure I've ever had homemade lasagna where someone made their own noodles. It's like a fresh flavor explosion in my mouth."

He laughed, sitting back in his chair with noticeable relief and delight. "It's a pleasure to cook for people who enjoy it," he said.

"I enjoy it," Martin mumbled, his cheeks fat with food. He swallowed. "And I don't remember the last time you made this."

Jerry waved a hand at him, dismissing him before picking up his fork and digging in. Everyone relaxed, enjoying the food, as the mood swung back to how it was the first time we'd met. If I could go out with Martin *and* his dad, it might not be bad. Martin alone was not as good.

Jerry began asking questions about my business, curious about how one starts something like that. He wanted to know where I got my recipes, how I knew what would sell, and how much time my baking took every week. He'd never had a dog and couldn't comprehend the billion-dollar industry that flourished around pets these days. Martin didn't seem nearly as interested, and after a handful of questions, I sensed him getting restless. Jerry also picked up on it and changed the subject abruptly to a new topic.

"Whatever happened about that artist lady who had the accident?" He looked from me to Martin. "Did you get her affairs settled? Did you figure out if one of the beneficiaries got ahead of themselves and helped her down the stairs?"

"Dad, you know I can't—"

"I know, I know. You can't talk about it." He turned to me. "You said she was a friend of yours? Are you doing okay?" He reached over and patted my arm.

"She wasn't exactly my friend—I'd only met her once, but I thought she was incredibly nice. I've been trying to help her sister with her dog. The poor thing is extremely traumatized."

"Oh, what a shame."

"It is. And the police are still investigating. They haven't been able to rule it accidental or not."

"Where'd you hear that?" asked Martin, scraping the side of his fork along his plate to get the last ground beef bits.

"Her sister told me. The police are keeping her up to date on the investigation. I forgot to mention that the other night."

"Does that change anything for you guys?" Jerry asked Martin. "If she was killed by one of the beneficiaries, I would imagine that changes the terms of the will. Otherwise, what's to stop all the beneficiaries out there from just going to town?" He looked sideways at Martin as if to ascertain his risk level.

"I dunno," Martin said, shoving another crescent roll into his mouth.

"Do you know anything about some jewelry that Christine was leaving to the dog rescue?" I asked. "Was that the addendum or codicil or whatever it's called that you were delivering to her? You'd said that you didn't think 'they' even knew they were named in the will. Was it this who you were talking about?"

"She left jewelry to a dog rescue?" Jerry asked, his eyes bright with interest.

"Yes, her sister told me she had an appraisal done on all the jewelry that her ex-husband had given her, and she was giving it to this dog rescue because he hated dogs." We both laughed.

"She sounds like she was a hoot. What a shame," said Jerry.

Martin set his fork across his empty plate and wiped his fingers on his napkin. "Dad, what's for dessert? Besides this pretty lady's good-looking cookies?" He reached over and ran a finger across my cheek.

Jerry beamed at us, openly enjoying the young love he thought was blossoming in his kitchen.

"I have a cherry pie and ice cream. Although, I have to confess the pie is store-bought."

"I'm sure it will be delicious," I said. "I love cherry pie."

"Another fact I now know!" Martin said, looking like he was about to touch my face again. I reached up and swatted preemptively at my cheek as if bothered by a gnat.

Jerry used two hands to lift the wine bottle, filling everyone's glasses with a generous pour like a bartender refilling pint glasses.

"Oh, that's too much," I said as the burgundy liquid sloshed nearly to the top of my glass.

"Drink what you want," said Jerry. "I'm sure Marty would happily give you his room if you overindulge. Wouldn't you, Marty?"

"Anything for you," said Martin, trying to move into my line of sight. I refused to meet his gaze, staring at my glass instead.

"Oh, I'm sure I'll be okay to drive," I said. "And there's always a ride-share. Or one of my friends lives not far from here. I'm sure I could get a ride. But I won't need one. All that food makes a pretty hefty cushion for the wine."

"We couldn't let that happen," said Martin. "What kind of hosts would we be if our guest had to call a friend?"

I looked at the clock over the door again and stifled an exasperated sigh. How could this evening be going so slowly? Jerry pushed back from the table and began clearing plates.

"Here, let me help you with that," I said, popping up.

"No, absolutely not. You and Marty go enjoy some alone time in the living room. I know how it is. I'm sure you didn't come here to spend an entire evening with an old guy."

"You're not old," I said. He reached over to wrest my plate out of my hands, but I held firm. "I insist. You went to all that work making such a delicious meal. It's the least I can do."

He smiled, but there was steel behind the smile. "Absolutely not."

Reluctant to get into a physical altercation over a dinner plate, I let go.

"I gotta..." Martin headed for the living room. "Dad? Could you keep Jessie company for a minute?" He raced away.

Jerry picked up Martin's plate and added it to his stack. "Oh, shoot," he said. "I was afraid the cheese in the lasagna might be a problem." I stood awkwardly in place. Jerry plunked the dishes into the sink with a clatter. "Marty has some..." His fingers wiggled as he searched for the right words. "He has some digestive sensitivities," he finally said. "I'm afraid we might have lost him for a bit."

I heard the bathroom door slam and was both relieved at the break and concerned that the bathroom might not be far enough away to buffer us from whatever was happening in there. Jerry looked at me, a look of consternation darkening his brows. He turned the faucet on, letting the water shoot out at maximum pressure.

"We weren't sure what you like to do, but we thought we could play some games this evening. Do you like games? Marty and I have always liked a good board game, but it's so much better with more than two people." He was talking loud and fast as if he shared similar concerns as mine about the acoustics in the house. "Did you see the games on the coffee table in the living room?"

I didn't recall seeing any board games, but I hadn't been

looking either. "I'm not sure." I poked my head through the door and quickly returned to the kitchen. "No, I don't see any."

"Oh, I'll bet Marty forgot to bring them in. He meant to bring several from his apartment so you could choose your favorite. I hope he left his Rock 'Em Sock 'Em Robots at home. That was always his favorite. I think the Blue Bomber got broken when he was in high school. We must have played that game thousands of times; it's a wonder it lasted as long as it did." He laughed. "Anyhow, hon, would you mind going out and bringing them in? His keys are there on the rack by the back door. The games are probably in his trunk." He was still talking too loud, plainly intent on getting me out of there before I overhead any noises that might kill whatever fleeting chance this relationship had left. I nearly told him there was no hope for this connection at all, so he could quit worrying. "Take your time. Marty might be a little while."

"Sure, no problem," I said, happy to be getting out of the house. I snagged the keys he indicated and left Jerry whistling as he ran a soapy sponge over the dishes.

I stepped outside, pulling the door closed behind me. Taking a deep breath, I felt my shoulders relax. A warm breeze had kicked up, and I closed my eyes, savoring the feel of it against my face, washing away the feel of Martin's touch. If I'd had any sense, I would have brought my purse out with me and made my escape while Martin was dealing with his digestive problems, but that would be rude, and I was only minutes away from Evan's escape call. I might as well get the games and be inside when my phone rang so that it would sound more believable.

Martin's car was an older sedan, and I flipped the keys around the chain, finding the right one. The markings were worn off, but I could discern the unlock button, which I hit, hearing the door lock click. It had been a while since I'd opened a genuine trunk rather than an SUV, and I opened the driver's door, looking next to the seat for the lever. I inadvertently popped the gas hatch first before realizing the trunk button was to the left of the steering wheel.

I slammed the door and closed the gas flap before approaching the trunk. Get the games, get Evan's call, and make my escape. The trunk lid was heavy, and I lifted it with two hands to ensure it wouldn't come crashing down on the back of my head while I was rooting around. Once I reassured myself it was solidly up, I looked inside. The trunk was huge. This thing could haul more than my little Subaru SUV, although getting things in and out wasn't as convenient.

Martin hadn't been blessed with his father's neat streak and piles of junk scattered around the space as if shifting and rolling with every turn. I stared at the collection, trying to find the board games, like a tricky game of I Spy. Gym bags, plastic bags, a case of Coke, a cardboard box stuffed full of papers, and a winter knit hat, and under the hat, I finally spotted several boxes that looked like games. There was also a nasty smell wafting from somewhere in there. I picked up the hat, pushed aside a partially unzipped gym bag, and reached for the first game box. Several flies buzzed out of the bag, and I stepped back, realizing the smell emanated from something inside.

I reached tentatively for the strap, both repulsed and curious. As I pulled the open zipper gingerly between two fingers, several more flies buzzed out, and I let out an involuntary scream, waved the hat at them, and dropped the bag onto the driveway. More flies flew off as it landed, and a bulging cloth bag the size of a large shoe plopped onto the concrete. I continued to wave the black knit hat around me, the nervous flapping more an energy release than an actual attempt to ward off the flies. The flies had no interest in me; they were more concerned with a second bag stuffed in the duffle, this one a stained paper bag that appeared to have gray chunks of meat matter breaking through the sides.

I was bending closer to figure out what I was looking at when the front door flew back on its hinges, and Martin sprinted out, his face flushed, his shirt untucked, and his breathing as ragged as if he'd just run a marathon. I glanced down again and caught the glitter of the setting sun reflecting off a delicate gold chain peeking out from the cloth bag.

CHAPTER THIRTY-FOUR

Martin skidded to a stop in front of me, his eyes unblinking and his mouth partially agape. "What are you doing?" he asked, his voice high and edgy.

I stood rooted to the spot, my brain making connections I should have seen earlier. He stared at me, his eyes scanning my face for any indication I'd figured him out, and I took a breath, trying to hide the revulsion that was undoubtedly reflected there.

"Your dad asked me to come get the games from your car," I said, my voice calmer than I could have hoped. "But this bag," I gestured to the driveway. "Oh my God, Martin. It's gross! Like, did you leave a hamburger in your gym bag or something?" I smiled, playing for time. My keys were in my purse inside. "I see how it is. You work out, reward yourself with fast food, and then forget about it. But geez. I think you'll have to throw the whole thing away." I could run away down the street and try to find help from a neighbor, but this story sounded nutty even to me. They would take one look at me babbling away and another look at someone they'd probably known for years, and I knew who they would believe.

He stared at me as if trying to read my mind before coming closer and snatching the hat from my hand. As he did, it unfurled, and I realized it wasn't just a knit hat—it was a ski mask. Suddenly, Bertram's words from last night made sense—a face hat. I'd found the face hat. A scene formed in my mind: Martin at the top of the stairs at Christine's house, a black ski mask hiding his identity. Christine leaving the gala early because she wanted to get away from her ex and spend a nicer evening at home with Lucille.

He seemed to relax, wanting to believe I was clueless. "You caught me," he said. He rolled the ski mask back up and tossed it into the trunk, where it landed behind the Coke case. "I've been working out. I want to look good for you, but those golden arches. You know, they pump the smell of fries out to entice you in. I fell for it, but I stopped myself before I finished the whole burger." He reached over and booped me on the nose with his index finger. "You're too smart for your own good." He leaned down, deftly pushing the cloth bag back into the duffle while using a finger to pull the sodden paper bag all the way out, leaving it on the pavement. "It is gross," he said. "I'm sorry you had to see that. I'm usually not that careless."

I pretended not to notice it wasn't a McDonald's bag. I pretended not to notice I didn't see any part of an old moldy burger. Instead, I saw bits of what looked like rancid steak cubes, and another piece clicked into place. He'd taken steak bits for Lucille. He would have met Lucille when he was there dropping off and picking up paperwork, but you could never tell how a dog would react to a relative stranger when the owner was out. So, he'd brought her meat chunks to ensure himself a smooth entry. I bit my lip, trying to remain impassive.

He zipped the duffle bag up and tossed it back into the trunk. "I usually don't have this much junk in there." He glanced at me again. "But with the workers coming in and out of my apartment, you can't be too careful."

Yeah, you wouldn't want your stolen jewels to be stolen, I thought. He leaned into the trunk, pulling out several cardboard game boxes.

"I wasn't sure what games you like, so I brought several." He balanced the boxes on the edge of the car while sorting them into a neater pile. "We have Monopoly, Clue, Trivial Pursuit, Pictionary, and Scrabble.

Let's play Clue, I thought. *It was done by Martin at the top of the stairs with a shove.*

"They're all good," I said, trying to work out what to do. I was pretty sure I was looking at Christine's killer. I was pretty sure the jewelry meant for the dog rescue was sitting in Martin's trunk. But I was also pretty sure I couldn't prove anything without having the jewels in hand to compare to the appraisal list, and I doubted Martin would just hand them over and confess.

"Well, you better make up your mind because you know my dad will insist that our honored guest decide." He repositioned the games in his arms, kicked the meat bag toward the street, then jerked his head to the open trunk. "Could you please close that?"

I glanced inside at the duffle resting on top of a junk pile. Even if I grabbed it and ran, I wouldn't get far without my car keys and purse. I reached up, slammed the trunk closed, and followed Martin inside.

The smell of lasagna lingered, warm and comforting like a big hug, and I felt better when Jerry emerged from the kitchen, wiping his hands with a dishrag.

"Oh good, you remembered them," he said to Martin with a smile. "I was afraid you might have forgotten, with everything going on at your apartment. I've cleared the table if you want to start setting up."

We followed him back into the kitchen, and Martin deposited the game pile on the table, his keys dropping from his hand beside them.

"What should we play?" I asked, glancing at the clock. Evan was late with his call.

"We'll let you decide," said Jerry. "You're our honored guest."

Martin slid me a look and smiled, gratified that he'd called it. I looked at the pile of games again. Which one was the shortest?

"Maybe we could play Scrabble?" I said. "I don't remember how the scoring works."

Martin's face twisted, and he trotted from the room again. "Be right back."

"Maybe I should go," I said to Jerry. "If he's not feeling well, I think it would be better."

"Oh, no! Don't be silly. He'd be heartbroken if you left now. I'm sure he's fine. I should have gone half-cheese on the lasagna." He knocked a fist against his own head. "Not smart, Jerry." He looked at me ruefully. "I wanted you to enjoy it. I hope I haven't ruined the evening. Please stay. Marty would be so upset. In fact, I'm sure he's already upset with you having to see this."

I sighed and glanced at the clock again. Where the heck was Evan?

"Okay, maybe a quick game then," I said.

"You can set the other ones on that sideboard there," he said, waving to the cabinet behind me. "Would you like some coffee with dessert?"

"No, thanks. I'm still very full." I shoved the Scrabble box to the center of the table and picked up the others, piling them onto the ledge behind me. Before I could stop myself, I palmed Martin's keys and slipped them quietly into my pocket. I'm not sure what I was thinking, but I knew I had to get that bag if we hoped to prove what had happened to Christine. My heart thumped wildly in my chest, and I looked as guilty as if I'd stolen a baby from a stroller. I looked up to ensure Jerry hadn't noticed, but he was rooting around a cupboard, pulling Tupperware containers from an upper shelf.

"I hope you'll take some of the leftovers home," he said. "I'm not sure Martin will be able to eat them all with me." I heard some sounds emanating from the far bathroom, and Jerry must have as well because he raised his voice again. "So there'll be plenty," he shouted.

"I'd love some," I shouted back.

"Great! I'll let it cool down a bit more." He turned and began drying dishes, banging them loudly as he put them away. "So, you like Scrabble?"

"It's been ages since I played," I said. I opened the box and dumped out the tiles, poking them around with a finger. I heard a toilet flush, and Jerry sighed with relief.

"Maybe we can play our first game before we move on to dessert."

Martin eased back into the room, and my guilty heart picked up its pace. "Come sit down," I said. "Help me set up."

I pulled out my chair and sat down, smiling for him to join me. I heard the slight clink of key on key from my pocket. His forehead creased as though listening intently, and I felt the metal poking my upper thigh. Surely he couldn't know I'd taken them, right? He'd just sat down when I heard a rumble emanating ominously from somewhere in his lower regions.

"Oh heck, I'm so sorry," he said. "I'll be right back."

Jerry came over and sat down beside me, looking close to tears. Just then, my phone rang, the volume so high I nearly shrieked out loud, and I sprang to my feet.

"I'm sorry," I said to Jerry. "I need to get this." I raced off through the living room and out the front door. I pulled the door halfway closed behind me and answered. "Evan?"

"Yeah, sorry I'm late. I lost track of time."

"You're not going to believe this," I whispered. "I think Martin killed Christine, and the jewelry is in his car trunk."

"What! Are you still there? Jess, you gotta get out of there."

"I know," I said. "Let me tell them I've got an emergency. Look, can you meet me somewhere? We need to figure out what to do."

He said he was on his way, and we agreed to meet at a Denny's Restaurant near the freeway. "If you're not there, I'm coming in to get you," he said.

I returned to the kitchen, where Jerry sat alone at the table, pushing tiles forlornly around on the plastic tablecloth. The Scrabble board sat still folded, and he looked up at me, his expression resigned.

"I'm sorry," I said. "I need to go." He stood, his shoulders sagging as he walked around the counter to pack my leftovers. "I can't tell you how much I appreciate this dinner. That was the best lasagna I've ever had." He pulled out a family-sized container and carefully scooped large chunks into it.

"Well, I'm glad you enjoyed it. I'm sorry I didn't consider what it might do to the evening." He sighed. "He's usually not this sensitive. Maybe he was nervous too. What all with wanting to impress you. I hope you don't hold it against us."

"Of course not!" I said. "Anybody that makes homemade pasta for me is pretty great in my book." Unlike his son, who was most likely a cold-blooded monster willing to kill a lovely person to get his greedy hands on her assets. I looked at Jerry in his fussy little apron, spooning homemade love into a Tupperware container, and I wondered what had gone wrong with Martin.

I noticed my hand circling in a nervous hurry-up movement,

and I shoved it in my pocket to still it. Of course, I came in contact with the stolen keys, which increased my edginess tenfold, and I pulled it out again, nervously tapping my phone instead.

"I hope everything's okay," Jerry said, finally snapping on the lid.

"Uh, yeah. It's a family thing. We've got, um, there's a...it's complicated." I've always been averse to telling lies about emergencies, fearful that I might jinx someone. Now, Bertram had me convinced the Universe was taking notes and might bestow the things I say, furthering this phobia. "But I do need to get going. I know it's rude, and I apologize for that."

"I don't suppose you could stay for a couple more minutes? I know Marty will be so upset if he doesn't get to say goodbye."

I snatched the Tupperware container from his hands, grabbed my purse and keys, and motored through the living room.

"I'm sorry, I can't." I turned to give Jerry an oh-so-brief but genuinely warm hug. "I really appreciate all the trouble you went to. Martin's lucky to have such a great dad," I said before rushing out the door. I didn't wait to see if he would follow me out; I took off at a quick trot, making a beeline to my car. I wanted to be long gone before Martin emerged because I knew he would come racing out as soon as his pants were up. I unlocked my car and slid in, dropping the lasagna on the passenger seat. I didn't even put on my seatbelt; I just pulled away from the curb with a chirp. The seat belt alert began bleating at the same time I saw Martin run out the front door, but I was already accelerating down the street. I didn't turn my head or even look for him in the rearview mirror; I kept my foot on the gas, hoping no small child would pop out from behind a parked car and impede my progress.

As I wound my way through the neighborhood, trying to get

back to Kirby Drive, I worried Martin would try to follow me. His keys were still poking me in the groove between my upper thigh and lower abdominals. I would probably end up with one of those bruises you can't remember how you got.

I clutched the wheel and began second-guessing all of this. What was I doing? Could I be arrested for stealing his keys? What if what I'd seen hadn't been a bag of jewelry at all? I *thought* I saw a gold chain, but it could have been anything. And why hadn't I stayed long enough to say goodbye? Then I wouldn't be worried about him trying to chase me down—he likely wouldn't have even noticed his missing keys till tomorrow, and I would have had a chance to toss them in the yard if I changed my mind. But, no. Here I was, committing some kind of crime because, face it, I couldn't stand the thought of him trying to kiss me goodnight with those fleshy lips one more time. I closed my eyes and groaned before realizing I was still driving. I needed to get a grip. I needed to meet up with Evan and talk this out.

CHAPTER THIRTY-FIVE

I arrived at the Denny's before Evan. The lot was moderately crowded, and I drove around twice, ensuring I hadn't missed his Jeep. Convinced he wasn't here yet, I backed into a space near the street where I could watch the main entrance. Picking up my phone, I jumped when it buzzed in my hand with an incoming text.

Why'd you leave? I didn't even get a chance to say goodbye.

My fingers hovered over the keys as I debated how to answer. Then I realized, had I been going home or to a family emergency instead of the Denny's a half a mile from the Amos house, I wouldn't have seen his text yet.

It buzzed again. *Can I see you tomorrow? I don't feel like our date is done. I need to kiss my pretty lady.*

I threw the phone back down on the passenger seat. The good news was he didn't appear to be intent on chasing me down tonight.

I saw Evan's Jeep turn in and I stepped from my car, inordinately happy to see him. I lifted an arm and waved like the old news clips showing crowds welcoming home sailors from war.

He spotted me, pulled into the empty spot next to me, and lowered his window.

"Are you okay?" he asked. He looked like he'd run out of the house without even checking himself in the mirror. His hair gave the impression that he'd spent the afternoon napping or driving around with his head out the window. He'd changed since he left my place, not that he'd been dressed up then, but now he was in a t-shirt with two visible holes near the shoulder, one mustard stain on the chest, and a ragged edge near the neckline that looked like it had been caught in a shredder. I've never been so happy to see such a mess.

I took a deep breath. "I'm okay," I said. "I did something."

Evan's eyes riveted on my face, and his mouth dropped open in anticipation. "What? What'd you do?"

"I stole Martin's car keys."

I watched an array of emotions flash in sequence like a facial expressions quiz: surprise, consternation, interest, admiration, and finally, excitement. "Awesome! Are we going to get the jewelry?"

"I'm having second thoughts about that. Maybe that's not what I saw," I said. I glanced around the lot, feeling exposed. "It could have been something else."

He turned off his engine and opened the door, swinging out and leaning against his seat. "So what do you want to do?"

I pulled Martin's keys from my pocket and twirled them around my finger. "Well. I guess since I have these, we might as well check. If that's not what I saw, no harm, no foul. Right? And if it is, then we've figured out who killed Christine, and the police can handle it from there."

Evan looked up at the sky. It was nearly sunset, but we were in the pale gray hour—dim enough that you had to squint to make out shapes in the shadows but light enough that two people standing in a driveway digging through someone's trunk would be easy to make out.

"We should probably wait till it's darker," he said. "Although, we don't want him to take the jewelry and hide it somewhere else."

"I have his keys."

"Yeah, but what if his dad has a set? He could go get the bag out of the car, stash it away, and we'll never find it. I say we go do some reconnaissance." His energy level ratcheted up, and he started tapping his fingertips together. "We could do a perimeter sweep and then set up zones for us each to patrol. You already know points of egress, right?" He bounced ever so slightly up and down, reverberating with energy.

"Evan, how come you were late calling? What were you doing?"

He stopped bouncing. "I got a new video game." All his talk of reconnaissance and perimeter sweeps suddenly made sense. "Anyway, he *could* move the jewelry. I think we should do this."

In lieu of a better plan, we agreed to go park on his street and watch his car until it was dark enough to check the trunk. Martin knew what my car looked like, so we decided to leave it at the Denny's and take Evan's.

"Do you think we have time to run in and get something to eat?" Evan asked. "I didn't have dinner." I told him I had leftover lasagna in my car. I retrieved the Tupperware and gave Evan directions to Martin's dad's house.

Within minutes, we were rolling slowly past the house. Martin's car was still in the driveway—no sign of a locksmith nor of Martin and his dad trying to raise the door lock with a bent hanger. The lights were on in the living room, and the drapes were open. I pressed myself against the seat, afraid Martin's sixth sense would feel me coming, but nothing happened. I also didn't get a good look inside.

Evan drove around the block, and we went by again. This time, I focused on the living room windows, and I could make out Jerry in his recliner while Martin paced back and forth, presumably blocking Jerry's line of sight to the TV because he was waving his hand as if trying to shoo Martin out of the way. Martin appeared to be clutching something, and I realized he was probably waiting for me to return his message.

"Should I respond to him?" I asked Evan after reading him Martin's last text messages.

"Yeah. Maybe he'll calm down then. The last thing we want is for him to be up all night, waiting and mad."

Evan wanted me to text him something sweet so that he'd go to bed happy and drift off to a deep, restful sleep. While I understood this logically, the idea of sending him something sappier than 'don't ever contact me again' made my skin crawl.

"Look, just because you say something nice doesn't mean you mean it, and it doesn't mean you ever have to see him again. We want him to settle down. You saw him—he's gonna walk around looking out that window all night if you don't respond. Heck, he might even borrow his dad's car and drive over to your house."

He was right. After multiple messages I started and deleted, I finally wrote: *Sorry I had to run out so fast. We had a family thing I needed to take care of. Dinner was amazing. Thanks so much.*

I'd barely hit the send button when my phone dinged.

When can I see you again? Can I come over tomorrow?

"Evan! He wants to see me tomorrow. What am I supposed to say?"

Evan had parked two houses up, giving us a clear view of Jerry's front door and driveway. He turned off the engine and shifted his seat back a notch, getting comfortable. Light glowed from the windows, but I couldn't see anything inside.

"Okay, again—you're trying to make him happy. You're not actually planning your future."

"So what do I tell him?" I hated the fact that he knew where I lived. If I ever went on another date again, I would only meet in public places until we were engaged.

"Tell him you'll let him know tomorrow. Hopefully, he'll be on Cellblock C by then, and you won't have to worry about it." I immediately felt better. Evan certainly had a way of putting things in perspective for me.

Why don't we connect tomorrow? I'm not sure my plans yet.

My phone dinged, and my skin crawled before I even read the message. *Sleep well, m'lady! I shall sleep holding thoughts of you against me all night.*

"Gross," I muttered. "I'm going to have to change my number."

"What's it say? What's it say?" Evan asked. When I didn't answer, he grabbed my phone and read the message. "Oh, my God! Who is this guy? Who says stuff like that?" He laughed so loud that I was afraid people would hear him, so I swatted his arm and told him to shush. "M'lady! He's going to hold you against him all night! You know what he means by that, don't you?"

"Evan, Stop! I'm disgusted enough as it is. And really, you need to keep it down. We're trying not to be noticed out here."

He handed my phone back and rotated, looking out each window in turn before settling back in his seat.

"So, seriously. Do you think he killed Christine?" His voice had lost all mirth, and his eyes were solemn when they met mine.

"I don't know," I said. "I can't imagine. He seems like such a weenie. Like, when we went to dinner, we ran into a bunch of his coworkers who were bullying him, and yes, they were awful... but he was such a victim. I hate to say it, but I could see why they were picking on him. It's hard to reconcile that with him deciding to rob and kill someone."

"I don't know. I've seen this on those criminal shows. Someone who's bullied and too chickenshit to stand up for himself goes off the rails and finds his own victim." He sounded like an authority.

A door banged across the street, and we hunched down into the shadows as an older man led an overweight beagle out the door. They lumbered down the sidewalk, the dog sniffing every bush he passed, occasionally lifting his leg at indeterminate intervals. They walked down two houses before turning around and slowly making their way home. The man never even glanced our way.

"Well, he did make a big deal about people leaving their assets to animals," I said, picking up our conversation where we'd left off. "And Christine left her jewelry to the dog rescue, where she got Lucille. Maybe he's got a thing against animals." Evan fidgeted, seemingly distracted. I thought he was contemplating how anyone could have something against animals, but no.

"Hey, you have that pasta?" He leaned closer in the dark car, sniffing and squinting toward my lap. "I'm starving."

"Oh, sure." I passed the still-warm container over, and he peeled the lid off, instantly making the car smell like an Italian restaurant.

"Do you have a fork?"

"Why would I have a fork?"

He huffed, then reached around and began feeling around the backseat. "Could you check the glove box? Maybe there's something in there."

I popped the latch, and it sprang open, a sheaf of wadded-up papers bulging out. "I don't think so," I said, shoving the door back in place. "It's getting warm in here. Could you put the windows down?"

He turned back in his seat, clutching a half-crushed Starbucks cup. Popping the plastic lid off, he curved it into a crude scoop, dipped it into the lasagna, and dug up a hunk. He took two bites before turning the key and opening the windows. "Whoa! That's good!" he said.

"Shh, don't be so loud."

Another bite. "Man, that's good!"

"Would you be quiet," I insisted. "Someone's going to call the cops on us."

"Then they could arrest this guy and get Christine's jewelry back," he mumbled around his mouthful.

"They couldn't get the jewels without a search warrant, and I'm almost positive they couldn't get one based on the fact I may or may not have seen a gold chain."

Evan chewed on. "So, say it was him," he said between bites. "How'd he get in? And why didn't the dog do anything? I'd like to think Henry would protect me if I were attacked."

I wasn't so sure Henry would protect anyone. Heck, I wasn't sure Addie would do anything more than stare intently at an intruder, and I hoped never to find out. "There's a couple of things I didn't tell you. Martin worked one summer with a locksmith. He was able to break in through my garage door before I could find my spare key."

"He broke into your house?" How had I never realized how loud Evan was before?

"Shhh!" I flapped my hand downward as if beating on my buzzer in a game show. "I'd dropped my keys and couldn't find them when we got home from dinner. So we went in through the garage using the code. I was looking for my spare key, but he got the door open before I found it."

"How'd he do that?"

"I don't know. He said he spent one summer working with a locksmith." He took another hefty bite. "Oh, and as for Lucille, that's the other thing." I shuddered, recalling the stench and the flies. "I think he took some steak or some kind of meat chunks when he went over that night. That's what made me look—these flies started buzzing out of this duffle bag, and there was this nasty smell. He forgot to throw out the leftover meat, and it's been decomposing in there."

He swallowed his mouthful. "Were there maggots?" My stomach constricted, and I gagged. "You're not gonna throw up in here, are you?" His voice rose again, and I fought to push the thought of maggots out of my mind. What if there had been maggots? How could there not be? With that many flies, they were probably crawling all over the inside of the paper bag *and* the duffle bag. Had I touched anything? Could there be one on me now? I began twitching, swatting at my arms and chest, terrified I would feel something gushy and squirmy crawling somewhere on me.

Mewling sounds broke from my throat, and this time it was Evan shushing me. "Shhh!" he said, shaking my shoulder. "Stop. Stop! I'm sure you're fine. You didn't feel any crawl onto you, did you?"

I did the best I could to subdue my vibrating vocal cords. Still shuddering, I took a deep breath and tried to soothe myself. "They don't jump, do they?"

"Nah, I don't think so. I think they're fly eggs that hatch. Although they crawl, I know that."

"Let's change the subject," I said.

Evan started droning on about some asset valuations he was doing at work, the details mundane and monotonous enough to distract me from my maggot-induced panic. He plowed through half the lasagna, talking around mouthfuls as he went. Finally, he sat back, patting his stomach and lowering his improvised utensil. "I'm full," he said. He snapped the lid back on and handed the container back to me. "Thanks." I set it on the floor near my feet and looked again at the brightly lit living room windows two doors up.

"What if they never go to bed?" I was tired, and the thought of sitting here much longer was not appealing at all.

"It's still early," he said, settling into a more comfortable position. "This is how the private eyes do it. It's all in the mind." He glanced over at me. "I can take the first shift if you want to take a nap."

"Geez, Evan, I hope we won't be here long enough to need a nap."

I looked towards Martin's house again. Someone was coming out the front door. I reached over and grabbed Evan's arm. We crunched down in our seats and watched Martin walk outside, move to the car, and try each door handle. He leaned down and held a hand to the driver's side window, trying to see into the darkened vehicle. Then he walked around to the back side and squatted down, looking underneath and feeling along the driveway with his hand. Finally, he flicked on a flashlight and scanned more closely underneath. He only came away with the maggot-infested bag, which he grabbed by an edge and flung into the neighbor's yard as far as he could.

My heart was pounding, nearly drowning out the sound of Evan's quickening breaths. Finally, Martin walked back to the door and stopped, holding his phone up and looking at the screen. It flashed through my mind a split second too late—he was calling me.

CHAPTER THIRTY-SIX

My phone, the ringer still set high, blared into the quiet night, the shriek reverberating through the car. I'd brought it up as the thought hit me, but I was too slow to silence it before the call connected. My bladder and heart squeezed in unison, and I swiped at the screen to decline the call while simultaneously pushing hard on the side volume button. I curled below the dashboard and silenced the phone within half a ring.

Evan had stopped breathing, his hand holding his chest as if he were having a heart attack. He'd slumped in his seat, but his eyes watched through the space between the steering wheel and the dash, unblinking and riveted.

"Is he coming?" I asked in the merest whisper of words.

He shook his head slightly. "He's looking, though."

I curled tighter, every organ attached to my nervous system screaming a warning to flee. Those movies where someone is hiding from the killer have always set me on edge, and here we were. If I didn't have Evan with me, I would probably pop out of the car and run screaming down the street. But Evan, while obviously rattled, remained stoically keeping watch, so I tried to calm my nerves.

"What's he doing now?" I whispered.

"He's staring at his phone." Actually, he was redialing because the screen on my phone lit up. I held it against my chest as tightly as possible to conceal any glow in the darkened car. I could feel a cramp tweaking my left calf muscle, and I closed my eyes and told myself to relax and loosen up. After what felt like an eternity, Evan let out a long breath. "Okay, he went inside."

I slid back up onto my seat and drew in a deep lungful of air. "Do you think he heard that? Do you think he knows we're here?"

"Well, he heard something. It's a good thing you got it silenced so fast." He pulled at the neck of his shirt, fanning his chest. I felt sweat trickling down my chest and back, and I hoped that wetness in my nether regions was also sweat.

"Do you think we should go?" I asked. The heavy meal, the wine, the heat, and now the post-tension crash was overriding my interest in seeing this through. "Maybe we should turn this all over to the police. Let them deal with it."

"We already talked about that," he said. "If you want this guy to get away with it—okay."

My phone showed that I had a voicemail, and I entered my code to retrieve it, sinking back onto the floor in case the light or sound attracted any attention.

"Hey, Jessie. Where are you? Did you take my car keys with you? I can't find them and needed to get something from my car." There was a pause, and I could feel him staring at our car during the lull. "Anyway, call me back."

"He wants to know if I took his keys," I whispered. "He wants me to call him back. What should I do?"

Evan swiveled in his seat and looked behind us. "Maybe it's a trap," he whispered. Tension flooded back through my body, and I scanned out my window looking for Martin, almost sure I'd see him bellycrawling his way to the car, his black ski mask on, and Jerry's chopping knife clenched between his teeth.

"Is your door locked?" I asked softly.

"I'm not sure that'll help with the windows wide open," he said. I felt for the lock on my door, checking that it was locked, but Evan was right—Martin could attack me right through the window without even needing to open it. I heard a click as Evan turned the key, and our windows rose simultaneously. "Better safe than sorry."

I felt immediately better once the windows were up, never mind that it suddenly felt like a sauna for two.

"Do you think I should call him back about the keys? What if he waits up to hear back from me?"

"Text him. Say you don't know what he's talking about."

I pecked out a short message. *I don't have your keys. Sorry.*

My phone lit up again, indicating an incoming call. "He's calling again!" I hissed.

"Don't answer it!"

We'd both slid down, but again, Evan stayed upright just enough to look out the windows. He swiveled and turned like a periscope on a submarine, keeping watch for enemy attacks. When the voicemail icon popped up, I retrieved my message.

"Where are you? Why aren't you taking my calls? Call me back."

This didn't sound like passive Martin. This was a petulant, controlling, red flag-waving, out-of-control man that all the articles warn you about. My fear was dissolving, and my anger was rising.

I can't call you right now. I'm busy.

This time, he texted back. *Busy doing what? You were supposed to be on a date with me!*

"Geez, who does this guy think he is?" I said.

"Where'd you find him again?" Evan asked. "What a loser." I refrained from mentioning Gabriella. Seemed like we both dodged bullets with these two.

"I'm not responding," I said. I sat silently, clutching my phone and seething as Martin continued to harangue me via text.

You need to answer me.

Where are you? Are you at home?

We made you a nice dinner, and this is how you repay me? 'We?' Jerry made me a nice dinner, and I thanked him and didn't owe anyone anything.

"Why don't you block him?" Evan asked.

"We need to know when he stops."

The front door opened, and Martin stormed out, moving to his car and jerking on the door handle. When it remained locked, he slammed a hand on the frame. Jerry appeared in the doorway, stepping into the driveway and placing a hand on his son's shoulder. Martin shrugged it off and turned, stomping rigidly into the house. Jerry's shoulders sagged as he followed Martin in, closing the door and turning off the porch light.

We'll discuss this tomorrow.

Not if I had anything to do with it. We sat in silence, the heat building. Now that they appeared to be in for the night, Evan cracked the windows a couple of inches. Twenty minutes went by before Martin texted again.

Look, I'm sorry if I sounded mad. I'm just disappointed that you left so fast. If I could find my keys, I would come over and cuddle. I want to make you happy. Don't be mad, okay?

If this guy wasn't arrested for murder, I would have to get a restraining order. Or a firearm. Or I'd have to get Addie a well-trained Belgian Malinois brother. Maybe all of that. Honestly, if dating was going to be like this, I'd have to rethink whether I even wanted a relationship.

As the evening dragged on, the street got quieter. Lights flicked off in the houses around us, and eventually, the living room light at the Amos house also shut off. Evan had nodded off and was snoring gently beside me, his mouth slightly open, his hand resting on his over-stuffed belly. I must have dozed off as well because I awoke with a start, feeling disoriented and frightened. My head bumped against the side window, and the evening flooded back into my memory.

Evan had slumped sideways, his head drooping so far to the right that it appeared his neck had lost one of its tethers.

"Evan," I whispered softly and shook his arm.

"What!" He woke with a jerk, his head flying up so fast I heard something pop. He looked around groggily, struggling to make sense of his surroundings. "Oh, Jess."

"Hey, it's almost midnight. We fell asleep."

Evan ran his hands up and down his face, smacking his cheeks a few times as if to jolt himself back to life. "Geez. I was out cold."

"I think we should get this over with." It was still overly warm in the car, but I felt a chill, my blood seeming to have gone sluggish during the interval.

Evan shook his head from side to side and rolled his shoulders. "Okay. How do you want to do this? Open the trunk, grab the bag, and take off? Or do you want to check it while we're here, and if it's nothing, leave everything as is?"

If I was wrong, I would rather not have anyone know what we'd been up to, but if I was right, I didn't want to advertise our presence while we leisurely perused the contents of Martin's trunk.

"Let's grab the bag, take it, and check it. If it's nothing, maybe we can bring it back."

"Or we just dump it. If there's nothing of value, why risk it?"

"What about his keys?" I asked. "Those are a little different. I don't want to get in trouble for stealing those."

Evan chewed his lip. "Okay. We open the trunk, grab the bag, and throw the keys in. Is it possible he could have dropped them in earlier?"

"Not really. He locked the car with them."

"He won't remember if he locked it or not. He was too busy thinking impure thoughts about you." He guffawed at himself.

"Gross. But okay."

We opened our doors, and the overhead light blinked on. Evan reached over and turned it off. "Don't shut your door all the way," he whispered. As if I hadn't already thought of that.

We crept side by side down the street, looking precisely like cartoon burglars—shoulders hunched, arms in defensive punching positions. The only thing missing was a pillowcase slung over one shoulder.

Even though Jerry had turned off the porch light, I felt exposed as we hunched behind Martin's car. I wondered belatedly about security cameras. I hadn't noticed any earlier, but that's not to say the neighbors weren't decked out with the latest and greatest systems. We'd probably be posted online to neighborhood security watch sites in black and white for all to see. I could only hope it would be grainy enough that we couldn't be identified.

I had the keys clenched in my hand, my nerves so tightly wound that my hand began to shake. Evan reached over and grabbed the keys, wrapping his fingers around them so they wouldn't jangle. He inserted the key into the lock and turned, keeping one hand on the top of the trunk to keep it from flying open. He opened it about half a foot, and we peered into the darkened interior. If there had ever been a trunk light, it was long burned out.

Evan reached in and began flapping a hand up and down,

feeling around. His fingers closed around something, and he pulled out a plastic bag, its side crinkling with more noise than I thought possible. I clenched my teeth and shook my head. We both froze, listening for signs that we'd alerted anyone. After a few seconds, he put the bag back in the trunk, setting it as quietly as possible near the corner, and reached in again.

I thought I heard a scuffling sound, and I grabbed his arm. Not even breathing, we squatted, immobilized, and listened for a repeat. In the distance, I could hear traffic on the South Loop and the breeze rustling softly in the trees, but I didn't hear anything else. I loosened my grip on Evan's arm but leaned in closer.

"It's a duffle bag. I think it was near the middle," I whispered directly into his ear. My breath must have tickled because he swatted his free hand at his ear, nearly whacking me in the face. Still holding the trunk lid, he reached back in and pulled up a nylon bag. The zipper was gaping open at one end as he pulled it up, but it was too dark to see anything. I could still smell the lingering scent of fetid meat in the humid air. I nodded vigorously when I saw it, then inched backward, mindful of lingering maggots.

I thought I heard another sound, a shoe scuffling on the pavement, and I pushed myself to my feet, turning to look behind just as someone launched forward, wrapping his arms around my middle and pinning my arms to my sides.

CHAPTER THIRTY-SEVEN

I yelped more than screamed as I thrashed against the iron hold. My feet were off the ground, and I was being pulled backward. I could smell the rank odor of oniony flop-sweat and struggled harder.

"Evan!" I yelled. My legs kicked out ineffectively, and I willed myself still, trying to formulate a more effective move. "Martin! Martin! Let me go!" I assumed it was Martin since I couldn't see who had me. "Let me go!" I pulled my shoulders together, forcing him to readjust his grip, and I twisted like a cork trying to free itself of a bottle. My feet were touching the ground now, but I couldn't balance. From the corner of my eye, I saw a blur, and suddenly, we all hit the pavement.

The hold around me loosened, and I skittered away as Evan wrapped one arm around Martin's neck, pinning his head tight against his chest. His other hand coiled in Martin's hair, pulling hard. It was a move more reminiscent of a five-year-old mutton buster at the rodeo than a wrestling champion, but it was effective.

"Stop it! You're hurting me!" Martin squealed. He scrabbled on the driveway, trying to get to his knees, but Evan was locked on for the ride. In the dark, it was a blur of movement—Martin trying to grab onto Evan's arms, Evan pivoting just enough to stay out of reach. "Let go a' me!" Martin sounded as if he was strangling now, but then he uttered a low growl, taking a deep breath and looking like he might erupt into something huge.

"Jess, a little help." Evan was panting, looking as if he was about to lose his hold or get his nose broken, as Martin began throwing his head back and forth. I moved around to Evan's side, reaching for Martin's arm. Grabbing onto his right wrist, I braced myself using both hands, trying to jerk his arm behind his back. He fought with more vigor than I expected, but he wasn't the buffest of guys, and once I grabbed onto his middle finger and pulled it backward, he stopped fighting. He screamed a little as I managed to reposition his arm, and I finally noticed what an odd angle I was holding it at.

"Stop moving, and maybe I'll stop hurting you!" I yelled in his ear. He lunged once defiantly, but his own movement nearly dislocated his shoulder, and he finally sagged against the driveway. I gave his arm one more tug, eliciting a yelp. Evan pulled his arm out from around Martin's neck, but he used his hand to hold his head down against the pavement. Porch lights flickered on in nearby houses, and Jerry shuffled out of the house at a quick trot, holding a baseball bat.

"Marty! Marty!" he called. "Are you okay?" He looked dazed, the bat wobbling in his hands as he rushed to his son. His baggy plaid pajama bottoms flapped in the breeze, and he stepped gingerly as if unused to rough outdoor surfaces. He hesitated, trying to make sense of the strange scene before him. Recognition lit his face when he saw me, almost immediately replaced by confusion. "Jessie? What are you doing?" He took in Evan, still holding Martin's head down. "Is this some kind of game? Please, let him up. I think you're hurting him."

"You want to tell your dad what you did?" I asked.

"I don't know what you're talking about," Martin said.

I let go of his arm and nodded to Evan to let him up. Evan let go but stood crouched like a cage fighter preparing for his next attack. Martin looked warily at him before pushing himself up. His face was scraped from the pavement, and he rubbed at the finger I'd pulled, flexing it as if to ensure it wasn't dislocated. Low-level dread hummed in my gut. What if we'd been entirely wrong? What if he pressed charges, and Evan and I were tossed in jail for assault and attempted theft? What other indictments might they be able to hit us with? I had a deep-seated fear of prison.

"What's going on here?" Jerry asked. He moved to Martin's side and put an arm around him. He wasn't as tall but stood protectively, rubbing a hand roughly up and down Martin's arm. "Are you okay?" He leaned closer, touching tenderly at the scrape on his face. "Someone needs to tell me what's going on here." His tone was severe, and he turned a disappointed face to me. "Who is this?" He jutted his chin toward Evan, still not taking his hands from his son. "And what are you two doing attacking my boy this way?"

A heavyset man with a scruffy white beard, wrapped in a tatty blue bathrobe, walked over from next door. His wife stood in their front doorway, her head poking out. "What's going on here, Jerry? Everything okay?" he asked. "Do you need us to call the police, or you got it?"

"We're just getting to it," Jerry said. "This young lady was our dinner guest this evening, but I don't know who this is or why they attacked Marty." He jerked his chin at Evan again.

"Are you kidding me?" Evan asked. He dropped his MMA stance and reached for the duffle bag that had been kicked to the side during the mini-brawl. My heart hammered as he grabbed the bag. If those jewels weren't there, I wasn't sure what we would do. Martin pushed away from his father.

"That's mine! Don't touch it!"

Evan turned sideways, blocking Martin from snatching the bag, while he reached inside and felt around. It was too dark for me to see any maggots affixing themselves to Evan's arm; nevertheless, anticipatory bile rose in my throat. I expected Martin to lunge for the bag, but instead, he sagged and leaned into Jerry's embrace. Jerry looked uncertainly from Martin to Evan to me as Evan drew out a dark object and dropped the duffle bag on the driveway.

"You want to explain this?" Evan asked. My teeth were clenched, hoping it wasn't just a bag of random crap that Martin had transported from his apartment to keep safe from the workers. We all stared as Evan pulled the drawstring at the top of the bag, stuck his fingers through the opening, and wrested it wide. He reached in and pulled at something, a tangle of items rising like a giant hair plug from a drain.

"What is that?" asked Jerry. His voice cracked uncertainly, and he dropped his arm from Martin's shoulders.

Evan slipped his palm underneath, and we leaned forward for a better look. All of us except Martin. He looked away, glancing up and down the street as if deciding whether to make a break for it. Even in the darkness, the jewels refracted the light, twinkling like tiny stars in Evan's palm.

"What is that?" Jerry asked again. "Is that jewelry? Martin, where did you get that? Is that a gift for Jessie?"

Evan slipped the jumbled mess back into the bulging bag. Apparently, he'd pulled up a fraction of the collection. I couldn't believe Martin had dumped these valuable jewels so carelessly into a tangled heap. Then I thought of Christine. I *really* couldn't believe he had killed Christine for her jewelry.

"You *killed* her," I said, moving toward Martin. I thought of her body at the bottom of the stairs. I thought of Lucille mourning beside her beloved companion. "You *killed* her!" I shoved at his chest, and he stepped back, throwing his arms up to defend himself.

"Marty? Marty? What is she talking about?"

"You didn't have to kill her! What, you killed her so you could buy your stupid muscle car? You killed her because the guys at work are mean to you? You killed her because you're such a damn loser? You're too much a victim to just go get a better job? You don't like who people leave their estates to?" I was shoving his chest now, over and over. I wanted to hurt him. I wanted him to pay for killing such a free spirit and for leaving a dog broken and traumatized. Tears leaked from my eyes, but I blinked through them. "You had everything. You've got a wonderful father who gave everything he had to make you happy, and it wasn't *enough*? What is wrong with you?"

Several more neighbors had emerged, and in the distance, I heard a siren wailing as it got closer.

"Marty?" Jerry looked suddenly old, his face caving into frightened understanding. "Marty? Please tell me. Please tell me this is all a misunderstanding," he pleaded. I'd stopped my tirade, exhaustion and depression washing over me. Martin slumped against the side of his car, refusing to meet his father's eyes. "You're a good boy. I know you're a good boy. This is all a misunderstanding, right?" His eyes flicked to the bag Evan held.

"It was an accident," Martin finally said, his voice a high-pitched whine. "I didn't touch her. It was an accident." Everyone fell silent, sidling closer to hear. "Dad, you gotta believe me. I didn't touch her. She wasn't supposed to be home. She was supposed to be out. But she had so much money! And she had all that jewelry she was leaving to dogs! I mean, come on! *Dogs*." His energy had flared momentarily, but then it was gone again. "I heard something. She wasn't supposed to be home, but I went to look, and she was coming up the stairs." He lifted his hand to his mouth and began chewing on his thumbnail. "She got scared when she saw me. I was wearing a mask. She didn't know it was me. And, then, she stepped back." Jerry's hand flew to his chest, and he let out a guttural sob. "And...and she fell. It was an *acci-dent*. You gotta believe me."

Jerry turned away as the police cruiser pulled to the curb, devastation wracking his frame. My heart thudded heavily for Martin's last casualty.

CHAPTER THIRTY-EIGHT

Evan and I sprawled across his sectional, the only nice piece of furniture he owned. It was late morning, and we were exhausted, having been up half the night over at the Amos house. The police officer who had arrived on the scene hadn't known what to make of our stories. It hadn't helped that Martin reverted to saying we'd assaulted him and were trying to steal his property. I couldn't remember the name of the detective I'd spoken to after Christine was killed, and in my overwrought state, I couldn't even come up with her last name. I finally texted Penny and woke her up, putting her on with the responding officer. He then radioed the detective in charge of the case, who said he would be right there. Turned out, his definition of 'right there' differed vastly from mine. In the meantime, I felt like a total heel when Jerry insisted on making us all coffee—even me, who was responsible for his beloved son being arrested.

The officer had taken charge of the bag of jewelry, and Evan insisted on getting his name and badge number to ensure he knew who to blame if anything went missing. He even took a picture with his phone for backup. We assumed everything from the appraisal list was in the bag, but we couldn't be sure because

Martin wasn't talking. The neighbors drifted away pretty quickly when it became apparent the excitement was over. By the time the detective arrived, I was lethargic and impatient to get home. I was sure Addie needed to go out, and I didn't want to tell this story one more time.

We'd been kept separated until we spoke to the detective. Evan napped in his Jeep; Martin was put in the back of the patrol car; Jerry waited inside, and I sat on the front steps, feeling my lower back seize up as the time dragged on. Even the responding officer seemed to tire of the wait and spent the interim scrolling on his phone.

"That was awesome last night," Evan said, rolling onto his side and tickling Henry.

"I don't know about awesome," I said. I tugged at the bandage on my elbow, trying to loosen the tape that pulled my skin. The scrapes I had paled compared to Evan's, but unlike me, he seemed revved up by his injuries. Addie raised her head and snuffled gently at the bandage.

"Yeah, but we got the guy! It was kind of like old times, don'tcha think?"

"Old times? Evan, it's not like this is something I want to be doing."

"You don't want to get killers off the street?"

"You make it sound like we're some kind of crime fighters or vigilantes or something. I think you've been watching too many movies." I ran my hand over Addie's head. "And actually, it wasn't awesome. It was awful. I feel so bad for Mr. Amos."

"Well, yeah. But he had to be at least partially responsible, right? I mean, he raised this guy."

I let my head fall back against the cushions and thought about that. "I don't know. Maybe. But if he was at fault, it was only because he tried to overcompensate for Martin's mom walking out."

"Yeah. And it sounds like he never made your boyfriend take responsibility for anything."

"He's not my boyfriend." I thought about how happy Jerry had been last night—literally beaming in his apron as he proudly watched his son, hoping I would see him in the same loving light. Okay, true, that was never going to happen, but it had been touching to see how much he loved Martin. Misplaced? Was a father's love ever misplaced? No. But maybe Evan had a point. Perhaps he had been so busy trying to smooth things out that he never taught him to take responsibility for his own life. Jerry had done everything he could to provide for his son, but ultimately, he hadn't ever made him accountable for his future, success, or happiness. And now they were both going to pay for it.

"Kinda funny," Evan mused. "You thought my girlfriend was bad. You thought she killed her aunt, didn't you? But no, it turned out to be your boyfriend."

"He's not my boyfriend," I repeated. Evan wasn't listening. He reached for the remote, flicked on the TV, and slid to his regular spot. Henry followed, pushing his way under Evan's arm and curling against his side in a well-practiced move. The volume was deafening, but neither of them seemed to notice. Addie tapped me with a white paw, pinching her ears against her head. "Could you turn that down a little?" I asked.

Evan complied, lowering the volume by approximately one notch. I looked at Addie and shrugged. I envisioned myself sitting across from Evan in a diner forty years from now, screaming out conversational tidbits while he held a hand cupped to his ear, yelling at me to speak up.

He flipped rapidly from channel to channel, not settling on anything for long. I glanced out the window to see if Kip was home, but his driveway was empty. I could only imagine how he and Bertram would react to the final development of this saga. I was sure Kip would be disappointed. Undoubtedly, he'd hoped Gabriella would be marched off in a huffy perp-walk. I admit that would have been pretty satisfying.

As for Bertram—shouldn't he have picked up on the fact I was going out with a murderer? Martin said he hadn't meant for anyone to get hurt, but at the end of the day, someone had died. Didn't my spirit guides think that was something I'd like to know? Maybe, being a baby psychic, Bertram just needed more practice or something. Or maybe it was all hooey.

Marty Anus. I heard the taunt of Martin's coworkers ringing in my head. Anus. Ass. Donkey. A donkey that liked shiny things. A bag of stolen jewelry. Twinkly, shiny jewelry. A man who was unhappy in his job but blamed everyone else. A man who'd rather steal from someone else than earn his own shiny things. Maybe it wasn't all hooey. Or, maybe I was looking for connections that didn't exist.

I tuned back in and noticed that Evan had landed on a romantic comedy. That was weird. He watched intently, his hand moving automatically along Henry's side as he gazed at the screen. It looked like it was near the end. The female lead ran crying through the rain as a finely chiseled guy galloped behind, calling out her name. They looked astoundingly attractive with wet hair. When my hair gets wet, it sticks in stringy wisps, making my head look entirely too small, like an old shrunken head I once saw in a museum.

"Hey, Jess?" Evan was still watching, his eyes never leaving the screen.

"Yeah?"

"Do you think we'll find someone like this someday?"

"Yeah, sure." The woman turned, and the couple embraced, the man uttering phrases no average man would ever say. "Well, this is a movie. So maybe not exactly like this."

"I've been thinking." He turned and glanced at me, running

a hand through his hair like I'd seen him do thousands of times before. Usually, he did this when he was nervous or tense. He looked away, and I felt a flutter of apprehension. "So, don't say no right off. Just think about it, okay?"

"Um, okay?"

"Do you think if we get to forty and we haven't found anyone yet...well, do you think we should make a pact that if that happens, then maybe you and I..." He drifted off and bent his head low over Henry as if hiding. "Maybe we could have a pact to get together if neither of us has found someone." The last part was muffled by Henry's fur.

The silence between us filled with romantic music as the couple on the screen twirled in ecstatic circles. Even from the corner of my eye, I could see deep red blotches suffusing Evan's face.

"Well, it's definitely a thought," I said. It was definitely a thought. Whether it was a good thought or not was an entirely separate matter. Seemingly satisfied, Evan flicked the channel, moving on to a grisly crime show. I looked away from the desiccated torso and closed my eyes. What was it Bertram had told me? There were words I was supposed to be saying to attract love. I wracked my brain until they floated into my consciousness. "Together reach divine love," I whispered softly into the ether. "Together reach divine love."